IMMORAL STEPS

MARISSA FARRAR

Immoral Steps

The Immoral Series
Book 1

Marissa Farrar

Castle View Press

© Marissa Farrar 2022
Published by Castle View Press
Cover Model Photography by Wander Aguiar
Typography by Covers by Combs

Written by Marissa Farrar
Interior Design by Silla Webb | Masque of the Red Pen

Dear Reader,

Firstly, I love you. Thank you for picking up one of my books, and giving it a chance.

Secondly, please note what you are getting yourself into.

This is a stepbrother and stepfather reverse harem romance and contains taboo themes. The heroine barely turns eighteen when things gets spicy, and there is a big age gap between her and her stepfather. It has darkness, which will become even darker as the series progresses, including scenes of SA.

If this is not your thing, please stop reading now.

But if you like your romance all kinds of twisted, then I hope you enjoy meeting Laney, Reed, Darius and Cade.

Marissa

1

Laney

I REACH for the front door of the trailer where I've lived my whole life and pause.

Something is wrong.

My fingertips brush the bubblegum pink paint peeling from the wood. I'm taken back to the day my mother painted it that color—one of her good days when, despite her issues, she'd been smiling and filled with vibrant energy.

There haven't been any of those days lately.

The door is already open a crack, and my stomach knots. I stare down at the dusty ground beneath my sneakers. The summer has been hot and dry—I can't remember the last time we had rain. My heart is racing, and my mouth runs dry. I swallow, hard.

"Mom?"

I allow my hand to continue its momentum, pushing the door open, revealing the inside of the trailer. I've done my best to keep the place tidy, but it isn't easy when the only other person who lives here doesn't give a shit about chores.

Once more, I hesitate.

What is it that's alerted me to the change? Some kind of spiritual connection, perhaps, my soul screaming out to me that the person who gave me life is no longer walking this Earth?

Or is it more practical than that? Can I sense there's no longer a heartbeat or another breath coming from inside? Or maybe the smell is different, already thick and cloying in the Los Angeles sun.

I shudder at the possibility.

Maybe I shouldn't go in there. My cellphone is in the back pocket of my cut-off jeans. I can take it out and call nine-one-one. I don't know how long it'll be before either paramedics or the cops get here, though, and I know I won't be able to just sit out here waiting until they arrive. What if I'm wrong and she's not dead yet? What if there's something I could do to save her, and instead of going in and helping, I do nothing?

There are several neighbors in trailers around me, and I wish I could go to one of them for help. But my mother's behavior over the years has ostracized us from everyone around us. I wouldn't mind so much, but it's not like they've been much fucking better.

"Mom?" I call again.

I'm not expecting a response, and I don't get one either. I step inside and peer down the length of the trailer, to our living area. It's made up of a narrow couch fitted to the wall, with a table in front of it that's on a pole and screwed into the floor. It all folds down to a bed, and that's where I sleep.

To my relief, she's not there, so I continue through the trailer and into the bedroom at the back. The bed is also empty.

Could I be wrong? Maybe she's just out with one of her boyfriends—though using the word 'boy' in reference to them is laughable when most are in their forties or fifties or even older. The slick sense of dread that's coated my skin since pausing at the door of the trailer hasn't left me.

I push open the narrow door to the bathroom, but it only swings a short distance before stopping. My diaphragm tightens and my heart seems to lurch up my throat. Tears fill my eyes, and I blink them back.

The toilet is positioned on the rear wall of the tiny space so when the door opens, it swings directly toward anyone who might be sitting on it, hitting their legs. There's no shout of protest from my mom, though I'm sure she's the one blocking the door.

"Oh, Mom."

I close my eyes and suck in a shaky breath. I don't want to touch her, but I know I have no choice.

Tentatively, I reach through the gap of the door and place my hand on what I can feel is her bare knee. It's cold, the skin somehow waxy. The position she's in means she's still sitting on the toilet and somehow hasn't fallen off. I don't have to give her a shake to know she won't respond.

Despair fills me but brings with it something else. Something I don't want to analyze too deeply. Is it relief? Relief that it's finally over. I'll no longer have to fear coming home, wondering what sort of mess I'm going to walk into. I'll no longer have to deal with whatever shitty excuse for a man she's brought back to the trailer, fending off their advances when she's already passed out cold on the couch.

I've been expecting to come home and find her dead for years. I remember turning ten, and being surprised it still hadn't happened, then I'd had my thirteenth birthday and she was still alive, and then I'd turned sixteen. My freedom had seemed so close then, and I'd started to think I might actually escape from home with my mother still living. Now I'm only a week away from my eighteenth birthday, and the moment I've been dreading for so long has finally arrived.

I straighten then drag my hand through my hair. Long, chestnut brown strands come away in my fingers, and I shake them off. It hasn't escaped my notice that I've been losing a lot of hair lately. It's the result of too much stress and not enough to eat.

I need to get her out of the bathroom. She'd never forgive me if I allowed cops and paramedics to find her body sitting on the toilet. It occurs to me that the police might consider this a crime scene now, and they won't be happy with me moving her, but I don't owe them anything.

My mother, however, is important to me, despite everything, and I don't want her seen like this.

With no choice, I push open the door, rotating her body along with it to make room. I'm able to open it enough to squeeze around the door, and I stand in the tiny space, fighting the urge to bolt.

She's slumped over, chin to chest. Both arms hang down, either side of the toilet, and, in her left arm, a needle protrudes from one of the veins, clinging on, even in these final moments. Around her bicep is a tourniquet made from red exercise band material. It's also hanging loose.

I cover my mouth with my hand and let out a harsh bark of a sob. Though my life has been far from perfect, and she hasn't been much of a parent to me for many years now, I still love her.

I *loved* her.

That I'm now completely alone suddenly hits me, and a tear trickles down my cheek.

I don't want to spend another minute standing inside this tiny bathroom with my dead mother. I need to get this done.

Holding back my tears, I brace myself for the feel of her body in my arms. I haven't had an easy life, but this is without a doubt one of the hardest things I've ever done.

"Come on, Mom," I say to her, though it's mainly for myself. "Let's get you out of here."

Like me, my mother is tall and skinny. The drug and alcohol abuse means she hasn't been eating much recently, and though it to go and live with my stepfather? A man I can barely even remember?"

"Not necessarily. It's just an option. I've made contact with him, so I'm just waiting to hear back."

"What are my other options?" I ask.

"To go into care until you turn eighteen."

I grimace. "You mean go and live with a whole heap of other people I don't know?"

She offers me a smile. "They're all carefully vetted and want to help. I'm sure they'll make you feel right at home, if that's what you'd prefer."

"I have a job," I tell her and gesture toward the trailer, "and I have a home. I don't need anyone to take care of me."

Despite what I'm saying, a part of me never wants to go inside that trailer ever again. The memory of her on the toilet, the thud her body made when I tried to haul her off it, the feel of her skin, cold beneath my palm, lingers in my mind. I shiver, frigid fingers trailing down my spine. Will I ever be able to use that bathroom again without picturing her sitting there? I doubt it.

"I'm sorry, but we can't simply let you live alone. You need to be eighteen."

Her phone rings, and she glances down at the screen then holds a finger up to me to say she'll be one minute and steps away.

I let out a sigh.

They say I'm a minor and I need looking after, but I've been taking care of myself for as long as I can remember. It seems ridiculous that these assholes are paying attention now that I'm almost eighteen.

I search my memories for any recollections of this elusive stepfather. I was only small when he came into our lives, but I have a vague memory of one man being around for slightly longer than the others. I wouldn't be able to pick him out of the long line of men my mother had coming in and out of her life, though. Why she decided to marry this one, I have no idea.

I don't want to end up with some loser. He might be even worse than my mother, and the thought of being in a similar situation with a man I don't even know is horrifying. I assume social services will do some kind of check before they just hand me over to a stranger. If he's another meth head alcoholic living in a trailer, they wouldn't expect me to live with him, would they?

A wave of sickness washes over me, hot followed by cold, and I'm suddenly dizzy. I plant my hands on my knees and fold at the waist, trying to inhale oxygen into lungs that have suddenly become tight and refuse to expand.

It's a panic attack. I've had them before. But that doesn't make it any less frightening or unpleasant. My entire world has just been swept out from under my feet, and I've lost the only person I've ever loved. It's hardly surprising that I'm not doing so well.

The crunch of feet approaching forces me to get a grip, and I look up to find the CPS woman standing over me.

"That was your mother's husband on the phone," she says.

"Estranged husband," I correct.

"We've explained to him who you are and what's happened."

This is the point where I expect her to tell me that he laughed and told them to fuck off, that he didn't want some seventeen-year-old girl he barely remembers hanging around.

But she smiles. "It's good news. He's in Los Angeles, and he'd like to meet you."

I sit up straight. Could that really be considered good news? "What? Why?"

Her brow crumples. "Because you're his stepdaughter and you've just lost your mother."

I realize she's misunderstood me. "No. Why is he in Los Angeles?"

I don't know why, but I'd never imagined that he'd still be in the same city. If he had, I was sure he'd have crossed our paths again at some point or another.

"Looks like he's on tour."

I'm still confused. "On tour for what? Is he in a band or something?"

"Umm…I'm not sure it would be considered a band. He's the manager for his son, Darius Riviera."

Darius Riviera? Where do I know that name from?

Ellen rambles on, seeming flustered. "Looks like your step-family is kind of famous. Darius Riviera is a violinist. He's been playing at a concert hall downtown for the last few nights."

My jaw drops. "Are you serious?"

"It's not something I'd joke about."

I snort. "Well, they're not going to want to know about me, are they? I can just picture that conversation." I throw up my hands. "What the hell are they going to do with me?"

"Actually, your stepfather is on his way here now. He really wants to see you again."

"I don't even know his name."

Her eyes widen with surprise. "Oh, right. Sorry. His name is Reed Riviera."

I harden my jaw and angle my head. "I hope he doesn't think I'm going to call him Daddy."

The knowledge that my estranged stepfather is rich punches me in the chest. I think of all the hours I've worked, the sleep I've lost, the exams I've come close to failing—not because I'm stupid, but because I've been too exhausted to study and almost fell asleep in class. This man could have stopped all of that in an instant, but he chose not to. He chose to walk away and forget about us.

Her tone softens. "You don't have to choose this option. We can find you a placement in foster care instead."

But my curiosity has been piqued. "I guess I can give it a try with Reed. It'll only be for a week, until I turn eighteen, right? If it doesn't work out, I can always contact you and go for the foster care option."

She nods and finds a business card with her number on it for me. "Of course. It's whatever is best for you, Laney."

Right now, I'm thinking about how I could just go with my stepfather and then run away. I can't imagine anyone will put too much effort into finding me again. Just another kid lost in the system.

I glance back at the trailer. "What about all my stuff?"

She follows my line of sight. Yellow police tape has been strung across the doorway.

"We'll have to get that sent on to you," she says.

One of the police officers approaches. "Miss Laney Flores? I'm afraid I'm going to need to ask you some questions."

My stomach drops. I knew this was coming, but I still don't want to speak to him. He's going to make me relive everything that's just happened, and that's the last thing I want. I'm also anxious that I'll be in trouble for moving Mom, or that the police will have found drugs in the trailer and will want to know if they're mine. What if they try to put Mom's death on me, framing things to make it look like I was the one who killed her?

Ellen stays with me—I think because legally I'm supposed to have an adult with me when questioned rather than because of any actual care for my wellbeing—but I'm glad not to be doing this alone.

I didn't need to worry. The cop is surprisingly kind, and it seems my mother's record is enough to back up my version of events.

I'm not sure how much time passes, but the crunch of car wheels approaching gets my attention and an expensive black Mercedes pulls up nearby. Is that him? Is my stepfather here already?

The driver's door opens. I hold my breath, my blood heating with anticipation, but the man who gets out is short, and in his sixties, and is wearing a driver's hat. He goes to the rear door and opens it.

A second man climbs out, unfolding his tall, lean body from the back seat. He straightens and smooths down his gray suit jacket. His dark hair is immaculately cut, just a few flecks of white at the temple, and his square jaw is smoothly shaven. He has the air of a man who other men take seriously, and he's drawn the attention of everyone nearby.

The sight of him has a physical impact on me. Is it memory? Do I remember him and that's why my heart is tripping, as though it doesn't know what sort of pace it's supposed to go, and my blood is suddenly on fire in my veins?

I have no doubt who this man is. It can only be Reed Riviera.

I'm about to be reunited with my stepfather.

I gesture vaguely at the trailer. "Do you want to say goodbye?"

Honestly, the place looks like a goddamn shithole. She should be pleased to get away from there. I know I never looked back.

I think she's going to say yes, but instead she folds her lips into a thin line, her nostrils flaring, and she shakes her head.

"Let's go," she says.

We say goodbye to the woman from CPS, and Laney follows me over to the car. The driver has been waiting behind the wheel, and he hops out to open the rear doors for us.

I feel guilty about the luxury of the vehicle. Even though I don't own it, it's a stark contrast to her trailer. I wonder what she's going to make of the five-star hotel and suite I've booked for her. Before leaving to pick her up, I made sure the hotel we're staying at had a room for her. She might be seventeen, but she's almost an adult, and I'm sure the last thing she'll want is to share a space with either me or her two stepbrothers.

She slides into the back seat beside me and sits primly with her bare knees pressed together and her fingers wound tightly in her lap. She doesn't glance out of the window at the trailer or the authorities surrounding it. I can't help but notice her smooth, tan skin or the way her long legs seem endless.

I catch myself and tear my gaze away. She's under my protection now, and even though she's not related to me by blood, there's a moral code that I won't cross.

The car starts up and, within minutes, we've left the trailer and the park behind. It hits me that I never asked if there would be a funeral for Estelle, if there is even anyone to arrange it. I guess she'll have an autopsy done, considering she died suddenly, so it'll be a little while before all those things will need to be put in place.

The vehicle crawls back toward the city, battling through downtown Los Angeles traffic until we get to the hotel.

I watch Laney for her reaction, but her expression remains impassive. Do I want her to be impressed by all this? Maybe. I can't read what she's feeling, though, or what she's thinking, for that matter.

A concierge steps forward to open the rear door of the vehicle, and Laney climbs out. She wraps her arms around her body, and I can see the tension in her neck and shoulders. Her gaze darts around at others entering and leaving the hotel, and she seems to shrink.

"Do you have any luggage, sir?" the concierge asks me.

"No, I don't."

Laney doesn't have any luggage either. In fact, she has nothing other than the tatty clothes she's standing in and the cellphone sticking out of her back pocket. I'll have to do something to change that.

In a couple of hours, we'll be going to see Darius play at the concert hall. She can't turn up in a pair of cutoffs, a long-sleeved tee, and a pair of sneakers. Despite who she is, and her relation to the star, I doubt they'll even let her in.

I'd already collected her room keycard before leaving to pick her up, so we head straight through the lobby and to the elevators. One is already waiting open for us, so we step inside. I punch the key for the top floor, and the doors slide shut, enclosing us within its mirrored walls.

The elevator glides upward, and I will it to hurry. I have no idea what to say to the young woman beside me, and she's making no effort to speak to me. Instead, she stands with her hands clasped in front of her body, her lips pressed together, not even looking up.

I take the moment to stare at her reflection in the mirrored walls that surround us. She's too thin, but that doesn't impact on her beauty. It only highlights her cheekbones and the fullness of her lips. I wonder if she's got any idea how stunning she is.

We reach the right floor, and the elevator draws to a halt and the doors slide open. We step out into the corridor, the carpet thick and plush underfoot, and expensive artwork on the wood-paneled walls. Laney's room is right down the hall from mine, and the boys are another couple of doors down from me—not that they're in right now.

They're already at the concert hall, preparing for tonight.

3
laney

THIS HOTEL IS like nothing I've ever been inside before, and I'm doing my best not to feel intimidated as hell, or like I simply don't belong here. I want to not care. My mother just died, and now I'm having to rely on someone who once walked out on me and Mom and who never looked back. I have a heavy stone lodged in my chest where my heart used to be. I don't know how I'm supposed to feel, so I prefer to feel nothing. It's safer that way.

I follow Reed obediently, and we stop outside one of the doors.

"This is your room," he says.

Reed presses a keycard to the device on the lock. It flashes green and clicks open, and he leans past me to push the door open. The scent of him, sandalwood and something citrusy, hits me, and it brings my senses back to life, if only for a second, and then the moment passes again.

He gestures for me to go inside, which I do, and he follows.

The room is huge—twice the size of the floorplan of my entire trailer. The floor to ceiling windows offer a view across the city, and the bed is so wide and deep, it looks like I could vanish into it.

"I don't know when you last ate," he says, "but feel free to order room service. Just put it on the room."

He looks me up and down, and an awkward smile tweaks the corners of his lips.

"You'll…umm…need some new clothes. I assume you're not exactly in the mood to go shopping, so I can have a personal shopper pick some stuff out for you. I guess you'll need…" He hesitates again and his cheeks flush. "Everything."

Finally, I lift my head and meet his eyes.

"If by everything, you mean underwear, yeah, I'll need that too. Unless you want me washing my panties in the bathroom sink, but then I'll have to go without until they dry."

The heat rises in his face, touching the tips of his ears, and I discover that I've enjoyed flustering him. Is he thinking about me not wearing any panties now? I bet that's fucking with his head.

"I'll send the personal shopper out to get you whatever you need," he says, pulling himself back together. "There's one other thing. You're going to need something a little more dressy than the sort of things you might be used to wearing."

I glanced down at my long sleeve t-shirt with the holes in the sleeves that I stick my thumbs through when my hands are cold and my threadbare denim-shorts and sneakers.

"What's wrong with what I'm wearing?"

"You can't exactly wear denim to a concert hall," he says. "Dax—*Darius*—has a show tonight, and we have to be there."

"I don't normally wear ballgowns," I say, doing my best not to sound sarcastic and failing.

He doesn't pick up on my tone, and instead, smiles brightly, revealing straight white teeth. "Not to worry. I'll get the personal shopper to pick you out something elegant. Money is no object."

Is this how he works? Throwing money at me to ease his guilt?

That's fine by me. It's exactly what I came here for. I never expected him to lavish me with affection or hold me and wipe away my tears. This man might legally be my stepfather, but he means nothing to me.

"Fine," I say firmly.

He holds the room keycard out to me. "I'll call on you before we're due to leave for the concert hall. My room is right down the corridor."

I take the card from his hand, and our fingers brush momentarily. A flush of heat runs up my arm and into my chest. I catch my breath. I refuse to let this man intimidate me. I try not to think about the fact that it isn't only him I'm going to have to deal with. I'll have his sons, too. Will they see straight through me? They don't have the guilt of walking out on me and my mother to use as motivation.

I struggle to picture what they're going to be like. Of course, I've seen pictures of Darius Riviera on billboards across the city. And I know from social media articles that he's blind. I've never really interacted with someone who's visually impaired before. Will it be strange? Though I know there is nothing wrong with his hearing, I still feel like it will be harder to communicate with him. So much of our communication involves our eyes and body language, like the way I'm staring at his father right now with cold indifference, deliberately positioning my body defensively, with my arms crossed as a barrier and one leg in front of the other, as though I'm going to bolt at any minute. These are the kinds of things Darius won't be able to read about me. I can't decide if that will put me at a disadvantage, or him. As for his brother, Cade, I know nothing about him. He's an enigma in my mind. I don't even know what he looks like.

Reed backs out of the room and closes the door behind him. I'm alone for the first time in what feels like forever. I feel like if

I stop and try to process what's happened today, I might fall apart, and that's the last thing I can afford to do. I've held myself together for so long, sometimes with no more than spit and mud, that I worry if I crumble, I won't know how to put my pieces together again.

So, instead of collapsing on the bed in tears, I turn my thoughts to more practical tasks.

I use my cellphone to make a call to one of my jobs and tell my boss I won't be in for a few weeks. I figure once I turn eighteen, I'll be able to return to the trailer and my old life, and I'll still need to work. He's about to give me some shit for missing my shift when I interrupt and tell him my mother just died. After that, he's a little more understanding, and I let him know I'll be in touch once things settle down. My second job isn't quite so understanding. Even with the news that I just lost my only parent, I'm told that they won't keep the job open for me for that length of time. There's nothing I can do about it, and the strange sense of emptiness inside me prevents me from even being upset.

Though I haven't eaten, my stomach still feels like a leaden ball. As much as I want to make Reed Riviera pay for leaving me and my mother in squalor while he lived the high life, and room services seems a good place to start, I don't think I can stomach even looking at food. Maybe I should order every item on the menu and have it delivered to the room only to just take a bite out of everything. The thought is tempting, but I've lived for so long with nothing that I can't bring myself to disrespect food like that. The thought of such gluttony, even if it isn't at my expense, turns my stomach.

Instead, I wander into the luxurious bathroom. The bath is long and deep with spray jets positioned along the sides. I wonder how long this personal shopper will take to bring me some clean clothes. As much as I'm tempted to soak in the bath, I don't want to be in there when she arrives. I'm also aware that lying in a bath will give me time to think, and I don't want that either. Figuring it will be quicker, I turn on the huge walk-in shower, and then I find my classic rock music playlist on Spotify and turn up my phone as loud as it will go. There's probably some kind of music system in the room that I could plug my phone into or connect to Bluetooth, but I don't have the patience to try to figure it out.

The hotel has provided all the toiletries I could need, and I click open the top of the shampoo bottle and inhale the citrusy fragrance. It takes me back to the moment outside of the hotel room door where I'd inhaled Reed's cologne. He certainly doesn't come across as a father figure, even though he's got two biological sons he must have at least partly raised.

I strip off my clothes and step beneath the steamy shower. I lift my chin and let the water drum across my forehead cheeks and eyes. Memories of finding my mother's body try to force their way into my head. I think of how cold her skin was to touch, how immobile her body had been when I tried to lift her, and I let out a cry of grief.

No, no, no. This is exactly what I've been trying to avoid. I don't want to feel this, don't want to process it. I knew it was coming—I had known for years. This shouldn't be a shock to me.

And yet it is.

I force my thoughts away and focus instead on the music. I open my mouth to sing along, but my voice sounds forced and mechanical. That panicky sensation fills me again, my heart fluttering, my breath hard to catch. Though I'm still in the shower, with steaming hot water coursing down my body, my skin prickles with goosebumps, as though I'm chilled.

I finish washing my hair and turn off the water, wanting to get out of there. I suddenly wish Reed had stayed. I realize he never gave me a way of contacting him. I don't even have his cell number. All I can do is wait until he returns.

Not wanting to dress in my dirty clothes, I find a thick white robe and sit on the edge of the bed, working the knots out of my hair with a flimsy black comb, also supplied by the hotel. I turn on the television, wanting to drown out my thoughts, and sit there, losing track of time.

A knock startles me, and I jump to my feet. I open the door to find a woman in her forties outside. She's well dressed and has a portable rail with a cover over it beside her. It takes me a moment to piece together who she is or what she might want.

"Miss Flores?" she asks.

I nod. "Yes?"

"My name is Anna. Mr. Riviera asked me to find you some clothes."

There's a hint of an accent to her voice, but I can't quite place it. I realize who the woman is—the personal shopper Reed hired.

I blink and then remember my manners. "Yes, of course. Come in. That was quick."

"I'm good at what I do." She frowns and glances me up and down. "I hope Mr. Riviera was accurate with his sizes."

It hadn't even occurred to me that he would need to pass on my clothes size to this woman. I suddenly realize that was probably the reason he'd been studying me earlier. My perverted mind had assumed he was thinking of me with no underwear on. I must be sick in the head. The man is my stepfather, and he probably just sees me as a little girl.

I shut the door behind Anna, and she unzips the cover from the rail, revealing a selection of clothes. She rifles through them, selecting certain outfits and tossing them to the bed.

"I suggest you start by trying these on," she says. "We want you to have a capsule wardrobe and then you can layer from that."

I look helplessly at the selection of clothes. A capsule wardrobe? I'm not even sure what that is.

"I'm happy just to have a couple of pairs of jeans and some t-shirts," I tell her.

She widens her eyes at me in horror. "You cannot wear jeans to a concert hall."

I sigh. "Okay, what do I need to wear then?"

I'll put myself in this woman's hands—she can do whatever she wants with me. I don't even care.

First she finds me a black, lacy thong and a strapless bra and waits while I put them on, still huddled inside the white fluffy folds on the robe.

She goes back to the rail and selects a couple of dresses.

She motions to the robe. "You're going to have to take that off."

I'm reluctant to let it go, but I have no choice. I stand like a mannequin as she slips various dresses and outfits over my head until she finds one she likes.

"This one goes perfectly with your coloring," she says and then stares at me. "Your eyes are the most unusual shade of blue."

My face heats. "Thanks," I mutter.

I'm not used to taking compliments.

She dangles a pair of high-heeled pumps from her fingers. "Now for shoes."

I shake my head. "Uh-huh. No way. I'll break my ankle in those. Flats only."

She sighs, as though I've disappointed her, but finds a suitable pair. I don't do heels, and it's not only because of my fear of breaking something. I'm tall, and heels only make me taller, which means I attract people's attention when I prefer to vanish into the background.

Anna glances around the room. "Do you have makeup?"

"No, I don't wear it."

She stares at me like I've just said I walk down the street

with my tits out. "Well, we must change that. Sit." She gestures to the stool in front of the dressing table.

I do as she says.

She fishes in her purse for her supplies and works her magic on me. Within ten minutes, I'm blinking back at someone who barely looks like me.

"There," she says. "You will wow him."

Wow him?

My ears burn. "Oh, God, no. It's not like that."

Does she think I'm dating Reed Riviera? He's old enough to be my father. I mean, he literally *is* my stepfather, even if he hasn't been in my life for as long as I can remember.

She pats my shoulder and gives me a wink. "I don't think any red-blooded woman would say no to Reed Riviera. And wait until you meet his sons."

My jaw drops and, before I can explain in more detail, she's already gathered her belongings and whisks back out of the room.

I feel hideously self-conscious in my floor length emerald dress. My shoulders are bare, as are my arms. At least I managed to talk my way out of being put in a pair of high-heeled pumps and instead have opted for strappy flats. Anna already pulled my hair off my neck and pinned it up. I don't look like myself. A part of me wants to rebel. Why do I have to dress myself up the way this man wants? But the other part of me doesn't want to look like the outsider—the poor one who doesn't fit in.

I wonder what the two sons are going to be like and how well they'll take to my sudden appearance. They are both adults, so it's not as though I'm having to get along with a couple of moody teenagers. I figure the best I can hope for is that they'll basically ignore me.

My head is still spinning, unable to process what's happened.

My mom is dead. My mom died. I'm never going to see my mom again. I'm an orphan.

I say the lines to myself over and over, as though trying them on for size, or testing out the pain they cause. None of it seems real. The reality simply hasn't sunk in yet.

I should be curled up in bed, sobbing my heart out, instead of standing here in a five-hundred-dollar dress, with my hair done and a full face of makeup. I don't want to linger on it, but I'm still relieved that it's over. I'll never have to come back to the trailer, wondering what sort of state I'll find my mother in, or if I'll have to deal with some asshole she's brought home. I had plenty of nights where I slept outside because I didn't want to go in there. Some of the men were so rough that they'd think I was easy game as well. I'd fought more than one of them off, with absolutely no backup from my mom.

A knock comes at my door, and I draw a breath.

I go to answer it. Reed is standing on the other side wearing a tux. Seeing him there jolts me like an electric shock. How have I not noticed how handsome he is? He's easily over six feet tall, and his shoulders fill out the tux beautifully. He's got a generous mouth and a strong jaw. From the surprise in his eyes, seeing me dressed this way has affected him as much as it has me.

"Laney," he says, his blue eyes widening a fraction, "you look—" he pauses as though searching for the right word before settling on— "the part."

I get the feeling he'd been about to say something else but changed his mind at the last minute.

"Thanks," I say. "You look *the part*, too."

He doesn't react to my sarcasm.

We stare awkwardly at each other, then he gestures down the corridor.

"Shall we?" he says.

I nod and grab my purse—also brand new and now containing my cellphone—from the console table and follow him out. I'm jittery, my stomach fluttering. I clench my hands by my sides to stop them from shaking.

Reed walks quickly, his long legs striding down the corridor, so I have to hurry to keep up. I'm so grateful I'm not in heels or I'd have fallen on my ass by now.

A car is waiting at the front of the hotel. The driver climbs out and opens the back door for us. I smile my thanks at him and climb in. Reed follows, taking the spot beside me.

I've never been in a car like this before—a stretch limo, all leather seats, and expensive interior. I feel so out of place, I just want to run back to my trailer and lock the door behind me.

I sense tension radiating from Reed as well. As awkward as I am with this situation, he's the same.

Is he expecting me to ask about my mother? To question why he left? To wonder out loud if he ever thought about me or what kind of life I was leading? I don't want to give him the satisfaction of trying to explain himself. I'd prefer to let him stew. He doesn't bring up the topic either, and I sit facing the window, watching downtown Los Angeles pass in a blur of color and lights.

There's a little traffic, but soon enough we arrive at the concert hall. The driver stops the limo and gets out, opening the rear door for us once more. We draw the attention of others as we get out, and I can see people angling their heads toward one another, whispering questions about who we are.

There's a stream of beautifully dressed people entering the concert hall, and we join them, stepping inside the breathtaking building. I feel utterly out of place, but I force myself to lift my chin and put my shoulders back. My stomach flutters with nerves and my blood fizzes through my veins. What am I even doing here? My mother died today. This is too much.

Why didn't it even occur to me to tell Reed that I'd just stay in the hotel room while he attended the concert? Instead, I got swept along with what Reed told me to do, and it didn't even occur to me to push back. I've been sleepwalking through this day, and I assume that's in part due to shock.

I eye Reed curiously. Does he realize that? Or is he so caught up in what he needs to be doing that he hasn't given my mental wellbeing a single thought?

I'm at least grateful he didn't allow me to show up in my jeans and t-shirt. At least, dressed as I am, I can blend in with the crowd. People are mingling, and many of them nurse tall glasses of champagne. Reed greets people with smiles and nods, as though he knows everyone.

"Ah, here's someone I want you to meet," Reed says, nodding across the foyer.

I follow his line of sight, and it's all I can do to stop my jaw hitting the floor.

I swear this guy is the biggest man I've ever seen. He's easily six-four, and it's not just that he's tall either. He's definitely been putting in some gym time, and he's not afraid to show it. He's dressed in black slacks and a black, button-down shirt, and shiny shoes. Like me, I feel he's dressed up for the occasion. The tattoos that crawl up the side of his neck and down across his hands and knuckles hint toward his normal style.

"This is your stepbrother, Cade."

4
CADE

My new stepsister is staring at me like the fucking
Abominable Snowman just stepped out in front of her, her lips
parted slightly, her eyes—a curious shade of blue—round.

She's young, but not as young as I had expected. I'm
assuming the getup Reed's put her in makes her look older. She
seems uncomfortable, tugging at the spaghetti straps of the dress,
so I highly doubt she's the one who has chosen what she's wearing. The dress alone probably costs more than her house. Does
she even have a house? I'm sure Reed mentioned something on
the phone about going to pick her up from her trailer.

My father tends to get what he wants. He files his controlling
ways beneath the header of 'watching out for us' or 'taking care
of us' or 'just doing what's best,' but the truth is that he wants
things to go his way. He's literally Darius's manager, for fuck's
sake. I often see Darius in him, in his need to control his
surroundings, but Dax has other reasons for that, ones I do
understand.

"Cade," Reed says, "I want you to meet Laney. Your
stepsister."

I stare right at her, and to give her props, she holds my gaze.

"I don't have a stepsister," I say, my tone indifferent.

"You do now. Be nice." A warning. "Her mother just died."

I smirk. "I'm always nice."

That's a lie.

Is this Reed's new project? Sometimes I think he focuses on everyone else so he doesn't have to think about himself. It hasn't escaped my notice that my father doesn't have much of a social life. There's been the occasional woman, but nothing like me and Dax. I'd put it down to his age, but he's only just turned forty, so it's not like he's ancient.

"You didn't think you should have warned us about a stepsister before now?" I suggest. "Maybe mention it at the dinner table, perhaps?"

Reed's expression is unreadable. "It never came up."

I raise an eyebrow. "Clearly not."

Laney turns those big, pale blue eyes on me. "You didn't know about me?" She seems surprised. "Did you know about my mother?"

I purse my lips and shake my head. "Nope. He never said a word."

We both glance in the direction of my father, who at least has the decency to shrink a little. I wonder what other secrets Reed has kept from us. He didn't come into our lives until I was eight years old, and Darius was six, so we're aware he had a life in between him breaking up with our mother and then coming back again when she got sick, but he's been seriously cagey about what he did during those years. Now I know.

Because I was already a defiant, angry eight year old by the time he was first introduced to us, I never fully got my brain to switch from him being 'Reed' to him being 'Dad.'

"She's definitely a stepsister?" I check. "She's not yours—biologically, I mean?"

Reed looks back to me. "Cade, Laney was three years old

when I met her mother. There's absolutely no way she's mine—
at least not by blood, anyway."

That pleases me, but I can't say exactly why.

I'm aware that we're drawing attention. I'm used to people
staring, but I doubt my new stepsister is. I almost laugh at the
fact I have a goddamned stepsister my father has completely
neglected to mention until now. The son of a bitch has been
married all these years and never bothered to mention it. What an
asshole. What did this girl's mother have that ours didn't? Why
did Reed decide to marry her instead of our mom? Maybe I
shouldn't give a shit—it was years ago, after all—but I still can't
help but feel the twinge of jealousy inside me. Did Laney's
mother look like her? Maybe that was what lured Reed away? I
suppose I get it—those big, pale blue eyes, the long reddish-
brown hair.

A hot piece of ass in an extremely short silver dress that
leaves absolutely nothing to the imagination saunters past. She
throws a glance over her shoulder and gives me a secret little
smile.

"Hey, you," I call out to her. "What you doing after the
show? You look like you'd look good on top of me."

"Cade!" my father snaps and shoots a glance at my new
stepsister.

I only laugh. The blonde has paused, unsure if I'm joking or
not. "Or would you rather ride my brother instead?"

My father glares at me like he wants me to burst into flames
right then and there. It only amuses me. I don't care if my father
thinks I'm out whoring around. Better that than he knows what
I'm really up to. I'm not afraid of my father, but I am afraid of
the consequences of my actions. Is that going to make me stop,
though? I wish it would. I wish it was enough.

The blonde tosses her hair behind her shoulder. "Your brother
is Darius Riviera, right? I would love to meet him after the
concert."

"I could arrange that. I bet he'd love to *meet* you, too." I drop the level of my voice a notch and lean in closer so she can hear. "I'm the one with the pierced cock, though," I tell her. "Wait until you experience that for the first time. You'll never go back."

I sneak a glance at my new stepsister, trying to assess whether my words have affected her. She hasn't budged but is staring at me with her eyebrows raised and her upper lip curled in disgust. The nostrils of her pretty little nose are flared.

"Seriously?" she says. "Don't you know what year it is? Since when has catcalling come back in fashion?"

"That wasn't a catcall, *sis*, that was an offer."

The chick in the sparkly dress throws me an extra smile and saunters away. I'm pretty confident she'll be hanging around after the show.

Laney rolls her eyes and gives her head a slight shake of disgust.

I can't believe my father has run to the rescue of this little orphan-Annie. That's what he does—thinks he can rescue all of us. I bet she couldn't believe her luck when she found out who her stepfamily were. Dollar signs probably flashed in her eyes like a fucking cartoon character.

Reed says she'll only be with us for a week or so, just until she turns eighteen, but I wonder how much she'll have gotten her claws into him by then. I don't know the full story about how or why Reed left our mother, but since hers came after, I can guarantee running around with other women played a part in it. She's not even blood, barely even family. I don't understand why we're the ones who've ended up shouldered with her.

At least she's easy on the eyes with that face and those never-ending legs. And then there's those eyes… She could do with putting on a few pounds, filling out those curves, but as they say, any more than a handful is a waste. I wonder how much experience she's had. Is she one of those slutty teens who has fucked half of the boys at high school, or is she one who thinks so much of herself she's untouchable?

It's hard to know for sure without seeing her in her natural setting.

It doesn't make any difference to me either way. If I decide I want her, then I'll take her, no matter what my father says. I picture those long, slim legs wrapped around my waist, and my cock tingles and lengthens. She's my stepsister, and that puts her off limits, but really that only makes me want her more. If it happens to also piss off my father at the same time, then it's a win-win.

"I need to get backstage," I say to my father. "Dax will be waiting for me."

"Of course. Your brother needs you."

Sometimes, I doubt that. Darius resents my presence; I'm sure he does. Maybe I feel the same way about him. If it wasn't for his talent, we'd all still be living in squalor, and he sure as hell likes to remind me about that.

But I'm like Dax's fucking guide dog—the one who watches out for him. When we arrive at a new place, I'm the one ensuring he can find his way around and making sure everyone supporting Dax's act knows exactly what's expected of them. If someone fucks up—leaves a chair in the wrong place or moves Darius's belongings—they hear it from me. So, I guess we're co-dependent on each other, which probably isn't a good thing.

"I'll see you later, then." I turn to Laney. "Nice to meet you, sis."

And I stroll away, leaving her gaping after me.

5

Laney

MEETING CADE HAS LEFT me shook. I had no idea my *stepbrother* was going to look like that guy. Honestly, if I'd met him down a dark alley, I'd have turned and run, and, by the darkness hiding behind his eyes, he'd most likely have chased me.

A little frisson of something I don't want to analyze too deeply goes through me.

Cade isn't even the famous one. If Cade is this imposing, what the hell is Darius going to be like?

Reed guides me through the foyer, his hand lightly placed against the small of my back. I'm painfully conscious of the position of his palm and of all the curious glances we're receiving. Do people know who he is? He nods and greets several people we pass, but I can't tell if he actually knows them or if he's just being polite. Either way, he doesn't stop to introduce me to anyone else.

We climb a grand staircase, which leads onto a bar area, and then climb yet another staircase, taking us even higher into the building.

"This is us," Reed says.

He guides me out into the concert hall, and I discover we're in a box with private seating. It gives a view across the rest of the hall, and all the people below us, and of course, of the stage itself. I don't know why I'm surprised. Reed is Darius Riviera's father and manager. If he can't get good seats, who can?

He gestures for me to take a seat and then drops into the one beside me. His thigh is touching mine, but he doesn't seem to notice, and I don't move my leg to create space. I like having a piece of him touching me.

Maybe I have daddy issues—since I've never actually had one—but I'm enjoying the sense of having a man be protective of me.

I give myself a little mental shake and remind myself why I'm here. This man owes me. He could have changed my whole life and chose not to. Now, I'm left with nothing and no one, and I'm determined to make him pay for that.

Negative phrases threaten to bombard me—gold-digger is one of them. Am I choosing to go with him because of money? Fuck yes. But I won't be shamed for it. My entire life has been a struggle, but it hadn't needed to be that way. Maybe he didn't feel any obligation toward me, since I wasn't his flesh and blood, but, as I've just discovered, he was legally my stepfather. Didn't that mean he should have had some kind of responsibility for me?

"You okay?" he asks.

I nod. "Just a little overwhelmed."

Movement comes behind us, and a waitress appears with a bottle of champagne in a silver cooler and two glasses. Reed waves it away. Is he going to tell me I'm not old enough?

"I don't drink," he says instead. "Not anymore. I've had a few slips, but I've been clean almost fourteen years."

Fourteen years. The length of time he's been away from my mother.

The length of time he's been away from me.

"Oh, right." I press my lips together and stare down at my hands. I want to ask a question, but I don't want to stir things. But I have to know. "Did you drink when you and my mom were together?"

He doesn't look at me but nods. "Drink, drugs…you name it, we took it."

"Did you stop because you left her?"

"Kind of. I got the call from the boys' mother to say she was sick. Cancer. She didn't have anyone else."

"So, you got clean for them?"

Jealousy curls through me at the thought of his two sons. He chose them instead of staying with me and my mom. He got clean for them, but he didn't for us.

"I didn't feel I had any choice," he says.

His words hang between us. My mother never bothered to do the same for me, and the pain of that knowledge makes my chest hurt. I wasn't enough for Reed to get clean for either. It's not as though I was ever his, biologically, and I guess in this situation, blood matters.

That hollow space in the middle of my chest expands. I'm not important enough for the people who were supposed to love me to want to make changes in their lives. Maybe I should be grateful Reed is stepping up for me now, but it's hard to be thankful when my mother is dead, and I now have the knowledge that this man had the ability to change my life for me but chose not to. He focused his attention elsewhere instead, toward the two biological sons he ended up raising.

A part of me wants to stand up and walk out, to tell him to go fuck himself and his money. I can't, though. If I do, he'll call the woman from CPS, and then God only knows what will happen to me. I don't even know if I can go back to the trailer, or if it's still considered a crime scene.

I remind myself that this is a better option than staying with some random family. These people have money, lots of money, and the way I see it, I'm owed. This asshole walked out on both me and my mother, and for the past fourteen years we've been living in poverty, while he and his sons have been staying in five-star hotels and eating fucking caviar for dinner every night. I think of all the hours I've worked while also trying to stay up on my schooling. I've slept barely more than five or six hours a night since I was twelve years old. I've busted my backside doing cleaning jobs until late and then getting myself up early in time to get to school the next day. I think how easily this man could have changed things for us. The sort of money that would have meant nothing to him would have changed our lives. Did we even cross his mind? Probably not, but I'm determined that by the time I turn eighteen, he'll feel so fucking guilty he'll sign over his life savings.

The lights in the concert hall dim, and I find myself catching my breath in anticipation. A curtain lifts at the front of the stage, revealing an entire orchestra. They didn't take up most of the space, though. They're all seated right at the back, with the front of the stage empty. The lights have illuminated them for the audience, but now they drop and are replaced by a spotlight. Every eye in the place is fixed on that circle of light. Then it sweeps away, toward the wings, and I catch my first ever glimpse of Darius Riviera.

He strides onto the stage, naked from the waist up. In one hand he holds his violin, and in the other his bow, and he lifts them both into the air as he walks. The audience breaks out into applause and whoops of approval. He comes to a halt in exactly the same place the spotlight had been moments before. If I didn't know, I'd have had no idea he couldn't see.

I lean into Reed.

"How does he know where to walk?" I whisper. "What if he falls off the stage?"

Reed shakes his head. "He won't. Darius has already mapped

out the entire stage before stepping onto it tonight. He counts his steps. He knows exactly where he is."

My gaze is drawn back to the man on stage. The audience has fallen silent again now, only the occasional clearing of the throat marring it.

Darius places the violin beneath his chin and then raises the bow with a flourish. It's as though the entire audience holds their breath.

The first note he plays is long and mournful, and then he eases into another, and another, each one layering on the first.

The notes seem to vibrate inside my chest, and crazily, I find myself close to tears. I know it's partly from the trauma of the day—I'm wrung out and exhausted—but as emotion swells inside me, at the same pace as the music, I can't convince myself that's the only reason. I've never listened to classical music before, and I'd never imagined it affecting me in such a way.

The music builds and grows, getting faster and faster. The way he plays is like he's taking part in a physical sport, or, dare I say it, even fucking. He puts his whole body into it. His muscular upper torso is already shiny with sweat. His long hair is also damp, coiled into separate strands and whipping around him as he moves across stage.

In the wings, Cade lingers, all six feet four of him, an intimidating scowl morphing his features. He's the only person in the theatre not watching his brother. Instead, he takes in the audience, perhaps watching for anyone who might pose a threat to Darius.

I wonder if Cade is ever jealous of his brother's talents. Who would they be if it wasn't for Darius? But then I remember that Darius is visually impaired, and it just seems wrong to be jealous.

I tear my eyes from the brothers for a moment to take in the audience. They're not like an audience of any concert I've ever been to. No one is rocking out, or moshing, or jumping with their fists in the air. They're all seated, civilized and nursing glasses of wine or champagne. They don't seem like the type of people who would want to listen to someone who looks like Darius, yet here they are. And they're captivated. The women in the audience are clearly affected the same way as I am, their eyes wide and lips parted. Hell, I think even the men would probably switch sides if the offer came up. But there's something else as well, something that reminds me of people watching a powerful animal at a zoo. This is safe for them, to watch him from their seats, to get a taste of this wild, beautiful, clearly talented man without actually getting their hands dirty. Like they're getting a glimpse into a different kind of life.

I wonder how Darius feels up there. He can't see his audience but is he aware of them in other ways—the scents of their perfumes, their breathing? Or does he feel like that animal at the zoo, like he's on the wrong side of a one-way mirror?

Darius has been playing alone all this time, but now the orchestra joins in. They do so gradually, first the other violinists, then the cellists, then some flutists layer in their sound.

Darius stops playing as the music around him takes over. His eyes slip shut, and he's completely absorbed, his body continuing to move with the flux and flow of the sounds. A conductor is directing the orchestra, but of course, Darius can't see him. The orchestra fades, and Darius lifts his instrument once more.

There must be thirty or more people on that stage, but every single gaze in the place is locked on Darius.

He's utterly breathtaking, and while he's playing, I forget everything that's happened that's brought me to this moment. I've even forgotten the man beside me until he covers the back of my hand with his palm.

Reed leans in, so close the heat of his skin and the scent of him washes over me. "Are you all right?"

I nod. "Yes. Why do you ask?"

"You're crying."

44

I lift my hand—the one beneath his—to touch my cheek and discover it wet.

"It's beautiful," I say.

It truly is, like nothing I've ever experienced before. I never understood why people paid huge amounts of money to come and see shows like this before, but now I do.

The concert is over far too quickly, and I find myself bereft. I want to experience it all over again.

"Are you ready to meet Darius?" Reed asks, getting to his feet.

Sudden nerves explode in my belly. "Umm... I think so."

"Good. He'll be waiting for us."

I'm nervous about meeting Darius in a way that I wasn't meeting Cade. Is it because I've watched him on stage and witnessed the magic that he creates with both his body and his violin? Or is it because I'm not completely comfortable with how I should conduct myself? I don't want to embarrass myself, or him, for that matter.

We leave the box, and I stick to Reed's side as we descend the staircase.

"Can Darius see anything at all?" I ask, wanting to prepare myself.

"He can see movement, shadows, but no detail. Imagine you're standing in the dark, but it's not pitch black, and someone waved their hand in front of your face. You'd be aware of the change of light and movement, without being able to make out any details. That's what it's like for Darius."

"Is he ever likely to regain his sight again?"

"Not unless there are some serious advances in medical science, no."

"It might happen," I say hopefully.

"There's no point in even thinking about it. All that does is stop him living his life as it is. He'd always be looking into the future instead of working with what he has now."

I nibble at a piece of dry skin on my lower lip. "I think I understand."

Everyone is leaving, and we join the throngs. Reed's fingers lightly wrap around my upper arm, as though he's worried he's going to lose me in the crowds. While everyone else is exiting through the front of the building, we push against them and head toward the rear. A separate staircase takes us to the space behind the stage, and then down a corridor, where individual doors lead to what I assume are dressing rooms.

We stop at one that has the name Darius Riviera on it.

Reed pauses and turns to me.

"Darius isn't exactly the warmest person you'll ever come across," he says. "So don't be offended if he seems a bit stand-offish at first. It's not personal. He's just far more reserved than his brother."

"Oh, okay."

He continues, "Also, don't touch anything. Don't move anything in the room, not even a chair. If he asks you to sit, then sit exactly where the chair is already positioned. Don't drag it across the floor or anything."

"Why?" I'm confused.

"Darius needs to be able to control his surroundings. Before he goes to a concert hall, he demands that both the stage and dressing room is laid out a certain way. He always has a chair a set number of steps from the door, so he can walk straight to it. He has a specific list of items he demands to have in his dressing room and has them laid out in exact positions on the table, like on the face of a clock. It means he knows exactly where every-thing is, so nothing is going to catch him by surprise. His memory is excellent—almost photographic—and he only needs to be run through where everything in once to have a vision of the space around him in his mind."

"Like the number of steps that are needed to put him center stage?"

Reed nods. "Exactly."

I picture how difficult that must be for Darius, traveling around like he does, always ending up in different places. Does he resent it, or does he enjoy the challenge?

I draw in a shaky breath and try to tamp down my nerves. I tell myself that Darius is just like any other man, except he's not. He's practically a rock star, minus the electric guitar or the growly singing voice. I don't want to find that intimidating, but I do.

Reed lifts his hand and knocks on the door, and from inside, a deep voice calls, "Come."

6

Laney

Reed opens the door and gestures for me to step inside.

Darius's dressing room is immaculate. The man himself sits at a dressing table. A bottle of expensive-looking mineral water is in front of him, and beside that is a bottle of Irish whiskey. There are also bunches of flowers, placed in vases—no doubt from admiring fans.

"Dax," Reed says. "I brought someone to meet you. The person I told you about on the phone."

Darius slowly turns in his seat to face us. He's bigger this close up than he'd appeared on stage. His presence seems to dwarf the already small room.

"A sister, huh?" he says. "Laney?

How can his stare be so intense, even when he can't see?

But then I remember how Reed said Darius was able to see shadows. Is that what he's seeing now? Me in the form of shadows? If he sees shadows, surely that means he can see light as well? Somehow, it comforts me to think that he's not in complete darkness. The thought of that would be terrifying.

"What did you think of my show, Laney?"

I swallow. "It was incredible. I've never seen anything like it."

I realize I've used the word 'seen' and immediately feel awkward.

He must sense something about me because he purses his generous lips. "Don't do that," he says.

"Do what?"

"Get weird whenever the subject of sight comes up. I am who I am. I don't need to be defined by my sight loss."

Well, now I feel even weirder.

He puts out one hand and beckons me. "Come here."

I glance over at Reed, who nods, and then I step closer. Darius rises to his feet, and I catch my breath. He'd looked imposing on stage, but up close, he's breathtaking. He's put a t-shirt on, thank goodness, but the material clings to the muscles of his biceps and pecs, and I'm pretty sure if I look hard enough, I can even make out his abs. He has a half sleeve of tattoos from his elbow to his wrist. His long hair is still damp and hanging loose. There's something pouty about his lower lip and the thought of biting it pops into my head.

Jesus. Where did that come from?

I don't know what to expect.

"I want to know what you look like," he says.

It dawns on me that he's going to touch my face, and my stomach flips, my pulse thudding in my veins.

He places both hands to my shoulders and then lifts one to the top of my head, his palm pressing to my crown.

"You're taller than I thought you'd be," he observes.

"Oh." I don't know what to say.

Does he think I'm a giant? Next to him, I feel tiny.

"Close your eyes."

I do as he says.

He lifts both hands and sweeps his thumbs lightly across my

eye sockets, tracing the line of my browbone, and then down to my cheeks.

"Your cheeks are warm," he says. "Am I embarrassing you?"

"No." *Yes.*

I'd expect his fingers to be soft, but they're not at all, and then I realize the strings of his instrument have hardened the tips with calluses. From my cheeks, he moves to my nose, learning the shape, and then his fingers are on my lips. I hold my breath as he outlines them.

"Pretty."

His thumb drags down on my lower lip slightly, and for a moment I think he's going to slide a finger between my lips and onto my tongue, but he doesn't. What would I have done if he had? Push him away, or suck on it?

A little flutter of arousal dances inside me at the thought, and my nipples tingle and harden beneath my dress. I hope he's not going to run his hands down my body, because he'll be able to tell the effect he's had on me. I'm also aware of Reed watching his son touching me, and that does strange things to my insides as well.

It's as though he's caught me in a trance. Just like when I'd been watching him on stage, I'm utterly under his spell. Does he have this effect on all women? I imagine he does. There's something incredibly attractive about such a talent, and it helps that he's also extraordinarily hot.

I remember myself and take a step back, breaking the connection. This is my stepbrother. We might be strangers, but legally, we are related.

I can also sense Reed's gaze on me. What's he thinking? Did he pick up on the spark I felt? I'm such an idiot. I bet any woman who gets within a few feet of Darius Riviera reacts in the same way. It doesn't mean anything.

The truth is, I don't have a huge amount of experience of being around men. Sure, I've been around plenty of high-school boys, but they definitely don't count as being men. Then there are the assholes my mother brought home, but I don't consider them men either—more like slimy, weaselly shitheads. They shared more genetics with pigs than humans, and honestly, that's an insult to pigs.

I remember that Reed was one of those assholes. Except he stuck around for longer than a few weeks—long enough for him and my mother to get married, in fact. I wish I could remember him better, could remember what their relationship was like, or how he treated her. I assume things didn't end well, since he didn't exactly stick around, plus, I note, he doesn't seem affected by the news of her death. But then, why would he be? She was probably nothing more than a fleeting moment in his past. Someone he'd long forgotten.

I think to my brief encounter with Cade. He's more like the men my mother brought home—cocky, smug, thinks the world owes him. I wonder where he is now. With the girl he'd tried to pick up before the show? I remember what he'd said about his cock being pierced. Was that true? The thought makes me feel all hot and flustered. Then I remember what he'd said about sharing with his brother. Did they really do that, or had it just been said for my benefit, to shock me?

The image of being sandwiched between Cade's and Darius's big, hard, naked bodies flashes into my head, and I quickly push it away. I don't know where that came from, and I vow to myself to not allow myself to think that way again. It isn't even just that they're my stepbrothers. It's that any girl with half a brain cell can see these men would only want women around for one thing. Cade probably doesn't even know how to spell the word respect.

"Are you coming with us back to the hotel?" Reed asks him.

Darius purses his lips and shakes his head. "No. Cade will be here shortly. He's got something planned for us."

I wonder if that something has anything to do with the girl in the short silver dress. A thread of bright green jealousy winds through me. Will she be the one who gets to be sandwiched between the two brothers? Will she have Darius's knowledgeable hands all over her body, and get to experience Cade's pierced cock?

"We're flying out to Montreal first thing," Reed says. "We need to be ready in the hotel lobby by seven. Got it?"

This is news to me. "Umm...am I coming?"

I don't know what I'll do with myself otherwise. Maybe he'll let me go back to my trailer? But even as the thought occurs to me, the image of my mother sitting dead on the toilet flashes into my head, and I feel like I never want to see the place again.

Reed shoots me a curious glance. "Of course you're coming."

"But I don't have a passport."

"Don't worry about that. I have my connections. You'll have an emergency passport by the morning."

"Oh, right." I wonder who his connections are to get a passport that fast. I guess with enough money and fame behind you, you can achieve just about anything. I've also never been on a plane before, but I don't tell him that. I don't want to appear inexperienced or childish in front of him, and my lack of experience with travel or just the world outside of my small corner of Los Angeles makes me feel both.

We leave Darius in his dressing room and exit the concert hall. The driver is waiting for us, and he takes us back to the hotel.

Reed walks me up to my room, and we stop outside of my door.

"Are you going to be okay?" he asks. "I mean, after your mom...and it being your first night alone..."

I raise my eyebrows. "You're not offering to stay with me, are you?"

He shoves his hands in his pockets and steps away, a frown

furrowing his brow. "No, of course not. That would be completely inappropriate."

"Yes, it would."

Yet there is a part of me that wishes he would stay. I don't really want to be alone, and I don't mean that in an inappropriate way either. Just that it would be nice to sit with someone. To know there was another beating heart in the room.

"If you need anything, call down to the lobby. I'll be back in the morning for us to leave for the airport together. Make sure you have everything packed."

I'm about to tell him that I don't have anything *to* pack, but then I remember the personal shopper woman and all the clothes she brought. I assume I'll also be able to take the toiletries from the bathroom. I might even pinch a towel. I figure I need it more than the hotel does. If the hotel notices it missing, I assume they'll either add it to the room or just ignore it.

"Okay, well, night, Laney."

"Night, Reed," I say and let myself into the room.

I'm grateful to be out of the emerald dress and into a pair of sweats and a t-shirt. I scrub the makeup off my face and brush my teeth with the toothbrush the hotel has provided.

I'm utterly exhausted, but my mind is racing. It darts toward memories of my mother, and tears threaten once more, so I force myself to think of more interesting things, such as my two new stepbrothers. What are they up to right now? Having the time of their lives, I bet.

The bed is the most comfortable thing I've ever slept on, but even surrounded by feather pillows and one thousand thread count sheets, I know sleep won't be easy to find.

7
REED

THE SUN IS BARELY over the horizon, but I'm already hovering outside of Laney's hotel room door, wondering if she's awake yet.

I've already made sure both the boys made it back to their rooms last night, though I suspect neither of them was alone. That's fine by me. They're adults and, as long as they're safe, they can bring back whomever they like.

I can't get any sense of movement from inside Laney's room, though. I hope she's already awake, and I'm not going to have to haul her out of bed. My mind briefly flits to picturing what she'd slept in, and I force the image away. I can't let myself think of her like that. She might be almost eighteen, but she's my responsibility. I probably look like an old man to her, though when I look in the mirror, I don't feel like I look any different than how I was in my twenties or thirties. Forty, fuck, how did that happen? With two grown sons, too.

The hotel room door suddenly swings open to reveal Laney standing there, a roller-suitcase in one hand, a purse in the other.

They're all things I asked the personal shopper to provide for my newly reacquainted stepdaughter.

"Ready?" she asks.

I blink in surprise. "Yeah, sure. I was going to ask you that."

She half lifts the suitcase. "Thanks for all this. I'll pay you back...someday."

I flap a hand at her. "It's the least I can do."

She gives me a strange look that I can't quite read. Does she agree? After all, it's not as though I gave her mother a cent toward raising her. I had my reasons for that—and those reasons weren't that Laney was never really my child—but I still can't escape the twinge of guilt that goes through me.

"Where are Cade and Darius?" she asks.

"They'll meet us down by the car."

I check my watch. We need to make a move.

The hotel room door swings shut behind her. I catch a glimpse of the ruffled bedsheets and quickly turn my head. I don't want to think about Laney half naked in bed either.

She's casually dressed this morning in ripped blue jeans and a cropped sleeved white tee. The white sneakers she'd been wearing yesterday are on her feet. Her hair is loose and hanging down her back.

I hope Cade and Darius aren't going to give her any shit. I'll have to jump on them hard if they even try. Maybe she should have gone to live with a foster family, or even a friend, but then she hasn't mentioned having any of those.

When we get down to the lobby and step out into the bright sunshine, I discover both the boys are standing beside the car. Darius is by the passenger door, his forearm resting on the roof, as he speaks to Cade across it. Cade has the rear door open, and he senses us coming, and looks past Darius toward us.

"Come on, old man," he says. "You're going to make us late."

He knows full well that we're not going to be late, but I

always try to keep everyone on track, so it's just his way of ribbing me.

Neither of them says good morning to Laney, and I sense her pressing in closer to me. A wave of protectiveness rises inside me. I guess it's better that they ignore her than they give her shit for me bringing her along. I can't imagine either of them particularly wants a little sister hanging around, cramping their style.

The driver appears, straightening his suit, and taking the bags off our hands to put in the trunk. Laney offers him a smile of thanks, and I tip him.

"Make sure we get to the airport on time."

He nods. "I'll do my best."

There will be five of us in the car, and since Darius is up front, and Cade and I both have to sit in the back, it makes sense that Laney sits between us. The boys have both got my height, and we're all well over six feet tall. Laney isn't petite for a girl but she's still substantially shorter. I do wonder about the length of her legs, and immediately snatch my thoughts away from them again.

We squash into the back seat together. Darius climbs in the front, but he still hasn't said a word—not that it's unusual for him. I'm aware of how closely squashed in Cade and I are to Laney, but there's not much I can do about that. She pins her knees together and folds her arms in her lap and stares straight ahead.

The driver starts the engine, and we pull away from the hotel and merge into the city traffic.

Laney frowns as we leave Los Angeles behind us and head north, toward the San Fernando Valley.

"Aren't we going to LAX?" she asks.

"We're not flying commercial," Cade tells her. "Private planes all the way for us, baby."

She blinks those big eyes at him. "I've never even been on a plane, never mind a private one."

"Then you're in for a treat."

It takes about an hour for us to reach the private airport. No one speaks much. Everyone scrolls through their phones or stares out of the window. I can't ignore the fact that the atmosphere is different with Laney in the car. Normally, the boys would be teasing each other or chatting about who they were with last night. I'm grateful to them for keeping those particular details to themselves, but I hope Laney doesn't think we're all unsociable.

I'm not sure why I care about what Laney thinks. In a little over a week from now, she can walk away from us all without a backward glance. What is it I'm even hoping to get from this next week? Am I simply trying to sate some deeply buried guilt about leaving her and her mother? I'd be lying if I said I'd felt guilty all these years. The truth is, I've barely thought about either of them. I had my hands full with Cade and Darius. But yeah, seeing that Laney had been living in those shitty conditions all these years does make me feel bad.

We arrive at the airport, and the driver hands us our bags. Though we're always on the road, we still try to travel light. If there's anything we need at a certain location, we just send someone out to buy it for us. A good hotel will make sure its highest paying guests have everything they need, no matter what.

As we walk toward the small terminal, a phone's ringtone chimes out. It's not mine, so I glance at the others. Cade whips his phone out of his pocket and checks the screen. Twin lines of concern appear between his brows and his tongue darts out and flicks across his lower lip. For a moment, I don't think he's going to answer it, but then he takes several steps away from the rest of us and presses the phone to his ear.

He speaks in low tones, quiet enough to be heard but not understood, at least by me. My son seems troubled, but that's not exactly unusual for him. My eldest son has always lived as though a black cloud is following him. He's been this way ever since I've known him. He carries the weight of the world on his shoulders.

Sometimes, I wonder if he was like this before his mother died or if this is the effect of losing his most loved parent. Of course, if I'd been in his life before his mother got sick, then maybe I'd remember. We were together long enough for Cade to be born, and for her to get pregnant with Darius, but I left shortly after. I never witnessed the birth of my youngest son. Maybe I should be able to remember Cade's personality from when he was a baby and toddler, but the truth is that I have very few memories from back then. I was always high on something, wasted on whatever booze and drugs I could get my hands on. So, I have no idea if this is just my son's personality or if it's the cruelty of the world that has made him this way.

I recognize myself in him from when I was younger—more so than I do Darius, though I catch flashes occasionally. The rage Cade uses as his defense against the world is familiar. Mine came from having a father who, when I did something wrong, sent me out into the yard to pick which stick he was going to beat me with. One time, he took it too far, and I literally thought he was going to kill me.

I don't know who Cade is talking to, but whatever it's about, it's serious. I recognize the tension in his shoulders, the way he reaches up with his other hand and rubs at the knots in his neck.

He glances over his shoulder and takes a few more steps away, putting even more distance between him and us. A ripple of worry goes through me for my eldest son.

What are you up to, Cade?

"Let's go, Cade," I call to him. "We need to get on this plane."

He lifts a hand to acknowledge he's heard me and then ends his call and rejoins us.

"Everything okay?" I ask him.

He scowls. "We getting on this plane or what?"

It hasn't escaped my notice that he hasn't exactly answered me.

We go through what security checks are needed. Each of us only has carryon bags—though Darius has both a bag and his violin case—so it's not like we need to put anything in the hold. A pretty flight attendant in her twenties rushes forward to help with the bags. She goes to Darius first, and he hands her his bag, but keeps hold of his violin. This doesn't surprise me. He's never far from his instrument and certainly wouldn't trust it in the hands of a stranger.

One by one, we climb on board.

I watch Laney's expression as she takes in the luxury of the plane—the individual, deep leather seats, with their separate tables with television screens that rise from inside them when needed. She's never been on a plane before, and it occurs to me that if she ever gets a commercial flight and has to travel economy, she's going to be deeply disappointed.

"Where should I sit?" she asks.

Darius always takes the seat closest to the door. It makes sense for him not to have to find his way up and down a plane aisle, though he is perfectly capable.

I nod to a seat across the aisle. "There is fine."

She nods. The flight attendant takes her bag and puts it into the overhead locker. Laney slips into the seat by the window and lets out a sigh of pleasure.

I watch her, and, just like when I saw her for the first time at her trailer, I'm struck by her beauty. It's like a physical blow, winding me. I see how she holds herself, like she's created a brittle shell around her exterior that's intended to protect her. There have been glimpses, though, where she's forgotten about that tough exterior. I saw it when she heard Darius play for the first time and tears had slipped down her cheeks. I'd even seen a hint of the real her when she'd opened the hotel room door and I'd been standing there in my tux. They were just moments, tiny snippets, but I was sure there was a vulnerable, emotional girl somewhere beneath it.

Vulnerable. I had to remember that. Just because she looks like a grown woman doesn't mean she is one, and I need to remember she's also just lost her mom.

I have to protect her. Even if that means protecting her from my two sons.

Even if that means protecting her from myself.

8

laney

THE PLANE TAKES off with a rush of power and noise, followed by sudden weightlessness. I grip the armrests of my seat and squeeze my eyes shut until the aircraft finally levels out.

Reed has chosen to sit beside me, while both Cade and Darius have selected seats on their own aisles, both positioned by the windows. As soon as the seatbelt light goes out, they all unbuckle and settle into the flight. I have no idea how they can be so chill this high off the ground, but they don't seem bothered at all. I force myself to breathe and try to emulate them.

Within minutes, the flight attendant is moving between us, presenting us with refreshments.

It's still breakfast time, so while we're offered champagne—which once more Reed turns down—we're also served freshly squeezed orange juice, coffee, and canapes of smoked salmon and a lightly poached quail's egg on something called blinis, which is basically just a tiny pancake. It's delicious, though, whatever it's called. I wonder how the men are getting on with such miniature food options. The three of them look like they could devour a whole pig between them. I can't imagine they're satisfied with the tiny offerings, but perhaps they ate before we left.

I take my time with the food, savoring each treat. Once we've worked our way through the appetizer course, sweet pastries and more coffee is served. It's like being at a fine-dining restaurant—not that I have any experience of that.

The meal is drawn out, but I love every minute of it, and am surprised to realize we're already a couple of hours into the flight. I've been distracted, and it's gone far quicker than I'd anticipated.

"Excuse me," Reed says, once the refreshments have been cleared away. He gets to his feet and makes his way to the rear of the plane, I assume to use the bathrooms.

I turn to face the window again. All I can see is cloud far below. I try not to think about how high up we are.

Movement comes beside me, and I glance toward it, expecting to find Reed has returned, but instead, it's Cade who's sinking his huge body into the seat. He tosses his phone onto the table in front of him.

"Oh," I say. "Hi."

He doesn't smile. "Thought I'd see how you're enjoying it."

"Enjoying it?" I assume he means the flight. "It's good, I guess. I mean, I've never been on a plane before so it's not as though I have anything to compare it to." I'm speaking too fast and waffling a little, but he makes me nervous. His bicep is huge, and my gaze runs over the multitude of tattoos covering his skin —a rose, a skull, a raven's wing. I feel like I'm being crowded out, compressed against the wall of the plane.

He picks up a napkin and folds it in half. "I didn't mean the flight. I'm asking how you're enjoying leeching off my family's money."

My jaw drops. "I'm sorry?"

"You heard me. This was your plan all along, wasn't it?

Getting your foot in the door. I bet it's a damn sight better than living in a trailer."

I speak slowly to ensure he understands me. "I didn't coordinate any of this. I'm here because your father married my mother when I was barely out of diapers, and now my mother is dead. It's not some crazy plan I hatched up."

"It's pretty convenient, though, isn't it? You certainly landed on your feet."

I can hardly believe this is happening. I look around, hoping for backup. But Reed's nowhere to be seen, and Darius is sitting with a pair of noise cancelling headphones on, most likely listening to music. I'm not sure he'd help me, anyway. For all I know, he shares the same sentiments as his brother.

"I don't want your family's money," I lie.

He curls his lip at me, his nostrils flaring. "Yeah, right. You're like one of those birds who take up residence in another bird's nest to get the parents to feed it. What are they called?" He thinks for a minute then jabs a finger in my direction. "A cuckoo. You're like a fucking cuckoo chick."

"Actually," I say, slowly as though I think he's stupid—which I kind of do, "the cuckoo chick is put in the nest by its parents while it's still just an egg, so it has no idea that the parents feeding it aren't its real parents. It's not the bird's fault. But then, thinking about it, I believe the chick also kills the real offspring of the stand-in parents, so maybe you should watch your back."

He snorts laughter. "Like I'm going to be afraid of you. You look like you could blow away in a high wind."

"Sometimes the smallest things are the deadliest. After all, the mosquito has killed half the people who have ever lived."

He stares at me like he's trying to figure out if I've made this up. I haven't. Documentary shows are my jam. They're how I wound down after a long night at work, knowing I needed to sleep to get up for school the next day.

"You're fucking weird," he tells me.

I press my lips together and hold his gaze. "So?" I glance down at the back of his phone case. "I'm not the grown man with a cartoon character on the back of his phone."

The picture is of a woman in a red dress, with an impossibly tiny waist, and her hair hanging over one eye.

"What?" he says. "That's Jessica Rabbit."

I arch an eyebrow. "Jessica *Rabbit*?"

He shrugs. "She's hot."

"It's a cartoon character," I repeat slowly.

"Still hot. And besides, that movie is a classic."

A figure appears in the aisle on the other side of Cade.

"Everything all right here?"

I wilt with relief that Reed is back. I wonder if I should tell him what Cade has just said, but I don't want to be the one to stir the shit. I guess I can't really blame Cade for being suspicious of me or for protecting his brother's fortunes. The truth is, I *do* feel like Reed owes me.

I flash Reed a smile. "All good. Cade and I were just catching up, weren't we, Cade?"

He smiles right back, but it doesn't reach his eyes. "Sure. We were just getting to know each other."

Reed gestures toward Cade's empty seat. "I can sit over there, if you want?"

That's the last thing I want. "No, it's fine. We're done, aren't we, Cade?"

He nods and gets to his feet. I suddenly feel like I'm able to breathe again.

I sit back and close my eyes, a part of me wishing I'd chosen to go with a foster family. My thudding heart gradually slows as the adrenaline caused by the confrontation with Cade ebbs away. I didn't sleep well last night, so I take the opportunity to doze.

I sleep deeper than I'd anticipated.

I don't know how much time has passed when the aircraft suddenly drops like a stone, jerking me from my dreams.

I gasp, instantly wide awake, and grip at the armrests again. I turn to Reed. "What was that?"

"Nothing to worry about. Just a bit of tur—"

His words are cut off as another drop leaves our stomachs way above us.

A male voice comes over the intercom. "Ladies and gentlemen, this is your pilot speaking. Due to weather conditions, we request you remain in your seat with your seatbelts on."

Anxiously, I glance out of the window again. A fog has come in—or maybe it's just white cloud—but either way, I can't see anything. It's a strange sensation, a cross between being cocooned and feeling claustrophobic. I try not to think too hard about how high above the ground we are. I'm pretty sure small planes like this one don't fly at the sort of altitudes commercial aircraft do, but it's still plenty high enough for me.

"How long was I asleep?" I ask Reed.

"I'm not sure. A couple of hours, maybe more."

The flight attendant moves up the aisle, checking our seatbelts. She seems a little unsteady on her feet and has to grip the backs of our chairs as the plane bumps again.

It drops out of the sky, sending the poor woman flying.

She lands in Cade's lap.

"Hey, darlin'," he drawls with a salacious grin.

She scrambles back to her feet.

"Sorry," she says, flustered. "Sorry. I'd better—" She motions to the back of the plane where her fold down seat is located.

My stomach churns with nerves. Is this normal?

The pilot's voice comes over the intercom again. "Sorry, folks. We seem to have some issues with some of the computer readings giving us an incorrect altitude, and the poor visibility isn't helping. We'll have things under control shortly."

"Incorrect altitude," I say to Reed in alarm. "Doesn't that mean he doesn't know how high we're flying?"

Is that why it's so bumpy? Because we're caught in some weather system close to the ground? Or have we gone the other way and we're too high? If the pilot doesn't know where we are, what's going to stop him crashing with another plane, or flying into the side of a mountain?

"I'm sure it's fine," he reassures me, but I'm not buying it.

My chest is suddenly tight, my palms sweaty. I want nothing more than to get off this damned aircraft, but I'm trapped. I reach out and grab Reed's forearm, appreciating how strong and solid it feels beneath my fingers.

As far as my first experience of flying goes, I can't say I'm enjoying it. Even with the comfortable leather seats and the posh food, I'd still much rather have both feet on the ground.

I look out of the window, hoping to see something that will reassure me, but there's nothing but white outside.

The pilot's voice comes over the intercom again. "I'm sorry, everyone, but we're going to need to make an emergency landing. Please ensure your seatbelts are secure and prepare to take the emergency brace position."

"What?" I gasp.

I turn to Reed, but his expression is rigid with worry and does nothing to reassure me. "Better do as he says."

No, no, no. This can't be happening. I feel like I'm stuck in a movie, or in a bad dream. Planes don't crash anymore, do they? Maybe not big airliners, but small private ones like this? The small ones probably crashed all the time.

My heart races and tears of terror prick my eyes. Do people

survive plane crashes? It seems highly unlikely. All the safety information we'd been given flies out of my head. The men all look terrified, too, and the flight attendant has strapped herself into the fold down seat at the back. An alarm is sounding somewhere at the front.

The nose of the plane suddenly tilts downward, and we're all thrown forward, only our seatbelts holding us into our seats.

I can't help myself; I let out a scream. My hold on Reed's arm moves to his hand, so we link fingers tightly. The plane is moving too fast, at too steep an angle to make a safe landing, and I have no idea if we're anywhere near a runway, or even an airport, for that matter.

I don't want to die. I barely feel like I've had the chance to live yet.

To my right comes an enormous bang, like we've struck something, and I'm thrown to the side, my head cracking against the wall of the aircraft.

I don't even have time to think about what's happened before nothingness claims me.

9
DARIUS

I OPEN my eyes to darkness, but there's nothing unusual in that.

What is unusual is that I have absolutely no idea where I am.

I normally have my exact location charted in my head. Though my eyes might not work, my brain visualizes perfectly. In every hotel room, I have the position of every item mentally marked down. In each new location, I learn the number of paces it takes to get from one side of the room the other, the number of paces it takes for me to reach the bed from the door, and again to the bathroom. It helps that I have my father and brother to ensure the staff know exactly where each item in the room needs to be placed, from the toiletries in the bathroom, to the remote control for the television, to the complimentary bottle of water.

But right in this moment, I have no idea where I am.

I catch a whiff of something in the air—pungent and bitter— and then I become aware of the sound. It takes me a minute to place it, the roar like being underwater, but then it dawns on me that it's something burning. The growl I'm hearing is that of a huge fire.

The moments before I blacked out suddenly hit me, and it all comes back to me.

Fuck. The plane went down. I remember Laney and the flight attendant screaming, and the yells of alarm from the pilots, and my father and brother. I remember being violently shaken, and things flying around me, and the entire plane vibrating.

After that…nothing.

I push myself to sitting and wince. Everything hurts. I test my limbs, opening and closing my fists, moving my toes. Everything appears to still be working.

"Cade?" I manage to croak. "Dad?"

Heat hits my face, and I remember the fire. How far away is it? I picture my family lying unconscious, about to be swallowed by flames. I have to get them out of here.

I force myself to remain calm, though I've never been so close to losing my shit in my life—even including the day I learned I'd lost my sight—and try to recall my position. Am I still inside the plane? Am I even still in my seat? I buckled up the moment it seemed like things were going wrong. I don't know if the seat has broken from the plane. Is the plane even still in one piece?

I remember the girl as well. Fuck. That adds an extra layer of complication to things. My father and brother can take care of themselves, but some seventeen-year-old who probably expects the world to revolve around her, and that we should all be taking care of her, is going to be an issue.

She might be dead.

They all might be dead.

I don't want to think about what that might mean for me. Alone, in a plane wreckage. Where were we when the plane went down? I'm not sure if we crossed the Canadian border yet, though we'd left Los Angeles behind us hours ago.

Movement comes to my left, followed by a volley of coughing. It's male.

"Dad?" I call out. "Cade?"

"Darius?"

Thank God. It's my father.

"Are you okay? I ask. "Are you hurt?"

"I—I'm not sure." There's a pause while he checks himself over, then he says, "Jesus, Laney."

"Is she alive?"

"I—I think so."

Should I be disappointed? I don't know how I feel.

"What about Cade?" I ask instead.

"He's bleeding and still unconscious."

"What about the crew?"

"I don't know. The plane has broken into three pieces. The front, where the pilots are, is on fire. The back is just…gone."

The back where the flight attendant had strapped herself into her seat.

Holy fuck.

"We need to get out of here," I say. "The fire might spread."

A feminine groan comes from my father's direction.

"Laney?" he says. "Are you okay?"

It's a fucking miracle we're not all dead.

"What happened?" Laney asks.

"We crashed," he tells her.

"Oh, my God." She sounds on the verge of tears, but that's hardly surprising.

I try to get to my feet, but something pulls me back again. I remember the seatbelt. I feel around for it, hoping it won't be stuck. My fingers find the catch, and I free myself.

"Cade?" I say, edging my way out of my seat and into what remains of the aisle. I have no way of knowing if objects are lying in my path, so I shuffle along, my arms raised to protect my face.

My fingers find my brother's shoulder, and I trace my way up his neck until I located the pulse point. It's slow but steady. I want to believe he's fine, but beneath the acrid tang of smoke, I smell blood.

"Cade? Wake up, bro. The plane went down. We need to get out of here."

I give his shoulder a shake, though I'm worried I might hurt him more. He lets out a groan, and I shake him again.

"Wake up."

His voice is gruff, but I've never been so pleased to hear it. "What the—"

I sense the moment he comes around fully and realizes what has happened. My hand is still on his shoulder, and he stiffens and then sits bolt upright. He lets out a cry of pain.

"Fuck. My fucking leg."

"What's happened?" I ask.

"There's some kind of metal pole…I think it's from the table. It's cut into my calf."

"Can you get it out?"

He needs to. It's not like we can just keep sitting here until help arrives. That might never happen, and from the way the fire is getting louder, I suspect we'll all burn to death if we remain where we are.

"Yeah, I'm going to have to, aren't I?"

He grunts and then lets out a gasp of pain.

"Here," Reed says. "Wrap this around it."

I don't know what my father has given Cade, but I assume it's some kind of tourniquet. There's a rustle, and I can hear Cade grinding his teeth, but then he lets out a breath.

"Okay, done," he says.

The weight of my father's hand rests on my shoulder. "Let's get the fuck out of here."

I wonder how we're going to do that. I don't know if the emergency exit is working, but then I remember Reed's description of how the plane has broken into three pieces and realize we don't need it. If both the front and the back of the aircraft are missing, we'll just be able to climb through the spaces that have been left.

I don't often rely on my father to guide me, but I do now. I have no way of knowing if the seats have shifted or if there's luggage in the way. I take hold of his bicep and follow him. I sense Cade and Laney close by as well, the four of us packed together—safety in numbers.

It feels like forever before we're out of the plane and stepping onto a dirt ground. I can tell by the change in shadows across what little remains of my vision that it's still daylight. My senses are overwhelmed by the stench of burning plastic and metal in the air, and the underlying scent of meat roasting. The fire is a roar, a hungry beast that is engulfing everything.

We put some distance between us and the plane, and I hear Cade drop to the ground beside me.

"Where are we?" I ask.

"I have no idea," Cade says. "All I can see are trees. We crashed right into them."

My father speaks next. "They probably saved our lives, slowing the velocity of the plane. If we'd gone straight into the ground, we'd be dead right now."

Laney's voice shaky. "What about the pilots? Shouldn't we check to see if they're still alive?"

Reed exhales a breath. "There's no way they're still alive, Laney. That part of the plane is burning up."

"Is anyone coming to find us?" She sounds panicky.

"I hope so."

I suddenly think of something. "We should get what we can off the plane, before the fire spreads. We don't know how long we're going to be here."

"Wait. What about our phones?" Laney says. "Is anyone's working? We can call for help."

"Mine was on the table in front of me," I tell her. "I've no idea where it is now."

"We can check inside the plane," she suggests.

I turn toward my father and brother. "What about yours?"

I sense Reed shake his head. "Mine's completely smashed, sorry."

"I have no idea what happened to mine either," Cade says. "I can try searching inside the plane, but it could be anywhere."

I clench my teeth. "Shit."

Reed takes charge. "Let's search inside the plane while we still can, try to find the missing phones, and grab what supplies we might need."

"Do you think we're going to be here for some time?" Laney asks.

He sucks air in over his teeth. "I think it's better that we're prepared."

I turn back toward the plane. Even through the fear and panic, I'd done my best to memorize the steps I'd taken and the position where I'd been sitting. "I'll go."

"No," Reed says. "You stay here with Laney."

One thing I hate is being told what to do. "Cade is hurt. He should stay here with Laney. You and I need to go back in."

My father knows me well enough to understand that I'm not going to back down.

"Okay," he relents, "but there's debris everywhere. I'll have to guide you back to the plane. No arguments."

I don't like the lack of independence, but I don't really have a choice. "Fine."

There's one item I definitely plan to get, and that's my violin. I refuse to see it go up in flames. The mere thought of that happening is enough to stir similar feelings as when I'd thought of either Cade or my father being dead in the crash. It would be a kind of grief for me. Maybe to others it's a mere object, but it's a part of me, and losing it would be like losing an arm or a leg.

Or how I'd felt upon learning I'd never see again.

I sense my father standing in front of me, and I place my

hand on his solid shoulder. Allowing him to guide me, we retrace our steps to the plane. We're lucky it broke apart and that it's the nose that's on fire. Even so, getting closer, I can feel the heat of the flames on my skin. It's bound to spread, so we need to work fast.

With Reed leading the way, we climb onboard. He guides me back to my seat. I hate feeling so helpless, but at least I'm here to help carry the bags.

"You get yours and Cade's stuff," he says. "I'll get mine and Laney's."

It's hard not to be overwhelmed by the heat and noise. My bag and, more importantly, my violin, are in the overhead lockers. I glide my hands across the surfaces, maintaining constant contact.

Smoke catches at the back of my throat, and I cough. I bruised my ribs—or possibly worse—in the crash, and the combination of coughing with this injury has me almost doubled over with pain. I grit my teeth and clench my fists, fighting the urge to cough again. I need to grab what I can and get out of here.

I find Cade's belongings as well and haul the bags onto my shoulder. I'm grateful that I'm big and strong, and carrying all of this isn't an issue. I'd prefer not to have to come back again.

Feeling around, I hope to locate my missing phone, but there's no sign of it. Damn.

I remember the blankets and pillows that were individually wrapped in cellophane and put my hands on those, too. It might be warm right now, especially with the fire blazing, but it'll get cold at night. Since we have no idea how long it will be before we're rescued, if we're out here for any length of time at all, we'll definitely need these blankets with the changing weather.

My father's footsteps come up behind me and he coughs. "I haven't been able to find any phones. How about you?"

I shake my head. "They could be anywhere. They could have

fallen from the plane when it broke apart for all we know."

"True."

I hold up the blankets. "If you see any more of these, grab them. It'll probably get cold later"

"Good thinking. Now, get out of here. The fire's spreading."

I take his shoulder again, and we stumble back out of the plane. Laney is there to meet us, taking a couple of the bags out of our arms. We go back to where we left Cade sitting on the ground.

"If the fire spreads," I tell the others, "we're going to have more to worry about than just being found."

Being caught in the middle of a forest fire will kill us, even if the plane crash didn't.

Laney is crying. I'd overheard what Cade had said to her earlier, about her basically being a gold digger. I'd also heard what she'd said in return. Cade could be an intimidating fucker, but she'd held her own. I think back to when she'd come to my dressing room, relishing for a moment in the memory of her soft skin beneath my fingertips when I'd traced the outline of her face, the scent of her shampoo or body wash, I wasn't sure which, and the gentle heat of her breath between us.

Now, she's trapped out here with the three of us.

I almost feel sorry for her. Stuck with three desperate men. My father introduced her as our stepsister, but it's not like we're actually related. Perhaps she'll be the one who turns to us for comfort and a little escapism? People act differently in dangerous situations than how they would in real life.

Cade is the one we'll have to worry the most about. He's not exactly known for his self-control. Plus, he's been acting strangely lately. It hasn't escaped my notice that he's claimed to be with me when he's been somewhere else. Clearly, he's hiding something from our father.

I wonder if it's a woman, but it's not like Cade to be coy about something like that.

10
laney

I CAN'T BELIEVE this is happening.

I'm shaking all over and my teeth are chattering, and I know it's from the shock. I've got a gash on my forehead and my neck is aching, but otherwise I don't think I'm injured. It's incredible the four of us have managed to walk away from this, though I can't say the same for the two pilots or the flight attendant. I'm doing my best not to look at the front of the plane, and I don't know where the back has ended up. It must have broken off somewhere in the air before we hit the ground.

A black plume of smoke billows into the sky. As much as I hate that the plane is burning, it'll definitely tell people where we are. Anyone searching for us is bound to see it for miles around.

That's if there is anyone for miles around.

I can only assume the reason we're not all dead is because we were already flying low when the pilot realized the computer was giving him the wrong altitude. The thick fog we were flying through meant he was unable to see the ground, so when the plane did go down, we were already close. That the plane broke into pieces meant the front of the plane—the part we were no longer attached to—took all the impact.

"The fire and smoke are bound to catch someone's attention, if there is anyone nearby," Reed says, echoing my thoughts, "but we're going to need to put some distance between ourselves and the plane."

Cade's brow furrows. "You mean leave the plane?"

I look around at the others. "What if someone does come looking for us and they find the plane all burned up and we're not here? They won't know there were any survivors, or to come keep searching for us."

I guess once they get a team out here to try to investigate what went wrong to bring the plane down, their forensics will figure out that there were only three bodies onboard, but it might be too late for us by then.

Reed seems to consider this. "We don't need to go far, unless the fire spreads, of course."

"Someone will find us, though, won't they?" My voice is too high pitched, an edge of panic to it. "I mean, aren't planes tracked? Someone will have seen the plane was in trouble and know where to look for us."

"Yes, I'm sure they will," Reed assures me.

Cade stares at him in disbelief. "You're fucking joking, right? Don't you know how planes work? They send off a ping every fifteen minutes or so to let them know of our location. If we were flying at five hundred miles an hour, we're looking at a search area of one hundred and twenty-five miles, and that's even assuming the computer monitors pinpointed our final location correctly. You heard the pilot say the computers weren't working."

"Enough!" Reed snaps. "You're frightening her."

"So fucking what? She should be frightened. She should be fucking terrified. We all should."

"We survived," Reed says. "Let's focus on that. Having a

positive mindset is vital right now. It could make the difference between us getting out of this or not."

Cade rolls his eyes and makes a *tsk* sound with his tongue and teeth.

Not all of us survived, though. I thought I'd already seen enough death after finding my mother, but it seems the universe had more in store. I just pray this will be the last, and our deaths won't be next.

"We need to stay near the plane," I insist. "If we're going to be found, it'll be right here. If we start wandering off into the forest, we could be lost for good."

"But what if we're near a town or city?" Cade says. "We could help ourselves rather than waiting for it to arrive."

"If we're near a town, someone will have seen the plane come down and will have alerted the authorities," I throw back at him.

He lifts his eyebrows. "Are you sure about that? In the fog? No one would have seen a damned thing unless they were right underneath us."

"How far were we from Montreal, anyway?" Darius asks.

Reed shakes his head. "I've no idea, but I think we'd passed Minneapolis. The flight path to Montreal takes us over a whole heap of wilderness from there. We're going to need food and water, and ideally shelter until help shows up."

"What about wildlife? Aren't there bears out here, and mountain lions, too? What if they smell the blood from—" I can't bring myself to say it.

He glances toward the crash site. "The fire will keep anything like that away."

Flames lick across the metal body of the plane. I do my best not to think about the bodies of the pilot and co-pilot inside, how they are roasting. Can I smell them on the air? I don't want to think about it.

What will happen when the fire reaches the middle part of

the plane? Will that go up in flames, too? Or worse? What if it explodes and we're close by?

Maybe Reed is right by suggesting we need to put a little distance between us and the plane.

"We need to get somewhere higher." Reed plants his hands on his hips. "If we're elevated, we might be able to see if there are any towns or cities nearby. I can go, and then I'll report back."

The fog that had at least partially caused the crash has started to lift. All I can see surrounding us are trees.

"We need to stick together," I tell him. "If you go wandering off, you might not find us again."

He points to the plume of black smoke that continues to billow into the air. "I'll find you. If the fog goes, I'll be able to see that from miles around."

"Let me come with you, then." I'm almost begging now.

Is it because I feel safer with Reed? Or is it that I don't want to be left alone with his two sons?

"No, you'll only slow me down. I won't go too far, I promise. It's better if you just wait here. Conserve your energy. We don't know how long we're going to be out here."

"Okay," I say, my voice small.

I'm thankful my bag survived the crash. Though the majority of what's in it didn't even belong to me before the previous night, it at least means I have clean clothes and the toiletries I took from the hotel. It also gives me something to sit on that isn't just the hard ground.

Reed faces me and tilts his head slightly to bring his eyes closer to the level of mine. He's solid and masculine, and I have to fight the urge to fling myself at him and wrap my arms and legs around his body like a little spider monkey and refuse to let go.

He must have sensed this need in me, as he touches my chin.

"I won't be long," he reassures me again. "You'll be fine. Cade and Darius will watch out for you."

I want to tell him what Cade said to me on the plane, that he thinks I'm a cuckoo, a parasite, but I clamp my mouth shut. I'm going to be stuck with these men for God knows how long, and I don't want to stir things.

Reed moves even closer, and I catch my breath. He wraps his arms around me, and I stiffen. Have I ever had a man hold me this way? I try to think. I'd had some of my mother's old boyfriends make a grab for me on the odd occasion, but it never felt anything like this—warm and safe and comforting. I never had time for boys from school. They saw me as haughty and standoffish—untouchable, one of them had said, as though that was supposed to be an insult. But the truth was that I was just too fucking busy taking care of my mother and working to bring money into the house to even think about getting involved with someone.

Reed holds me a little tighter, and he drops his nose against the top of my head. Finally, I allow myself to relax, and I breathe him in. He smells of smoke from the fire, but I don't even mind.

He releases me, and I try not to be disappointed. Then I remind myself that I'm supposed to hate this man. He abandoned me and my mother. He's been wealthy for years, while we'd been struggling, and he hadn't even given us a second thought.

Just because he's tall and handsome and older does not make him some kind of hero or rescuer. If he was that kind of person, he could have saved me years ago.

"You okay, Laney?" He frowns in concern.

I nod, but I don't meet his eye. "Just go."

Behind Reed, Cade is sitting on a tree trunk, his leg elevated on the wood. He's staring right at me. No, not even staring—glaring at me. What the fuck is his problem? Is he worried I'm going to steal his daddy from him? Poor baby.

I can't help glancing over to Darius. He can't see Reed hugging me, but I wonder if he knows. His face is angled toward the trees, the daylight slotting between the trunks. Can he see the contrast of light and shadows?

Reed clears his throat. "Right, I'll be back as quick as I can, okay? Hopefully, I'll bring help with me."

Tears fill my eyes, and I wipe them away and sniff. "Be careful, okay?"

I still don't think this is a good idea. There are wild animals out there, and he doesn't have any way of defending himself. But I know he's not going to listen to me. He looks at me and sees a girl, not a young woman who has been looking after herself most of her life.

He leaves me to go over and say goodbye to his sons. I expect some handshaking and back slapping, but he hugs them both just as tightly as he hugged me.

I allow myself a moment to hope. Maybe Reed will return with help. Or he'll spot a town in the distance that will be close enough for us to walk to. I have to cling to the hope that we will be found.

Reed strides off into the trees, and each of us remaining retreats to our own spaces, allowing the shock and disbelief of what has happened to sink in.

Cade has found a large tree branch, which he's using as a crutch. He has a torn t-shirt wrapped around the injury on his calf, but blood spots have appeared through it. I wonder how much pain he's in. For a moment, I think perhaps that's the reason he's being such a dick—well, that and the fact we've just been in a plane crash and are stranded in the middle of nowhere —but then I remember he was acting that way long before he got hurt.

Darius holds his violin in his hands, but he doesn't play. I'm somewhat glad for that. The thought of his music slipping through the trees while the plane continues to burn would have been so surreal, I'd have worried I'd lose my mind.

His long fingers trace the outline of the instrument, running up the neck and across the top and back down again to follow the curves of its body. I wonder how he feels about it surviving the crash. The way he's touching the instrument is with such tenderness that I can't help thinking he's as much relieved to still have his violin as he is to have his brother and father.

Does it bring him comfort to have it close?

The way he's touching it is as though it's a lover, and he's tracing the outline of her body.

The thought takes me back to the moment in his dressing room where he'd run his fingers over my face, the way he'd stopped at my lower lip and dragged it down slightly, my saliva wetting the tip. He's a strange contrast of pure masculinity and refined tenderness. Sitting out here now, with his long hair hanging loose and his t-shirt torn, his face dirty and bloodied, he looks the epitome of a mountain man. Big and brooding. The one thing that shows he's not is the instrument he's holding so carefully.

An hour passes, and then another.

Cade picks up the bottle of water his brother rescued from the plane and lifts it to his lips. I watch his tattooed throat work as he drinks deeply. He lowers it again and screws the lid back on without offering any to either me or his brother.

"Don't you think you should make that last?" I say. "We don't know how long we're going to be out here."

He shrugs. "There's no point in saving it. A few extra mouthfuls of water won't make the difference between us living or dying."

"You could at least offer it around. Maybe Darius is thirsty."

Cade glances over his shoulder at his brother. "He'll tell me if he's thirsty. He doesn't need to use all this passive aggressive, manipulative bullshit."

Is he talking about me?

"How am I being passive aggressive and manipulative?"

"Pulling out the poor little me act with Reed. You think he's the fatherly type? That he's going to take care of you? I guarantee he's already thought about getting in your panties."

I burn up with humiliation. "Shut the fuck up."

He gets to his feet, using the stick as a prop. "You gonna make me?"

I glance over to his brother, hoping Darius will step in, but he just seems to be listening intently, perhaps using our fight as entertainment or a distraction.

Cade takes a step closer. "I mean, you're stuck out here with three men who have nothing else to do. You might as well make yourself useful."

I glare at him in dismay. What's he expecting of me? That I'm going to spread my legs and let them pass me between them to keep them entertained?

He's close enough now to touch me, and he runs his finger down the side of my cheek, leaving a sensitive trail in its place.

"I see you, Laney," he growls. "I know what kind of person you are. You're a fucking martyr, and you want everyone to feel sorry for you. So life handed you a bag of shit? So what? Plenty of people have tough lives—they don't go around blaming everyone else for it."

"I don't blame everyone else, and I'm not a fucking martyr."

"Really? You sure about that?"

I knock his hand away. "What right do you have to criticize me? Like you're fucking perfect or something?"

"Leave her be, Cade," Darius finally says. "You're not helping the situation."

"You wouldn't say that if you could see her." His brother smirks. "She's a little on the skinny side for my liking, but she's still hot. You got a feel of her, didn't you? Ran your hands over her face so you know what she looks like. Maybe she should let you do the same for her body. Small tits, but any more than a handful is a waste, right?"

"Fuck off," I tell him.

I don't want to cry, but I'm mad and I'm frightened. Where is Reed? What if I end up stuck out here with Cade and Darius? That's almost more terrifying than being alone.

Yes, alone. That's what I need to be right now. I don't want to be anywhere near that bastard.

I turn, away from the plane and both the men, and head toward the tree line.

"Where are you going?" Cade shouts after me.

I ignore him and keep walking. I won't go far—I'm not so stupid that I'll risk losing sight of the plane—but I simply don't want to be around him right now. When I feel I've put enough distance between us, my legs give way beneath me, and I crumble to the forest floor. I put my face in my hands and give way to the tears that have been building ever since Reed left.

I cry for the loss of my mother, for the deaths of the two men and woman in the crash, for fear for myself.

I cry until I feel like I can't breathe.

The last of my energy ebbs from my body, and I take a couple of hiccuppy breaths and wipe my eyes. I need to go back. It's not safe for me to be in the middle of nowhere, all alone. Besides, Reed might be back by now.

I force myself to my feet and try to remember which way I need to go. All I can see is tree after tree. I'd thought it would be easy to pinpoint the location of the plane, but the foliage hides everything.

A shot of panic goes through me. Oh, God. What if I start walking and I can't find my way back again? What if I'm heading in completely the wrong direction, putting more distance between myself and the others. I've heard of people walking in circles when they get lost in the woods, unable to orient themselves.

I spin around, fighting my building terror, and collide with a big, solid chest. For the briefest of moments, I think it's Cade, but then I realize it's Darius.

"How did you find me?" I gasp.

"I followed the sound of you crying."

"Oh."

I'd thought I was far enough away that neither of them had heard me. I exhale a slow, shaky breath, and blink away fresh tears. I'm so relieved to see him, but I don't want him to know that.

He places his hand to the side of my face and wipes a fresh tear away with his thumb.

I sniff. "This must be even more frightening for you, not being able to see."

"We're all frightened in our own way. Cade is injured, and that scares him. That's why he said those things to you. It stops him worrying about himself."

"Cade said some pretty shitty things to me on the plane, too, long before the plane crashed."

"He's protecting his family. That's his job. Cade's sense of worth comes from protecting us, and it unhinges him when he's the one who needs helping."

"Aren't *I* supposed to be family?"

He seems to consider this for a moment. "Family in Cade's mind has nothing to do with shared surnames or marriages that took place half a lifetime ago. It's about loyalty."

I press my lips together. "How can I be loyal to someone I didn't even know existed a couple of days ago?"

"I'm just saying you need to bide your time with him. He'll come around."

Do we even have that kind of time?

"Come on," Darius says. "Let's go back."

I'm surprised that he's now guiding me, but he seems to know where he's going a hell of a lot more than I do. I'm also amazed at how close I am to the crash site when I'd believed I was lost. Darius moves slowly and cautiously, one hand in front of him to protect his face, but he leads us straight there.

Cade isn't alone. His father is standing with him.

Reed has made it back to us.

11
CADE

THANK FUCK REED IS BACK.

Darius and Laney are making their way through the trees as well, so Darius clearly found her. At least with our father here, he acts like a buffer between us all.

I don't know what it is about Laney that winds me up so fucking badly, but something about her just sets me off. I have no idea how I'm supposed to act around her. Most women are easy enough to read. Generally, if they're hot, I'll simply be aiming to get in their panties. But Laney is my stepsister—apparently—and though she is undoubtably hot, she's also out of bounds. She's also not yet eighteen, and though there's only a few years between us, that she's underage is also no-go territory.

"How did it go?" I ask Reed, hoping he won't ask why Laney and Darius weren't with me. "Did you see anything?"

"I managed to hike to a higher point," he says, "a ridge that gave a view over the tops of the trees and into the distance. There aren't any towns anywhere nearby, but I think I saw something. I'm not sure what, though. It looked like the sun reflecting off glass, and if there's glass, it means there's something manmade."

The fog has cleared since we've been here, or else he wouldn't have been able to see anything.

"How far away?" Darius asks.

Reed rubs his hand across his lips as he thinks. "Hard to tell. Maybe ten miles."

Darius nods with certainty. "We can make that."

Laney's gaze darts between us, concern written all over her pretty face. "But it'll mean leaving the plane behind. Is that a good idea? Any rescuers won't know where to find us."

"They'll see that our bodies aren't in the plane and that our bags are missing," Reed says. "They'll keep looking."

It would be so much easier if she wasn't here. I hate the way my father is fawning all over her, treating her like some precious little princess. He hasn't even mentioned her name over the past fourteen years, and now, all of a sudden, she's important? I wonder if he'd be acting this way if she wasn't all long limbs and big blue eyes. He's such a fucking hypocrite.

I guess he's not the only one.

I slip my hand into my pocket and touch smooth metal and glass. A pulse of guilt goes through me, but I keep my mouth shut.

I don't want to die out here, in the wilderness, but I don't want to die in regular society either. The way things have been going lately, either possibility is on the table. I think of my father and brother, and of this new stepsister I've suddenly been lumbered with. Don't they deserve to live?

My gut twists. Fuck. What a fucking mess.

We will live. Someone will find us. All this is doing is buying a little time. It might even be good for us—give us a little bonding time away from the bright lights and expensive hotels of the city. We're getting back to nature.

I almost laugh at myself. I doubt the others will see it that way. But I feel like I've been handed a gift of sorts, and even though none of us would have chosen for this to have happened, or for the pilots to have died, it is what it is.

Laney's expression is still creased with worry. "That's if they even send out a search team for us. We don't even know that anyone is looking."

"People are going to miss us." I point in my brother's direction. "That's Darius fucking Riviera. He's supposed to be playing to sold out concert halls for the next five nights. People are going to notice when he doesn't show up, and they'll start to ask questions. Hell, someone is going to notice that our plane fell out of the fucking sky and they'll send help. Yes, it might be a big search area, but they'll put out a big search team. It'll be all over the news. They're not just going to let us die out here."

"They might think we're already dead," Darius says. "We probably should be. People don't normally survive those kinds of crashes."

I bristle. "Yeah, well, when they find us, they'll learn that we did, won't they?"

"That's *if* they find us," Laney says.

I note that her eyes are rimmed with red. She's clearly been crying. A little bubble of something swells in my chest, and it's not sympathy. What is that feeling? Power?

Reed shoves his hands in his pockets. "What are we going to do, then? Wait for help to come, or see if we can find help for ourselves?"

I don't like the idea of just waiting around. I prefer action.

I give voice to my thoughts. "How long would we end up sitting here, waiting, only for no one to come? Right now, we're in decent physical shape to be able to hike."

Reed jerks his chin down at my calf. "What about your leg?"

"It's painful, but I can manage." I raise the large stick I found. "I can use this as a crutch. Also, we don't have any supplies here. We don't even have much water."

"We *had* water," Laney throws at me, "but you drank it all."

I roll my eyes. "How long do you think a few mouthfuls would have lasted between us all?"

She folds her arms across her chest. "Well, my vote is that we stay near the plane."

Her presence is pissing me off now. "Who the fuck says you even get a vote? What are you even doing here? You're not blood. You're a fucking stranger."

"That's enough, Cade," Reed warns.

"Or what?" I throw my hands out to either side of my body. "I'm just saying that she doesn't get an equal vote, in my opinion. She's not one of us."

Laney flinches.

Reed steps in again. "We'll take a vote, and everyone gets an equal say, got it? We all matter." His gaze passes across us all to make sure we agree. No one says anything. "Good," he continues. "Now, who votes to stay with the plane?"

Only Laney puts up her hand.

"And to see if we can find the place I've seen?"

The three of us men all raise hands.

Reed claps once. "That's decided, then. Let's gather up as much as we can carry, and then we'll go for help."

12
laney

We gather as much as we can carry, including our bags, plus the blankets and small cushions from the plane. More importantly, we bring what water and food we're able to scavenge. I've tossed out one of the pairs of strappy sandals and a couple of the dresses I'll have zero use for out here in order to make space for the more practical items of blankets and water. The lack of water and food is concerning, especially the water part. The day has grown warm, and now we have to hike, which means we'll need the water. My throat is dry from inhaling smoke, and a headache is throbbing behind my eyes. I don't know if it's from when I hit my head, or if it's because of the smoke.

I'm not happy about the decision to hike away from the plane, but I've been outvoted. That we're hiking to some unknown destination with one man with an injured leg, and another who is visually impaired, seems like utter madness to me. There's nothing I can do about it, and I'm not going to stay here alone.

Besides, the plane is still burning. This time tomorrow, there might not be anything to stay near.

Sweat prickles in my hairline and trickles down my spine. I'm losing both fluids and salt, and that isn't a good thing. The annoying whine of an insect buzzes close to my ear, most likely attracted by the sweat, and I flap it away.

"Ready?" Reed asks.

We all nod.

I glance over at Darius. He's put his violin in his backpack and zipped it up around the neck, so the top sticks up over his head. It means his hands are free, and he's going to need them. This whole thing is terrifying, and I don't even have his disability. I remember what Reed told me about how Darius always wants things placed in certain positions so he knows exactly where everything is. It's clearly helped him navigate his way in the world, but that's not going to help him now.

Looking at him, he doesn't seem fazed by the thought of what lies ahead. He stands with his shoulders back, so his t-shirt, damp with sweat, clings to the muscles of his pecs and biceps. There is a determined jut to his jaw, and his chin is lifted. There's no way I'd know he couldn't see unless I'd been told. I hate to think of him tripping and falling, of that pride he carries being stripped away.

"This way," Cade says and heads up the front.

Darius is directly behind him, his hand on his brother's shoulder for guidance, while I'm behind Darius, and Reed brings up the rear.

Though I'm unsure that we're making the right choice, I'm grateful to be leaving the crashed plane and the stink of metal and rubber and bodies burning behind us. It's something I never want to smell again. What lies ahead is incredibly daunting. I'm also thankful I'm wearing my sneakers and not something flimsier.

The hike isn't easy. There is no path, so we literally have to fight our way through the foliage. Cade leads the way, though his limp is obvious. He uses the large stick he'd found partially as a crutch, but also as a tool to thrash as much of a path as he can through the woods. He breaks low hanging branches with his hands and, as he walks, warns us of fallen trunks and large boulders.

At first, I think he's doing it for my benefit, but then it dawns on me that he's directing Darius. Darius is quite literally stepping into his brother's footsteps.

We keep going, one foot after the other. I'm relieved to have Reed behind me. I'd have been worrying about being picked off by some wild animal otherwise. The deepness of his breathing and the crunch of his footsteps reassures me that he's still there. I don't risk turning around to check. If I do, I guarantee that it'll be the time a branch will swing and hit me in the face, or I'll end up tripping over something.

My body is battered and bruised from the plane crash. Every movement hurts, and I don't want to add any more injuries. I'm fearful of spider or snake bites, aware that there's no possibility of treatment way out here.

Time passes, but I have no idea how much. I've entered a kind of trance, just moving forward. We stop to take a drink of the small amount of water we have left and wipe the sweat from our eyes, and then keep going.

Cade draws to a halt, and Darius almost collides with his brother's broad back.

"There's something ahead," Cade calls over his shoulder.

"Is it the thing Reed saw?" I ask.

"How am I supposed to know?" he snaps back at me.

But Reed shakes his head. "I don't think so. It's too close."

My heart thrums with hope. Could this be our rescue? But I can't hear any engines, and we're not on anything like a road. We start walking again, and something bright catches in the sunlight.

We break through the trees and bushes and draw to a halt. I

catch sight of metal and glass, and suck in a breath. Could it be a vehicle of some kind, or dare I hope a building?

"Oh, shit," Cade breathes.

What I'm looking at dawns on me. We've found the tail end of the plane.

I take another couple of tentative steps toward it, and the buzzing of flies and other insects grows louder.

I see why.

In the opening of the tail end, where it was torn from the middle part of the plane, the flight attendant is dead in her seat, still strapped in. A tree branch has punctured her chest, pinning her in place.

"Oh, God."

I cover my face with my hands and turn away. I don't want to look at her, knowing the image of her face will be imprinted on my brain. I don't want it to haunt me when I close my eyes at night. I've already been struggling with the memory of my mother's cooling dead body in my arms, and now I have this to add to it. How much more death will I see before this is all over?

Will I experience my own?

"There might be supplies," Reed says, moving closer to the tail. "Food. Water. They were kept at the rear of the plane."

"They'll be in the section behind her," Cade said.

Reed nods. "I'll check"

I turn back, feeling I should face the plane. It's only sheer luck that it isn't one of us with a tree branch punctured through our chests. The thought makes my breath come quicker, and even though I want to support Reed, I can't do it. I can't watch.

I stumble away to pause at a tree a short distance off. I place my hand to the trunk, the rough bark beneath my palm helping to ground me.

A low voice comes from behind me.

"You okay, Laney?"

Darius has joined me. I don't know how he knew I'd walked away.

"I can hear your breathing," he says by way of an explanation. "It's fast and shallow."

"I-I'm sorry."

"Sometimes," he says, "I'm thankful I can't see certain things. I can imagine it, though."

A tear slips down my cheek, and I sniff. I close my eyes briefly and angle my face away. How can I feel sorry for myself when that poor woman died? I'm the lucky one.

Gentle fingers touch my cheek, and I glance up to find Darius frowning at me. It's strange to know that even though he's facing me, he can't see me, but then his fingers sweep over my face, taking my tears with it, and I realize he's seeing me now, building his image of me in his mind.

"It's okay to cry," he says.

I shake my head, my cheek pressed to his palm. His skin is warm and dry, and emotion swells in my chest. It feels like all I've done is cry. To my surprise, his other arm wraps around my shoulders and he pulls me into him. I find myself pressed against his broad chest, my nose, forehead and lips touching the softness of his t-shirt, the solidness of his pectorals beneath. He holds me tight, and I do my best not to think about our situation.

Finally, he releases me.

"Better?" he asks.

I nod then realize he can't see me. "Yes, I am. Thank you."

I've been held more in the past twenty-four hours than I've been for most of my life. My mother had never been the tactile type, apart from the odd occasion when she'd been happy drunk, and then it had felt more like she'd been hanging off me than holding me with any true affection. But Darius's touch makes my body hum with pleasure, and I crave more. How touch-starved am I?

I'm pathetic.

Reed calls out to us. "You guys are going to need to carry some of this stuff."

Still doing my best to avoid looking at the dead woman, I turn my attention to Reed. He and Cade have thrown anything of use that they found onto the ground. I'm relieved to see several unopened bottles of water, and even a first aid kit.

"These might come in handy," Cade says with a grin. He holds up a handful of miniature bottles of booze—whiskey, champagne, vodka and gin.

"Seriously? You're going to start drinking?" I can't believe him.

"Alcohol is good for cleaning wounds, little Cuckoo," he throws back at me.

I'm not so sure champagne would be much use for that, but I keep my thoughts to myself. The last thing we need is for us to fight.

"What about food?" Darius asks.

Cade huffs out a breath. "Not much substantial, bro. We should have crashed before we had breakfast. There's some snack stuff—olives, nuts, jerky, and crackers—and some cookies and muffins, but not anything that's going to make a decent meal."

"It'll keep us going until we're found, though," Reed interjects. "We'll have to ration it out."

The three men I've ended up stranded with are all well over six feet and have God-knows how many pounds of muscle on them. They're going to take some feeding, and I don't think a few miniature packets of honey-roasted peanuts are going to hit the spot.

It won't matter, as long as we're rescued soon. A rescue team is bound to be searching for us by now. Someone will have realized we haven't landed and will be doing whatever checks it is they do on these small, private planes, charting our route or figuring out where our last signal came from.

"We could stay here," Cade suggests. "We can take the body down and move it away. We can use the tail of the plane for shelter."

"What about the place Reed saw?" I look to my stepfather. "If it's a house, someone might be there. They might be able to contact help for us."

He nods. "I think it's worth a shot. We've come this far."

"Or we could leave Laney and Dax here," Cade suggests, "and you and I go for help."

I fold my arms across my chest. "No way. We're not separating. Don't you watch movies? That never ends well."

Deep down, I'm thinking that I don't want to be left with a dead body nearby. What if a wild animal smells the blood and decides to take us down with it? And while I'm aware that Darius is perfectly capable and will probably hear danger coming long before either Cade or Reed sees it, I still believe in safety in numbers.

"Laney is right," Reed says. "We need to stick together. I wouldn't feel right leaving them with no protection."

"She has me," Darius growls.

He drags his hand through his long hair and plants his hands on his hips. I can't help smiling at him, even though he can't see me. Cade might hate my guts, but it seems his brother doesn't dislike me quite so much. I remember that hug and wish I could repeat it.

Cade relents. "Okay, we stick together, then."

13
REED

I HOPE I haven't made the wrong choice by not leaving Laney and Darius behind at the tail of the plane.

We're on the move again, but already our pace has slowed. Cade does his best to clear a pathway for us, but the forest and undergrowth is thick in places. We're all battered and bruised from the crash. I haven't mentioned to the others that I believe there's a good chance I've fractured a rib, maybe even two. Every breath is painful, but they've all got enough to worry about. Cade's leg means he's walking with a limp. Laney has dried blood in her hairline where she must have hit her head, and Darius has a cut lip and grazes down the side of his face. From the way he's holding his side occasionally, I suspect he's hurt his ribs as well. It's incredible that these are the only injuries we're sporting considering others died in the crash. We've been lucky, and I can only hope that luck holds out.

I'm also praying that the place I saw from the hillside is an actual house and not some kind of mirage or trick of the light. What if I'm leading them deeper and deeper into the forest, and we get to this place only for it to turn out to be nothing? What if we can't find our way back to the plane again?

The responsibility I feel for these three young adults is a heavy weight on my shoulders, and it makes each step harder and harder.

"Are we almost there?" Laney calls out in a singsong voice.

"I hope so," I reply.

She glances over her shoulder to give me a smile. Good. It's important we try to keep our spirits as high as we can, given the situation.

I'm concerned about her and Cade. I'm fully aware that Cade isn't the easiest of people to get along with, but he seems to have taken an instant dislike to her. Is it jealousy? Is that the reason he doesn't want her around? I'd thought it might do him some good to have a younger stepsister around, might soften him up a little, give him someone to look out for other than Darius and himself, but the opposite seems to have happened. He's even spiker than normal. Admittedly, these aren't exactly normal times, but he'd been that way even before the plane had taken off.

If we're going to survive this, we need to pull together. It won't help anyone for us to be fighting among ourselves.

I do acknowledge, however, that I made a mistake by taking Laney in. When social services called and explained the situation, I'd imagined her to be some gawky teenage kid, not this beautiful young woman with heart-stopping, pale blue eyes. She'd have been better off going to a foster home. It would only have been for a week, and at least she'd have been safe. She would never have been on the damned plane.

We stop to drink some water, though I'm concerned about how much we have and how long it's going to last. Water is going to be far more important than food, at least initially. I want to believe we'll be found and rescued in the next twenty-four hours, or the place we're heading to now will contain someone who can call for help or who will have their own supplies, but we can't take that for granted. Assuming we're going to be rescued soon could prove fatal. We need to prepare for the possibility that we won't.

I wonder how much daylight we have left. I don't want us to still be wandering around out here when it gets dark. What if we went in the wrong direction and we've completely missed whatever place I caught sight of?

But finally, the trees head of us thin, and a log cabin appears between the trunks.

"We found it!" Cade calls over his shoulder.

My heart hitches. Thank fuck for that.

"Hello?" Cade yells, picking up his pace. "Is anyone here?"

The minute I get closer, I can see we're out of luck. The windowpanes are still in place—which was what made the cabin visible to me from a distance, but they're cracked and filthy. A wooden porch runs around the outside of the cabin, but the forest is doing its best to claim it back again, creepers winding around the balustrades like snakes around a charmer's arm. The roof still looks like it's in one piece, and a chimney protrudes from between the moss-covered slates. Even though there is clearly no one living here, it will provide shelter, and we might even find some more supplies

"It doesn't look like there's anyone here," Cade says.

Darius draws to a halt. "Is there a vehicle around?"

Cade purses his lips. "Can't see one."

"There must be a road or some kind of trail," Darius says. "How else would whoever owns this place get here?"

I look around. "It's probably a hunter's cabin. They wouldn't live here full time, just use it as a base while they're in the forest."

"That's a good thing, though, right?" Laney's tone is pitched higher with hope. "If people come here, then they might find us."

"Hunting season begins mid-September. We've got a while to wait if that's the case, and we don't even know if this place is still used. It doesn't look as though anyone's been here for some time."

Laney bites her lip. "We should have left a note of some kind back at the plane. We should have told people we were coming here."

"What on?" Cade's tone is cutting. "A piece of paper? Which we could have then left with a burning plane? Sounds sensible."

She shoots him a scowl. "I don't know, but we should have tried something. If rescuers arrive, how will they know where to find us?"

"If rescuers arrive, we'll see helicopters or something flying above the forest. We'll know to go back."

She throws up her hands. "We've been walking for hours. If we just happen to see or hear a helicopter in the distance, do you really think we'll make it back there before they give up and leave again? If the fire has spread to the middle of the plane, it'll burn up any evidence that shows we weren't in the plane when it burned."

Cade stares at her. "Are you stupid? They're not going to just arrive and leave again. A plane went down. People died. There will be a whole investigation around it to find out what happened."

Laney's cheeks flame red, twin spots appearing. Her eyes go glassy, and she blinks several times.

I keep my voice low. "All right, that's enough, Cade."

He spins to me. "Why? Am I wrong?"

"No, but this is a stressful situation, and calling people stupid isn't going to help anyone." I look to the girl. "You okay, Laney?"

Cade makes a tsking sound with his tongue and teeth. "She's the favorite now, is she, Reed? Except you're not exactly looking at her like a daughter, are you?"

I harden my tone. "That's *enough*."

Tossing a beautiful young woman into the wilderness with the three of us, fuck. What had I been thinking?

I hadn't known we were going to end up in a plane crash and stranded away from civilization. I'd thought both Cade and Darius would be out doing their own thing, entertaining themselves with other women, and not paying Laney much attention. Now there are no other women for miles around, and we have no idea when we're going to be rescued. This is already a boiling pot of tension, and it's only going to get worse as the days go by.

The truth is, I don't know if I can fully trust my son.

"Let's go inside and see what we've got to work with," I say, redirecting our attention.

Cade leads the way. He calls out to Darius as he goes. "Fourteen paces, two o'clock, then two steps onto the porch."

Cade has his faults, but he's nothing if not devoted to his younger brother.

He tries the door. "Not locked."

It creaks open, and there's a flurry of dust and dried leaves in its wake. I fully expect that we'll be sharing the cabin with multiple insects, rats, and mice, but then we'd be sharing the forest with far bigger creatures.

Cade disappears inside, closely followed by Darius. Laney throws a glance over her shoulder, and I give her a nod of encouragement. I hope I haven't just delivered the lamb into the lions' den.

The cabin smells musty, but it seems dry and solid enough.

Everything is covered in a fine layer of dust and dirt. I glance over to Laney to try to judge what she's thinking, but she's just standing there, her expression unreadable. I scan her injuries— her poor bruised face and the blood that's now crusted in her hairline. I haven't seen my own face, and I'm not sure I want to, either. I feel like crap, and I bet I look it, too.

"This will do us, right?" I dump my bag onto the table. "It's shelter."

Cade looks around. "Are you kidding? It's a fucking shithole."

I ignore him and explore the rest of the cabin.

A couple of rooms lead off the main living area. I open one to discover a bathroom. This place clearly isn't hooked up to a town sewer—the toilet is compost—but the presence of a bathtub and a sink indicates that this place must be served by water from somewhere. Could there be a well? Or did the previous inhabitants just bring water up from a creek somewhere nearby? Either option is good. Water was my biggest concern, and if there's somewhere nearby, it solves that issue. There's no mirror, but I'm taking that as a good thing.

I try the faucet, but it doesn't even make a noise, never mind produce any water. It's almost as though someone had plans to connect it to a well but didn't bother. I'm disappointed, but I hope we'll find another water source nearby. There clearly was one, once, and I doubt it'll have completely dried up.

I go back into the living area of the cabin and tell the others what I've found. "We have enough bottled water to last us until tomorrow, but then we're going to need to find a water source. Even if we do find one, there's no guarantee the water is going to be clean enough to drink. It'll need to be boiled first, so we'll need to get the wood stove going."

"Hang on," Cade says.

He digs into his pocket and then he places something into my hand. A lighter. I'm not sure he was supposed to have that on the plane, at least not in the cabin, but now's not the time to start laying down rules.

"Good. We can start a fire, at least, and then we can keep it burning. A fire means smoke from the chimney. If a rescue crew is somewhere nearby, they're going to spot it. If we hear an engine, then we can throw some greenery onto the fire and the smoke will turn black. Plus, it'll keep the cabin nice and warm and will give us the chance to boil our water whenever we need to."

We explore the rest of the cabin and search the place for supplies. There isn't a lot, but some of it will be useful. The other room is a small bedroom containing two single beds. There are four of us, but I guess we'll sort out the sleeping arrangements later.

The cabin has an elevated position, which is why I was able to spot it from a distance, and it allows a view across the trees, in the direction of the crashed plane. I want to see how far away from the crash site we are. I'm betting that I'll be able to see the smoke still rising from the plane.

I step outside, and it suddenly hits me just how dark it is. I can barely see beyond the clearing where the cabin is situated, never mind anything else.

Movement comes from behind me, and Laney joins me on the porch.

"Why has no one come looking for us yet?" she asks, clearly worried.

"They'll be looking," I assure her. "They just haven't found us."

I think to what Cade had said about how often the plane would have sent out pings to signal our location and the distance we might have traveled since that final ping. The pilot had said the equipment wasn't working, so how can we even be sure we'd remained on course? The search team might have an area the size of Florida to cover, and we were just one small plane.

"*Will* they find us?" she asks.

I risk a smile, though the movement hurts my face. "Of course they will. Let's go back inside. It's getting dark now." I place my hand on the base of Laney's spine to guide her back inside the cabin. "Things will seem better in the morning."

She turns those big eyes up to me, and my stomach flips.

"Shouldn't someone keep watch for the search planes overnight?"

I shake my head. "They won't be searching while it's dark. It would be too easy to miss something."

"Yeah, of course. Another stupid comment, I guess."

I catch her elbow and tug her to face me. "Don't let Cade get to you. He opens his mouth before he thinks."

She purses her lips, and I have to fight a sudden urge to cover her mouth with mine. I swallow, hard, and that's not the only part of me that's hard. Fuck. I can't react like this around her.

I drop her elbow and hurry back inside before she gets the chance to see the effect her proximity has on me.

14

Laney

WHAT THE FUCK JUST HAPPENED?

Reed has left me standing out on the porch, surrounded by the rapidly darkening forest, all on my own. It was like he couldn't get away from me fast enough.

I don't want to go in the cabin with those three men, but something in the undergrowth nearby rustles—too loud to be something as innocuous as a rabbit—and my heart catapults into my chest. My skin prickles with goose bumps, and I lunge for the cabin door, bursting inside as though something is chasing me.

Darius lifts his eyebrows in my direction. "Everything all right, Laney? You sound like you're in a hurry."

"Sorry. Just got spooked." I don't look at either Reed or Cade.

While we were on the porch, Darius and Cade have pulled the two single mattresses into the living area.

"We thought it was better if we all slept in the same space," Darius says.

Reed nods. "Good thinking. Safer that way."

"Safer? Do you think we're in danger in some way?" I ask, alarmed.

He still doesn't look at me but busies himself by shaking out one of the thin mattresses. "Probably not, but I'd still prefer us to all be in one room."

I'm not sure how I feel about sleeping in the same room as all of them, but then I also don't want to be alone. As well as the mattresses, there are also a couple of sagging couches.

"Me and Darius will take the couches," Cade says. "You two have the mattresses on the floor."

The floorspace isn't exactly huge, and the mattresses are side by side.

"I can take one of the couches, if you want the mattress, Dax," Reed offers.

Darius shakes his head. "Nah, I'm good."

I ready myself for bed as best I can.

We have toiletries in our bags, and I'm relieved that we also have a toilet, even if it is a compostable one. At least I won't have to shit in the woods. I risk wasting a little of the bottled water so I can brush my teeth. Maybe it's silly of me, but I can't stand the thought of going to bed with dirty teeth.

What if we're out here for weeks or even months, and we run out of all this stuff? Right now, I have bodywash and toothpaste, and a brand-new razor, but they won't last. It should probably be the last thing I should be worrying about, considering our situation, but I still don't want to end up gross.

I don't bother to change out of my clothes. I'd rather be fully dressed if help arrives.

We have the thin pillows from the plane and the blankets. I lie on my side on one of the mattresses and try not to think about the very real possibility that it's infested with bugs. I normally can't sleep in strange places, but I'm so exhausted from the stress of the day that my eyelids seem weighted, dragging downward.

I'm almost asleep—veering on that edge where my reality is half dream, half real—when an arm sneaks around my waist. It pulls me from sleep for only a fraction of a second, but the weight and warmth gives me comfort, and I find myself pushing back on the solidity of the body behind me before I drift off to sleep.

Sunlight hits the backs of my eyelids and I flicker them open.

I have absolutely no idea where I am.

The first thing I become aware of is that every single inch of my body hurts. The second thing is that something hard is pressing against my ass. There's also a weight around my waist, and when I glance down, I see a bare mattress and a distinctly male hand.

It all comes back to me in a shock. The man with his arm around me is my stepfather, which also means that's his erection digging into my butt.

I jerk away from him as though I've been burned. Adrenaline shoots through my system, and it takes my mind away from the fact that I feel like someone has been hitting me with a sledge-hammer during the night. I dart a glance back at Reed. He lets out a groan and rolls onto his other side.

I catch my breath. He was still asleep.

I turn back and let the air out of my lungs, only for my eyes to lock with Cade's on the other side of the room. He's awake and is staring right at me, an amused glint to his eye.

"Got an early morning wakeup call, did you, little Cuckoo?"

"Stop calling me that," I hiss.

We both speak in low tones to avoid waking the others.

He smirks. "You look pretty when you blush. Did you know that?"

"Shut up."

He snorts and gets up from the sagging couch. He stands and stretches, his t-shirt lifting to reveal the ridges of his abs and the dark line of hair that runs downward, beneath the waistband of his pants.

"I'm going outside to take a piss," he announces.

"We have a toilet, you know. Or is that too civilized for you?"

He shrugs. "I'm marking my territory. Testosterone in men's urine keeps animals like bears away."

I have no idea if this is true or if he's just bullshitting me so he can call me stupid again. I decide I don't care. I'm just happy he's leaving the cabin so I don't have to look at him.

The door swings shut behind him, and I edge my feet off the mattress and plant them on the dusty wooden floorboards. I put my head in my hands and try not to think about how it felt to have Reed pressed against my back when I woke up. It had felt so natural, his knees tucked into the backs of mine, his arm hooked around my waist. He most likely hadn't even realized how he'd been sleeping.

"You're awake."

I jump at the voice and turn to find Darius sitting on the edge of his couch.

"Yeah," I say. "Sorry. Did we wake you?"

He lowers his head between his knees and then flips his hair up and out of his face. "I'd kill for a coffee right now."

I sigh. "Same. A tall vanilla latte with an extra espresso shot." I smile at him. Though he can't see, I bet he can hear it in my voice. "I bet you drink it black, no sugar."

He grins. "What are you? Some kind of coffee psychic?"

"Did I get it right?" It's silly, but I can't help being pleased.

"Totally right."

Reed is awake now, too, and he sits up. "Where's Cade?"

I can't bring myself to look at him. "He went outside to take a piss."

I wonder if today will be the day we're rescued.

"We need to find out where the water supply for this place is," Reed says. He lifts a bottle of water and gives it a shake. It's almost empty. "This isn't going to last."

Darius agrees. "Let's make it a priority, then."

We still haven't explored the cabin properly either. It was already getting dark when we arrived, so we only did a cursory glance at the rooms or in the cupboards.

Cade reenters the cabin, looking annoyingly fresh, considering what we've gone through over the past twenty-four hours. He's still limping, though.

"How's it looking out there?" his father asks.

"Like we're in the middle of the wilderness."

"Did you see any lakes or rivers?"

Cade shakes his head. "Sorry, I didn't go that far, but there's a woodshed around the back of the property. It's got a decent amount in it, but we'll get through it quickly enough. I think it makes sense to replenish what we use and even stock up."

"You think we're going to be here that long?" I dare say.

He shrugs. "It's better to be safe than sorry. There was an axe embedded into one of the tree stumps, which will come in useful, but we need to explore farther afield."

Reed goes to his bag. "Let's eat first. We need our strength."

Does Reed have any idea that he had a hard-on this morning and that he was pressing it against me? I sneak a glance at him. He doesn't seem to be acting any differently this morning, but then what do I have it to compare to?

We share out some of the food we'd scavenged from the plane. It doesn't seem like much to me, and I assume it must feel like even less to the men.

"We've got enough to last us a few days, if we ration it," Reed says, "but we're going to need to find more food."

Darius nods. "We're incredibly lucky to have a roof over our heads. Imagine if we hadn't found this place. We'd be screwed."

"I think one of us needs to keep an eye out for any signs of a plane during daylight hours." Cade looks to Darius. "Sorry, bro. You'll need to sit out of this one."

Darius scowls. "I might not be able to see a plane, but I'll guarantee I'll hear one before any of you lot spot one."

"Yes, he will," Reed agrees. "We can take it in a couple of hours stint until it gets dark. Darius can go first, then Cade, then me, and then we'll start again."

I straightened my shoulders and lifted my chin. "Hey, what about me? I'm perfectly capable of taking a slot, too."

"There might be wild animals out there," Reed says.

A raised an eyebrow. "What, on the porch?"

"If they're hungry, they might come up on the porch."

"So, you're saying you or Cade or Darius would be able to fight off a bear, but I wouldn't?"

To be fair, looking at Cade, I suspect he probably can fight off a bear. He's certainly big enough.

"I'm supposed to be taking care of you, Laney," Reed says, irritated.

I can't help my sarcasm. "You're doing a great job so far."

He winces with pain at my words, and I instantly feel guilty.

I soften my tone. "I've been looking after myself for as long as I can remember. If I can survive Los Angeles as a kid practically on my own, I'm sure I can sit on a porch for a couple of hours. If I see a bear or cougar or anything, I'll shout. It's not like you're going to be far."

"Okay, fine," he relents. "You can take a shift, too."

The authorities will definitely know that we're missing by now, and that the plane never made it to its final location. There will be teams of people searching for us. They're bound to find us soon.

Darius gets up to take the first shift and crosses the cabin to the door.

He appears to have already mapped out the locations of the various items in the room, and where the door is. It amazes me how quickly he learns his surroundings, but I guess he's used to it. He's spent months, if not years, traveling from place to place, staying in different hotel rooms. He's had to adapt.

I notice how he always keeps his violin close. Is it a kind of security blanket for him? He hasn't played it since we've been here, though. He's taken it from its case and smoothed his fingers across the polished wood and strings but hasn't tried to coax a sound from them. He's so different from his brother. Is it because of his disability? Or is it because he's a musician? Or is it simply his personality? Where Cade is all pent-up rage and sarcasm, Darius is calm and introspective. He's only a few years my senior, but he seems a decade older.

No matter how Cade is treating me, these men are my family now. I don't have anyone else.

I don't think it's even sank in fully that my mom has gone. The idea that I'll never see her or speak to her again feels completely unreal. Maybe that sensation would be normal, but after everything that's happened since she died, I have no way of knowing for sure, or if I'm just in a state of shock. I probably am. I'm sure I read somewhere that it's never a good idea to make any drastic life changes or decisions during the months after a bereavement, because you're not in the right frame of mind to make any important choices, but here I am, lost in the wildness with three men who were effectively strangers until a few days ago. I can't trust my reactions to them, or my emotions for them, or the thoughts I have about them. In a way, I find that a comfort. It gives me a kind of out—an excuse for thinking or doing or reacting in a way I might not feel completely comfortable with. It means the reason I keep remembering how big and hard Reed's cock was against my back, and the reason I'm picturing how long and thick it must be, is simply because I'm grieving and in shock. *Normal* Laney would never think such a thing.

Reed gets to his feet and brushes down the front of his jeans. "I'm going to try to find a water source. We're going to need to figure out something to eat, too. These supplies won't last."

"I saw some berry bushes on our way here," I tell him. "I'm pretty sure they were blueberries. We could try foraging."

"Do you know the difference between edible berries and ones that are poisonous?"

I twist my lips. "Honestly, I'm not sure, but I think I know a blueberry when I see one. They're my favorite."

They were what I treated myself to whenever I'd come across some spare cash. A whole tub of fresh blueberries that I'd sit and eat by myself, popping one after the other into my mouth. I never took them back to the trailer to share because Mom would berate me for wasting money—money she could have spent on booze. A wave of guilt passes through me about that. I should have shared with her.

"I'll keep an eye out when I go farther to try to find a water source." He eyes me for a moment. "You going to be okay here?"

I wonder if I should offer to come with him, but then I remember waking up in bed with his erection pressed into me and decide not to.

"Of course, I'll be fine."

15
DARIUS

THE SOUNDS of the forest are beautiful.

I've lost count of the number of different bird songs I've heard. I don't even mind the buzzing of insects around me, though I slap at my skin when a mosquito tickles. The breeze in the canopy of branches shushes like ocean waves on the shore.

I feel better now we've found somewhere to settle.

The hike through the forest had not been a good experience for me. I'd lost count of the number of times I'd almost tripped or had been struck in the face by a low hanging branch. I'd never concentrated so hard in my life, putting everything into focusing on Cade's movement. Occasionally, I'd been forced to put my hand on his shoulder to allow him to guide me, but I'd hated doing it. With every stumble and bump, my anger had grown, but I'd buried it inside me. If I lost my temper, I worried I wouldn't be able to rein it back in again. I pictured myself tearing at the trees and roaring at a sky I couldn't even see.

Perhaps I should be more grateful that we're even alive. The pilots and flight attendant weren't so lucky.

I might not be able to see them, but that doesn't mean I

haven't noticed the tension Laney's presence has caused. Is it because she's off limits? Reed says she's our stepsister, but how the hell are any of us supposed to think of her like that? She's a stranger.

Well, we're all going to get to know each other a hell of a lot better now.

At least sitting here, on the porch, it is peaceful. I can't remember another time when I couldn't hear the constant hum of traffic or of sirens going off or even planes flying overhead. I can picture in my mind the porch I'm sitting on and the cabin at my back and even the apparently never-ending forest surrounding us. It's one thing I imagine would be different for someone who'd been blind since birth—how would they be able to picture such things? I'm grateful to be able to remember the color of the sky and what trees look like.

Are we ever going to be found?

My fingers itch to create music. I'm sure the others will ask me to play at some point, but I won't. The next time I play will be when we're back in civilization, safe again. If I play before then, it'll mean I've given up, that I've accepted this is our new normal and we have to live like this—like mountain men.

The sunlight shining through the trees is creating a strange stripey shadowed effect across what little remains of my vision. I have no ability to see depth, but I can see the contrast of light and shadows.

I hate my impaired vision here. I'm in completely unmapped territory. I don't want to be reliant on anyone, but how can I know where anything is out here? A fallen tree or boulder threatens to trip me. A tree trunk is just waiting for me to smack straight into.

One thing I hate more than anything is looking foolish. I don't want to be that person, stumbling around, their hands held out in front of them. I like to be calm, cool, controlled.

It's not going to be easy if we end up having to spend any longer than a couple of days here.

Things will be even harder when the only woman around is also out of bounds. I don't know how long we'll be here, but I can sense frustration already mounting—and I'm including myself in that. Will Laney be safe with us all? I'd like to think we're civilized people who can control ourselves, but what if we've had civilization stripped from us? What then? And as the nights grow longer and colder, will we be looking for other ways to keep ourselves warm?

I wonder what Laney thinks when she looks at us. Does she see us as strangers, or family?

"Hi."

Speak of the devil.

"Hey, Laney. I don't think it's your turn yet."

"No, I know. I just thought you might like some company."

"I'm fine."

Despite me saying this, she doesn't get up and leave.

I pick up a slight tremor in her voice. "Are you nervous?" I ask.

Her feet shuffle on the floorboards. "Oh, umm…it's just you're Darius Riviera."

I huff out a laugh. "Yeah, I know that."

"And you're kind of intimidating."

"I'm really not."

"Yeah, you are. You're kind of…unapproachable."

"And yet you've just approached me."

It's her turn to laugh. "I did. I figured I needed to get over it, considering we're going to be stuck in this cabin together for goodness knows how long. I thought we should get to know each other a bit better."

I nod and lace my fingers between my knees. "Okay. What do you want to know?"

She settles into the wooden chair beside me. "When did you know you wanted to play the violin?"

I smile to myself. "The first moment I put my hands on one."

"It was when you touched one? Not when you heard it?"

"It was like touching a beautiful woman. It still is. The moment my finger connected with the wood, my heart beat faster, and my blood rushed through my veins. It was like my body came alive."

She draws a breath. "You felt a connection."

"Exactly."

"Do-do you feel that same connection when you touch people?"

"I guess that depends on the person." I shift my position slightly and put my hands out.

"Wh-what are you doing?" she asks.

"Seeing if there's a connection."

I wait to see if she jerks away, but when she doesn't move, I reach out and place my palms against her cheeks. Her skin is hot to the touch, and I know she is blushing. I'm unsure why that causes a swell of emotion inside my chest, but it does. I like that I've affected her. I run my thumbs across her cheekbones, her skin incredibly soft, like velvet.

"Well?" she asks, her voice almost a whisper.

I nod. "Yes, I think there's a connection."

"Is that because we're family?" She still has that breathy tone, as though she can't quite fill her lungs.

"We're not family, Laney. You said yourself that we don't know each other."

She pulls away, and my hands slip from her face. I said the wrong thing. Does she want us to be family? Why?

It dawns on me, and I feel like a fucking idiot. She doesn't have anyone. Her mom died only a couple of days ago, and she's alone in the world. She's so desperate to have someone that she'll even put up with assholes like Cade and me, and our father. Reed Riviera is not father material. Sure, he got his shit together for us when we were younger, but we'd already spent a large chunk of our childhoods believing we didn't have a dad. He had no idea how to be one, and we had no idea how to have him in our lives.

Reed only raised me the way he did because he saw my potential. I'm not saying that's a bad thing, but I'm fully aware that I'm the only reason both he and my brother have been able to lead the lifestyles they have. What would either of them be doing if it wasn't for me? It might seem like I'm being boastful or resentful by thinking such a thing, but that's not how it is at all. I wonder, have always wondered, that if it wasn't for my talent, who would I be? Would my family continue to stick around if I wasn't able to provide them both with an income? What reason would they have to help me? Cade would be off doing whatever the fuck it is Cade lives for—drinking, fucking, and fighting as far as I can tell—and Reed would have decided he'd done his duty by getting us to adulthood and would be getting on with his life.

Out in the real world, I have value. Here, in the middle of nowhere, I'm good for nothing. While the others can go out and forage, I'm stuck in the cabin. I hope we won't be here long enough for me to need to learn the surrounding forest. Plus, nature is unpredictable. I'm not suggesting that trees uproot themselves, but they do fall down, and wind and rain help to move and erode the forest floor. I don't want to repeat the hike through the forest to get here, especially not on a daily basis. It's one thing I always try to control—my surroundings, even when we were staying in different places. Here, that's nearly impossible.

Getting injured also concerns me. I could offer to help chop wood, but even I'm not proud enough to pretend like it's not a hell of a lot safer for either Cade or Reed to do it. One badly aimed swing could take off a foot or hand, and it's not like we can race off to the nearest ER.

They don't need me.

What about Laney, though? She's a clean slate.

There are more ways to become a family than being related from birth.

We settle back into silence again, sitting side by side, just listening to the forest.

"Do you remember Reed?" I ask, curious. "From when you were a kid, I mean."

"I think so. I was really little when he was with my mom, but he's the only person I remember sticking around for any time. I remember him being huge and being frightened of him."

"Oh." I frown. "Why were you frightened of him?"

"He was big and loud, and he and my mom always fought."

"He would have still been drinking back then," I say.

"Yes, I suppose so. No one sober would have been able to handle being around my mom for any length of time."

The sadness inside her echoes from her soul.

"You were," I point out. "You were around her your whole life."

"Up until two days ago." Her voice thickens, and she sniffs. "Do you think we'll be found?"

"I hope we will."

"Me, too."

I find myself reaching for her again. This time, my fingers find hers and I squeeze them, trying to both take and offer comfort. The tension in her muscles and joints radiates through mine for a moment, but then she relaxes and even squeezes my hand in return.

"Is there anyone you'll miss from back home?" I ask.

Her shoulder brushes mine as it rises and falls. "Not really. Some work colleagues, I guess."

"School friends?"

"I didn't really have any."

"No? How come?"

"I was always too busy trying to keep our household running, making sure I could eat. I was always the weird kid, the one no one ever invited home, or even had birthday parties. I guess I was a bit of an outcast."

I picture the map I'd traced of her face, the full lips, the slightly pointed chin, the small, upturned nose. Her long lashes had brushed my fingertips when she'd blinked.

"What color are your eyes?"

"Blue," she says. "Pale blue. In some lights they look almost gray."

"They sound beautiful."

She doesn't reply, and I can tell I've embarrassed her again. I imagine she's not used to getting compliments.

I lift my other hand and touch her hair. I twine a chunk of the strands around my fingers, and revel in its silkiness. It takes every bit of self-control not to lean in and lift her hair to my nose to inhale the scent. "What color is your hair?"

"Brown." Her voice is so close, right next to my ear, and I'm sure I can feel the warmth of her breath on my face. "With reddish tones in the right light."

I picture the combination, building an image of her in my mind. At least in my head, she's beautiful.

Footsteps approach, and then Cade says, "You two look cozy."

16
laney

AT THE SOUND of his brother's voice, Darius snatches his hand away from mine.

I glance over at Darius.

I have so many questions I want to ask him about when and how he lost his sight, but I don't want to look like I'm prying. Not that he seems to be holding back on what he's asking me. I know it's stupid to treat him any differently than I would anyone else, but it's not even because of his disability. It's because he's Darius Riviera, and I watched him perform on stage with an entire orchestra and full house completely absorbed by him.

"Don't you have anything more productive you could be doing?" Cade's eyes narrow and dart between us.

Darius sits back and folds his arms over his chest, apparently unbothered by Cade's presence, despite how he'd jumped away from me. "I'm on the lookout stint."

"I wasn't talking to you. I'm talking to her."

He jerks his chin in my direction.

I let out a sigh. "I didn't think it would matter if I sat down for ten minutes. It's not as though we don't have plenty of time on our hands."

"You're the one who talked about the berries. The least you could do is help."

I always thought that I was a spikey, anger-filled person, but compared to Cade, I'm practically a little ray of sunshine.

Is he jealous? That's definitely the vibe I'm getting off him. I assume he's jealous that I'm taking up Darius's attention rather than him being jealous of Darius talking to me. I believe he's jealous of Reed and me as well, and the thought brings back the memory of waking to find Reed's hard cock jammed up against my spine. I know it wasn't his fault—men wake up that way, and with the floorspace being so small, he had no choice but to have his mattress right next to mine. I tell myself it didn't mean anything.

I get to my feet. "Okay, fine. I'll help gather some."

If it'll keep Cade happy, I'll pick berries until my fingers drop off. All I want is to keep the peace. We have enough to worry about without fighting each other.

"Where did Reed go?" I ask, leaving Darius behind and stepping down the couple of steps that lead off the porch and onto the surrounding land.

"To search for a water source. He's got it in his head that we're going to need one."

"Do you think we're going to be here that long?"

He shrugs. "How the fuck should I know? Your guess is as good as mine."

Nerves flutter in my stomach as we put more distance between us and the cabin. I'm fairly certain Cade won't actually do anything to hurt me—his bark is worse than his bite—but his tongue can be cruel.

We reach some of the clumps of bushes I'd spotted during our hike here. I hadn't paid much attention to them previously, but now I do, checking the small, deep purple berries and the shapes of the leaves. They look exactly like blueberries to me, but it's not as though I'm an expert.

I hesitate, and then quickly pick one, pop it on my tongue, and chew. I hate the thought that I might be poisoning myself right now—the thought of getting an upset stomach out here embarrasses the hell out of me—but only the familiar and comforting taste of blueberries coats my tongue.

I grin at Cade. "Definitely blueberries."

"Not that they're going to go any way to filling us up."

God, he is such an asshole.

"At least they're something," I spit.

He doesn't reply, so I turn my back on him and use the lower half of my t-shirt to gather the berries to take back to the cabin. For each one I gather, I put another in my mouth. They don't come any fresher than this, and even if Cade is turning his nose up right now, if he's right in saying that we might be here awhile, he'll be grateful for them.

To my right, a large bird rustles and flaps through the undergrowth. I stop and squint after it. "Did you see that?" I ask Cade.

He nods. "I think it's a type of grouse?"

"Grouse?"

The name is vaguely familiar.

"Yeah, we can eat them. Be a hell of a lot more filling than some berries."

I lift my eyebrows. "Are we really going to get to the point where we're going to need to eat the local wildlife?"

"You saw what supplies we've got. You might be able to survive on a handful of olives and a cracker, but the rest of us are men. We need our calories."

I'd had the same thought myself earlier. They are going to struggle harder than I will when it comes to food, though once we've demolished the supplies we've taken from the plane, I'll starve just as quickly as any of them.

"We'd need to catch one first."

He drags his hand over the lower half of his face. "True. But there must be a way, and it's not like we don't have the time to figure it out."

"You keep talking as though you think we're going to be here for some time."

He doesn't look at me.

"I just think it's better that we're prepared."

I understand where he's coming from, but that doesn't stop me hoping and praying that I'll hear the thrum of helicopters approaching, searching for us. Back at the crash site, he'd seemed convinced that people would be out searching for us because of who his brother is, but now it's as though he's going the other way.

I think Cade will just say and think whatever the opposite is of everyone else.

"Let's take these back to the cabin," I say. "Reed might be back by now."

Cade stops and stares at me. "You know, my father doesn't owe you anything, just because he happened to sleep with your mother fourteen years ago. It's not even as though he got her pregnant. You were already born then."

I harden my gaze, refusing to let him intimidate me. "He didn't just sleep with her. He married her. That's a whole different thing."

"Is it? Is it really? Why? Because society has told us that if we say certain words at a certain place in front of a certain person then that means something? If we have a piece of paper, it makes that thing legal? It's all just bullshit. I doubt either of our parents can even remember the actual wedding. They both would have been shitfaced at the time."

I shake my head. "You don't know that."

"I think I know Reed better than you do. He's our actual father, not some wannabe for some teen with daddy issues."

Every muscle in my body tenses. "I do not have daddy issues!"

"Yeah, right. I've seen how you are with him. You're getting him wound around your little finger. Reed got our mother pregnant again when I was still a toddler, then ran off to fuck women like your mother instead. Your mother was the home breaker, not the perfect wife you seem to think she was."

I snort at that. "You have no idea. Seriously. That's the last thing I'd think."

"But you think he owes you something, just because he and your mother said I do?"

I straighten my shoulders. "He chose to walk away from us. At any point over the past fourteen years, he could have checked in, but he didn't. Do you have any idea how hard life has been for me?"

He curls up his lip. "Oh, boohoo. Poor little Laney."

"Fuck you, Cade."

"I bet you'd like to, wouldn't you?"

Suddenly, he's crowding me in with his body. I find myself with a tree trunk at my back and Cade directly in front of me. I've still got the berries nested into the hammock of my t-shirt, but a handful spill out and scatter across the forest floor.

"Cade!" I protest.

With my empty hand, I shove at his chest. He's solid as rock and doesn't budge. He reaches up and grips my jaw between his thumb and forefinger, and then drags his thumb over my bottom lip.

"Shame you're still only seventeen."

I scowl. I don't know why, but it feels like him saying that minimizes me somehow, like he thinks it makes me less important. One thing I always want is to be taken seriously, and the fact he doesn't just because of my age pisses me off.

"I'll be eighteen in a few days," I snap.

He smirks, and it dawns on me that I might have just said the wrong thing.

He doesn't move his body. "A few days, huh? Think we'll still be here then? Lost out in the middle of nowhere, with no one around to judge us or to report anything."

What's he saying? That he can do whatever he wants because there's no one around to hold him accountable? The thought shoots fear through me, but also something else. A thrill of excitement. No, I don't want to think like that. Cade is a fucking asshole, and not only that, he's my stepbrother. That he's also huge and a little scary and right now he has his fingers on my lips, sending a dark thrill and tingle down through my core to coalesce between my legs, means nothing. Or so I keep telling myself.

I swallow, and I wish my voice would come out stronger than it does. "Reed won't like this."

He smiles again, the corner of those perfect lips curling. "You really think I give a fuck what Reed likes or doesn't like? Besides, I've seen the way my father looks at you. He might be acting like he's the perfect stepfather right now, but it's all an act. That isn't who he really is."

"You're lying."

"Am I? You think he's all reformed or some shit, but think about it for a minute. This is a man who walked out on his pregnant girlfriend when she had his other baby to look after as well. He's the sort of man who married some other woman he barely even knew, and walked out on her, too."

"He's different now," I insist. "He's changed."

Finally, Cade creates space between us. He releases me and steps back, and, to my surprise, I find myself missing the solid shield of his body. While he'd been crushed against me, for once I hadn't given any thought to the never-ending expanse of forest that stretched all around us. I hadn't thought of the bugs that seemed to constantly buzz in my ears and land on my skin, leaving me itchy, or the possibility of wild animals stalking us. All I'd thought about was him, the proximity of his body to mine, the way he'd stared into my eyes, and the touch of his thumb on my lips. While I was focused on that, I wasn't thinking about how we might die out here.

"Sure, you keep telling yourself that," he says. "Maybe certain parts of him are changed, like he's not abusing alcohol and drugs anymore, but that doesn't make him a different person."

I still refuse to believe him. I need to believe Reed is a good man. I'm relying on him to save me. To protect me. But what if Cade is right?

"He raised both of you," I say. "He turned his life around for *you*. Look at the lives you're both living. He must have done something right."

"The first time he heard Darius play, it was like dollar signs appeared in his eyes."

"You've done pretty well out of your brother, too," I point out.

"Darius and I, we watch out for each other. You think he'd live half as well as he does without me?"

"Darius is perfectly capable of taking care of himself."

"I watch his back. I'm his eyes. You think his level of fame only brings with it adoring fans? There are people out there who are all kinds of crazy. Because he's in the public eye, they think they know him. They think they have a right to him. And I'm not just talking about women, either. One time, he got back to his dressing room to find a guy in there. He said Darius was his muse and, in his head, had convinced himself that they were best buddies. Darius had replied to one of his comments on social media at some point, and this guy had taken that to mean they knew each other now. He claimed that he should be on tour with Darius and refused to take no for an answer. When we asked him to leave, he got violent and produced a gun. I was the one who took him down, who prevented anyone from getting hurt. You think Darius would be able to handle shit like that without me?"

I raise my free hand in defense. "Okay, okay. You don't need to explain yourself to me."

"No, you're right. I fucking don't."

He turns his back on me and stalks away, leaving me standing there, my heart still racing, a pool of half squashed berries held in my t-shirt.

17
REED

I DON'T LIKE LEAVING the others behind, but finding water needs to be a priority.

I haven't seen any signs of a well having been dug near the property. I can only assume whoever built this place had intentions of digging one at some point, but then never followed through.

Working on the theory that water runs downhill, I follow the downward slant of the hillside. I keep an eye on my location, ensuring I'll be able to find my way back again. It won't do any of us any good if I end up lost out here.

Like Cade did the previous day, I use a large stick to whack my route through the foliage. Not only does it help clear my route, it also gives me a path to follow to get back again.

I just have to hope I'm heading in the right direction.

I hope Laney is all right back at the cabin with the boys. She's going to have to get used to handling them if we're stuck here for any length of time. I can't be with her twenty-four-seven. Besides, I worry about myself as much as I do the boys. My reaction to Laney last night is playing on my mind, and then this morning I woke up with an erection. Luckily, she was nowhere near me, so she hadn't noticed, but I definitely did. I need to focus harder on marrying the young woman she is now with the chubby toddler I used to know, but I'm finding it impossible. I don't know if it's because she seems so completely different, or if my memories from back then are just so clouded from all the booze and drugs, but when I look at her, all I see is a beautiful young woman I met only a couple of days ago.

I hear the water before I see it, the gentle rush of a river.

I pick up my pace and push my way through the foliage.

The river is wide, but not too fast. The areas closest to the bank are almost pool-like, still and clear. I move closer and squat at the edge and dip both hands into the water. I bring it up to my face, splashing my skin with the cool water and exhaling a breath.

It's good the water is moving—it's more likely to be clean than finding a stagnant water source—but we'll still have to boil it before drinking it. There's no way of knowing if an animal has fallen into the water and died farther upstream, plus feces from the wildlife—bird and fish included—will be in the water. As I think of fish, there's a splash somewhere to my right, and I catch a flash of silver. There are probably trout in these waters.

My stomach growls at the thought of grilled fish.

Of course, I'll have to catch it first. I'm no fisherman, and I don't remember seeing any kind of fishing rods or nets back at the cabin, but that doesn't mean they're not hidden away some-where. Or maybe we can improvise, though with what, I've no idea.

I realize I'm thinking as though we're going to be here long enough to worry about things like the food running out. There isn't a lot, and, after raising Cade and Darius through their teenage years, I'm fully aware that they need a lot of food.

I glance up at the blue sky, praying to hear the thrum of

engines. There's nothing, though, except the twittering of birds and the buzzing of insects.

Pushing myself back to standing, I turn back to the cabin. I should have brought something to collect the water in, then I could have gotten it straight onto the woodfire to boil and would have saved myself a trip.

I take a long inhale, savoring the peace and trying to quiet the torrent of worries that are crashing through me. I want to believe we'll be found in the next day or two, but what if we're not? How long can the four of us survive out here? We have shelter, and a fireplace, and if we can figure out how to hunt and fish and forage, we won't starve. But we're at the tail end of the summer now, when all those things are plentiful. What will happen when winter comes and the snow falls and the river freezes? How will we make it through then?

No, we'll be found long before that happens. I'm sure of it. Like Cade said, it's Darius fucking Riviera who is missing. Maybe if it was just me, Cade, and Laney, people wouldn't care so much about us and they'd stop looking after a few days, but Darius's plane crashing will be all over the news and social media. His fans will keep pushing for him to be found, or for them to at least get answers. There will be social media and GoFundMe campaigns. They won't just let it go.

With these reassurances, I leave the river and make my way back to the cabin. I continue to clear a path as I go, ensuring it'll be easy for either myself or one of the others to find their way back.

I get back to the cabin to discover everyone is there. Laney has been picking blueberries, while Darius keeps watch. I'm not sure what Cade has been up to, but it's not worth questioning him. He's had a stick up his ass ever since I mentioned bringing Laney into our lives—albeit temporarily.

"Everyone okay?" I ask, assessing them.

Laney flashes a bright smile. "I found blueberries."

"That's great, Laney."

There's something about the smile that's too forced. I know we're not exactly in a smiling situation, but I can sense the tension on the air.

"Well, the good news is I found a river, and it's only about a ten-minute walk from here. I've done my best to clear a path as I went, so it should be easy enough to find again. We need to find containers bigger than the small bottles we currently have for water so we can bring it back up to the cabin."

"There are some pots in the kitchen," Laney says. "They're metal, so we'll be able to use them for boiling the water, too."

"That's great."

"I found a couple of flashlights, too. They're working, but God knows how long the batteries will last, and I didn't find any replacements."

"We'll keep them for emergencies."

When it gets dark, the only light we'll have will be from the fireplace and the few candles that are around the cabin. We really will have to get back to nature—wake when the sun rises, and sleep when it sets.

I want to believe we won't be here long enough for it to be an issue, but a gnawing deep inside of me won't let me.

18

laney

We've made several trips to and from the river, carrying what water we can. Though there are logs in the woodshed out the back, we also gather any fallen sticks and branches we find.

I'm filthy from the crash and sweaty after the hike through the forest the previous day, and from the physical work. It's not that I'm unused to working hard, but being in a forest is very different than the city.

The thought of plunging into the cold river, being able to wash, and then changing into clean clothes sounds like heaven.

"I think I'll take a walk down to the river," I announce. "I'd like to wash. I'm gross."

Reed purses his lips at me, his brow drawing down. "You shouldn't go down there alone."

"I'll be fine."

"You might not find your way back again, or what if there's a bear or something?"

"We haven't seen any bears."

He's not giving up. "What if you misjudge the flow of the water and fall in and get swept away?"

Jeez, he really is imagining every possible bad scenario. I want to think he's overreacting, but then we have recently been in a plane crash.

"I won't go in that deep, I promise."

Reed folds his arms across his chest, the sleeves of his t-shirt straining against his biceps. "It's not safe, Laney. Please. I don't want to have to worry about you on top of everything else."

I relent, but only because I'm distracted by his arms. "Okay, fine." I guess this means I won't be able to strip off completely. "You won't look, will you?" I check.

He arches an eyebrow at me as though he thinks I should know better, and I throw up both hands.

"Okay, okay. You can't blame a girl for asking."

"I'll keep my back to you the whole time," he promises.

"Though then you won't be able to watch out for bears." I'm only teasing him, but his expression falls.

"I'll be fine," I repeat, exasperated, but also a little pleased.

I've never had anyone care about my safety or welfare before, and there's something about this older man wanting to watch out for me that warms me from the inside.

It seems strange to think that Reed was only reintroduced into my life a matter of days ago, and that it's been the same length of time since my mother died. It feels like so much longer —a time period that should be counted in weeks, or even months, rather than days. I wonder if he thinks the same.

I gather my belongings—a towel I'd stolen from the hotel, some body wash, and a clean set of clothes. I can smell smoke in my hair, and I'd like to wash it, too, at some point, but I won't do that today. I don't know how easy it's going to be to get clean in the river, and I feel like I'm quite literally testing the waters. If it proves to be straightforward, then I'll go back tomorrow and deal with my hair.

That's assuming we're even still here tomorrow. With any

luck, a helicopter will fly overhead at any minute, and we'll be saved.

Somehow, I can't get that scenario to sit right with me.

We leave the cabin and make the ten-minute walk down to the river. Now we've made a number of trips, we've created a clear pathway. There would be no chance of me getting lost if I came down here on my own, but I appreciate Reed's concerns.

We reach the water, and I dump my belongings on the ground.

"I'll be right over here," Reed says, heading a short distance away, toward a cluster of trees.

"No peeking?" I check.

"I'll keep my back turned the whole time."

I feel self-conscious as I stand on the riverbank and strip out of my clothes. I keep my underwear on, though I'd have really liked to rid myself of those as well. It doesn't feel like I'll be properly clean with them still on.

I risk a glance over my shoulder. True to his word, Reed is facing away. He's resting one forearm on the trunk of a tree, and his neck is bent. I don't think he'll try to get a look at me naked, and I'll get in the water quickly, so it's not as though he'll see much, anyway.

Hesitating a moment longer, I made a snap decision and strip off my bra and panties too. I step into the shallows, sucking air in over my teeth as the cold water hits my skin, and then wade in. I have the bottle of bodywash in one hand, and, as soon as I get deep enough, I duck down, submerging my body. I gasp and splash my face. It's freezing, but invigorating.

I want to soap myself down, so I stand straight again, lifting myself back out of the water. My skin is covered in goose bumps, and my nipples are hard and tight. I can hardly believe I'm standing in the middle of nowhere, in a river, completely naked. I suddenly feel wild and free, and more alive than I have in years, and I have to resist the urge to lift my head and whoop at the endless expanse of sky and trees. But I know doing that will only bring Reed, and possibly the other two, running, and I don't want them to find me here like this.

The thought sends a little thrill through me. What would they do if I yelled and they all came down to the riverbank only to find me wading from the water, completely naked? Would they be shocked? Darius wouldn't be able to see me, of course, but I'm sure his brother would fill him in on the details. What would they do with me then? Would they rush with a towel to save my modesty, or would they enjoy the view?

I blow out a breath and try to clear my head. If Cade found me naked, I highly doubt he'd even consider my modesty.

I finish washing myself then turn back to shore. Reed is still in the same position, so I grab my towel and hurriedly dry myself, and then put on my fresh clothes. I gather my belongings and make my way back toward the trees where Reed is waiting.

"I feel so much better," I say.

He barely glances at me. "Let's get back to the cabin."

He starts walking, and I hurry after him.

"Everything okay?"

"Fine. I just didn't know you'd take so long."

What the hell has got into him?

"I wasn't that long. It's not as though we have somewhere we need to be. Why are you mad at me?"

"I'm not. You're the one who should be angry with me."

My skin prickles with unease. "What do you mean?"

He raises his hands to gesture either side of him. "I'm the one who got you into this mess."

I huff air out of my nostrils and stop walking. "If I'm mad with you about something, it won't be that."

Reed stops as well, and he faces me, eyes narrowed. "It won't?"

"No. I was angry with you long before the plane went down."

"Why?"

"You left us," I say to him. "You left us both."

He shakes his head. "No, I left *her*. You have to try to understand the headspace I was in back then. My mind was fucked up. I barely even registered that she had a daughter. The times I was there, you were always asleep—"

"No," I argue. "I wasn't. I remember you being there."

He eyes me, trying to tell if I'm lying. "You can't. You were practically a baby."

"I was three. I was young, yes, but I remember you. You left, knowing you were leaving a young child with the mess that my mother was."

"I was as much of a mess. I couldn't take care of myself, never mind you or your mother. I was wasted all the time—from the minute I woke up to the minute I passed out again."

"But you straightened yourself out. You did that for the boys."

He nods. "I had to. They lost their mother. They only had me left."

"But you never thought to do the same for me?"

My eyes fill, and I blink the tears back angrily. I don't know why I'm so upset—so hurt, so betrayed. I shouldn't feel this way. I barely know this man. What difference does it make what choice he made fourteen years ago? It's not like either of us can go back and change things.

I try not to think about the life I could have had, growing up with Cade and Darius as two older brothers, living a life of luxury. Then I remind myself that this money is a new thing. They didn't grow up this way. They grew up in poverty, much like I did.

They had each other, though. That was the difference. They took care of each other.

The only person I ever had taking care of me was me.

"You were with your mother," he says. "I thought you were

okay. Looking back, I should have done something different, but it honestly didn't even occur to me back then."

"You married my mother. Surely, you should have felt some responsibility toward me."

"Yes, legally I was your stepfather—"

"You still *are* my stepfather," I remind him.

He glances at the ground as though that reminder embarrasses him. "Okay, but I was never a father to you. I was never anything to you. I was the person who occasionally came to the trailer and got wasted with your mother. That was all. I wasn't going to come back into your life and whisk you away. You barely knew who I was."

All I'm hearing coming from his mouth are excuses.

I shake my head. "You must have known that we'd never amount to much. When Darius started getting successful and you had all this money, did you never even think of coming and bailing my mom out of whatever shit heap she was living in?"

He holds my gaze. "What would have happened if I'd given your mother a whole heap of money? What do you think she would have done with it? You think she'd have found you somewhere nice to live and saved for your college fund? No, she'd have put it up her nose, or injected it into a vein, or drunk the whole damned lot. You know I'm telling the truth."

The worst part is that he's completely right. That's exactly what she would have done.

I speak honestly. "It hurts to know that I've struggled all my life when you could have made a decision to change it."

He stares at me, lines forming between his dark brows, his blue eyes, so much darker than mine, narrowing a fraction.

"Do you think this is how we've been living for the past fourteen years?" he says. "Do you think I walked away from that trailer, straight into this life? You can't be farther from the truth, Laney. I was a fucking mess when I walked away from both of you. I was addicted to drugs and alcohol. I was violent and full of rage. I had to leave because I knew I'd end up doing something terrible, and I didn't want that for either of you. Then the boys' mother contacted me to say she was terminally ill and didn't have anyone to take care of them. I hadn't seen Cade since he was tiny, and I'd never even met Darius. She threw me out when she was pregnant because of my shitty behavior. I knew she must have been desperate to turn to me. Then she died, and all of a sudden, I was a single father to two grieving children. They were six and eight, and suddenly forced to live with a father they couldn't even remember while having just lost the only parent they'd ever known."

I wanted to say 'sounds familiar,' but I kept my thoughts to myself for once. I wasn't a young child anymore, completely dependent on someone else for her survival. And I hope the two boys' mother had been a hell of a lot better than mine had.

"We struggled, Laney," he continues. "I can't tell you how much we struggled. I lost count of the number of times I almost went back to using. I had no idea what I was doing, and both Darius and Cade were angry and grieving. Then Darius got sick, and things got even worse. I didn't think we were going to make it, to be honest, but I didn't want the boys to end up in foster care. Darius lost his sight, and I had no idea how to help him."

He draws a breath, and I can tell how hard this is for him to speak about. I reach out and place my hand on his forearm. I realize how I've only thought about things from my side. I never gave a single thought to the possibility that he was struggling during those years as well.

Reed continues. "It was only when Darius became a teenager, and out of sheer luck, picked up a violin, that we discovered he had such a talent for the instrument. A genius for it, in fact."

"How did he accidentally pick up a violin?" I'm curious. I've wanted to ask Darius all these questions myself but haven't been able to build up the courage.

"He had an aid back then who helped him get around, and they went into a music shop with some buddies 'cause they were looking for an electric guitar, and there happened to be a violin on display. Of course, it wasn't as though he could see the instrument, but he said he was drawn to it. He put his hands on it, traced the shape and the strings, and he picked it up, together with the bow, and played it then and there. No lessons, nothing. It was like magic.

"The old shop owner watched it happen, and he was so taken aback by Darius's playing that he insisted on funding lessons. I said we had no money for anything like that, but he wouldn't hear of it. He said we could pay him back when Darius was playing to huge audiences in Vienna. Sadly, he died before we could do that, but I know Dax brought him a lot of joy while he'd been alive."

"He just picked up a violin and played?" I said.

"That's right. Of course, he's always loved music, especially after losing his sight, but never classical. I think it was as much a shock to him as it was to us, but he's never looked back." Reed gives a small smile. "Good thing for us. I can't imagine what any of our lives would be like if it weren't for Darius's talent."

I'm still trying to figure out how Darius has made *all* of them wealthy. "But surely it's Darius's money? I mean, he's a grown man. It's not like he has to share."

"I manage him, which means I take my cut, and Cade is head of his security. He couldn't do it without either of us, and he knows it, which is why he pays well."

I wonder if Darius ever wants to be rid of his father and brother. Doesn't he ever want to branch out on his own? Hire his own people? Or does he believe it's better to keep his family close? Maybe he thinks they're the only ones he can fully trust? I can't imagine how it must be for Darius, traveling from city to city, always in unfamiliar places, surrounded by strangers. It would be difficult enough to live that way as a seeing person, but being blind must throw up a whole heap of different challenges.

Maybe that's why he keeps his family around.

I offer Reed a smile. "I'm sorry I was such a bitch to you."

He glances at the ground. "No, you weren't. Certainly no more than I deserve. I should have thought about you, especially after Darius's career took off. I'm sorry I didn't."

I step into him, and surprise myself by wrapping my arms around his neck. His hands slip around my waist, holding me close. I find myself with my cheek against his chest, and he lowers his face and presses his lips to the crown of my head.

I'm not sure how long we stay that way, but, when we part, there's a new kind of understanding between us.

"We should get back," Reed says, nodding in the direction of the cabin. "They'll wonder where we've gotten to."

We continue on our way, back to the cabin, where we'll spend what remaining light we have sharing out our food rations and either waiting for rescue, or for darkness to fall...

Whichever comes first.

19
REED

THE DAY HAS PASSED with no sign of rescue. Now, our second night here has fallen, and I lie on my back on the thin mattress and stare up at the ceiling. Beside me, Laney's soft breaths deepen as she falls to sleep. I'm painfully conscious of the exact position of her long limbs, of the way her hair fans across the tiny pillow.

I *did* look at her, naked, in the river.

I hadn't planned to, but her offhand comment about me not being able to see a bear coming if I wasn't looking had been playing on my mind. I'd honestly thought she'd have at least kept her underwear on, but when I glanced over, just to make sure she was safe, I discovered her completely naked. She was standing, thigh deep in the river, her back to me. Her long hair had been twisted up into a knot on top of her head, so she'd exposed the elegant line of her neck and back. I couldn't help but follow her spine down, to the curves of her ass and the length of her thighs, before they vanished beneath the water.

She was so breathtakingly beautiful, I completely forgot my promise for a moment, and just stood there, staring.

Combined with the gorgeous scenery of the river and surrounding forest, she's like something out of a screenshot of a movie.

It wasn't that I was thinking about her sexually, though I had to admit—not out loud—that it was a struggle. It was just like admiring a beautiful photograph. I managed to tear my eyes away from her and turn back around, but it took every ounce of my self-restraint not to sneak another glimpse. I'd pictured her using the bodywash and running her soapy hands over her breasts and flat stomach, and then down between her thighs. I'd felt myself lengthen and harden as the images danced in my mind, and I'd done my best to force them away.

She's my stepdaughter. She's seventeen. She's out of bounds.

Except now I can't get the image out of my mind.

20
laney

THE DAYS TICK by with no sign of help coming.

We're all starving, our stomachs growling audibly. We're down to the final few packets of nuts and crackers, and I hate to think what the atmosphere is going to be like in the cabin when they're gone.

I can already see the difference in my body shape from the lack of food. My jeans hang from my hips. I try not to let it get me down, but it's not easy. I've never been particularly curvy—probably due to my lack of food during my developing years—and that I might lose what few curves I have is depressing. Each time I find myself feeling down about it, I remind myself of the flight attendant and how she'd have happily lost a few pounds if it meant she got to keep her life.

I try not to cry in front of any of the men. I don't want them to see me as a burden or as being weaker than them, even though I am, physically. There isn't much I can do about that, though. If I need to cry, I go down to the river and tell them I'm going to wash, or I lock myself in the bathroom. Maybe they notice my red eyes and blotchy skin, but if they do, none of them says anything.

The men seem to find their release in the physical tasks that need doing—the chopping and hauling of logs in for the fire. Darius has taken that job—not the chopping of wood, but the clearing and setting and feeding of the fireplace. It keeps the cabin cozy and means we can signal for help if we do hear or see signs of a helicopter.

We probably could have put the mattresses back on the beds by now, and maybe one or two of us could have taken the bedroom, but there seems to be a silent agreement between us all that we don't want to be separated. There's a comfort in us all sleeping in the same room.

In the bedroom, I find a set of shelves filled with paperbacks. They're slightly swollen with damp, the pages yellowing, but they're legible. Most of them appear to be old eighties and nineties horror books by authors like James Herbert, Dean Koontz, and Stephen King. They're not the sort of thing I'd normally choose to read, but beggars can't be choosers.

I pick one up, and the slightly terrifying face of a drawn rat with red eyes stares back at me. I hurriedly shelve it again.

Maybe I won't be reading that one. I hope there aren't too many real rats or mice around. I'm not a fan.

I flick through the other books and discover one is a woodsman's guide to edible plants. That could come in handy. I carry it out onto the porch and take a seat to continue the lookout for a search team. I have the book open on my lap, but I'm not really reading it. I don't feel I can pay proper attention to the skies if I've got my nose buried in a book. It's been days now, though, and my hopes that anyone is coming for us are dwindling.

Movement comes from the bushes, and I straighten, muscles tense, senses alert. Cade appears, and I relax, but only a fraction. He strides up to the cabin with all the bravado of a street fighter who's just won a brawl. From one hand dangles a good-sized bird that's clearly dead.

"Anyone hungry?" he calls.

"You caught the grouse!" I say in delight.

"Didn't I tell you I would? Boil some water so we can pluck and gut it. Dunking it in boiled water will make the feathers easier to pull out."

I don't normally appreciate Cade ordering me around—especially not for things that involve the kitchen—but I'm so delighted at the thought of getting to eat some meat that I don't care. I hop out of my seat and hurry inside the cabin.

Darius is sitting on the couch, his violin in his hands. His head is down, shoulders rounded.

"Cade caught a grouse," I tell him, excited. "We're going to eat well today."

"Yeah? That's great."

Despite his words, his tone doesn't sound like mine.

I pause. "Everything okay?"

He raises his eyebrows. "As it can be."

"You're missing home."

"Am I? I'm not even sure I know where home is."

I think back. "Didn't Reed say you have a house in Maine?"

He gives a strange chuckle. "Yeah, we might own a house there, but I couldn't tell you when we last went back to it. It's just a roof and four walls, no different than staying in yet another hotel room. I don't have any kind of attachment to the place."

"I'm sorry," I say.

I remember the water I'm supposed to be putting on the stove for Cade. He's in a good mood, for once, and I don't want to piss him off.

"What about you?" Darius asks. "Do you miss home?"

The largest pan is already filled with water, and I carry it over to the stove.

"Honestly, I'm not really sure. The trailer is the only place I ever lived, but I never felt about it the way people are supposed to think about their homes. I didn't ever go home expecting to find a sanctuary or comfort or even love."

"Your mother didn't love you?"

I chew my lower lip. "She probably did, in her own way, but she didn't know how to show it."

"But you loved her?"

I swallow past the emotion that suddenly forms in a painful ball in my throat. "Yeah, I did."

We wait as the water heats, and then carry it outside to the porch. Reed has been gathering more firewood, and he appears with his arms full of sticks.

"What's going on?"

Cade holds up the carcass, the feathers bloodied and matted. "I caught this. I just gutted the bird away from the cabin. I didn't want it to attract any wildlife."

Reed grins and smacks his son on the shoulder. "Good work."

"I think I've figured out a trapping system now," he says. "I found some string, and I've been testing different knots. Looks like we won't starve after all."

He dunks the bird in the water, and then plucks it. Then we take it back into the cabin, and he roasts it on the fire. It smells incredible, and my mouth waters. When it's ready, Cade shares it out equally between us.

I push my portion back at him. "You three are bigger than me. You should get more."

He doesn't take it. "No way. We might be bigger, but that means we can afford to lose more weight. There's barely anything left of you."

I wait for Reed or Darius to protest, but they don't say a word. They're too busy digging into their own food.

"Thanks," I say.

I am starving, and I'm grateful for the meal. My mouth is

watering so much I think I might actually drool. I lift the chunk of hot meat to my mouth and take a huge bite. The meat is darker than chicken, a bit more like duck, only nowhere near as fatty. As I chew and swallow, and then take another bite, I'd swear I can feel the energy returning to me, like I'm coming back to life.

I speak around my mouthful, my voice coming out muffled. "This must be the best thing I've ever tasted."

The cabin is filled with the sound of meat being torn from bone and people chewing. It's a noise that would normally grate on me, but honestly, in that moment, I don't even care. All I'm focused on is getting that hot, sweet flesh down my throat and into my stomach. The heat of the grouse burns my fingers, but again, I ignore it.

I suck on the bones until they're clean and then sit back and let out a loud burp. I cover my mouth and laugh. "Excuse me."

Cade raises an eyebrow and chuckles. "Such a lady."

I toss the bone at him. "Never claimed to be one. If you can catch another grouse sometime soon, I'd be most appreciative."

"Would you, now? How appreciative?"

There's a teasing, flirting tone to his voice, and I shoot a quick look at Reed to see if he's picked up on it. He seems to be too engrossed in his meal to have noticed, but Darius has angled his head in Cade's direction.

"Not *that* appreciative."

Cade only laughs. "Well, I didn't see any more grouse, but I've noticed a few rabbits hopping around at dusk. I reckon I could catch a couple of those if I set my mind on it."

"I've never eaten rabbit either," I say.

"I guess this is going to be a whole raft of first times for you, then."

Cade catches my eye and holds my gaze. My heart suddenly trips and heat blooms in my cheeks. I hate how he has this ability to make me blush with just a few words or a single look. He has no way of knowing for sure that it would even be my first time—

assuming he is referring to sex, and not the eating of various forms of wildlife. The problem with Cade is that he just exudes sex appeal. It's like his body was made for it, and it's all he thinks about, and he's probably got pheromones blasting out of him in waves. It makes it feel like everything he's doing and saying is referring back to sex.

I don't bother reminding him that I'm his stepsister and that I'm still seventeen—albeit by only a matter of days—and that he shouldn't really be talking to me like that. He'd probably feign innocence and then would claim it was me who had the dirty mind.

Perhaps he'd be right.

Refusing to be the first one to look away, I lift my greasy fingers to my mouth and suck them off, one by one. The smirk creeps into a full-blown smile, and I can't help myself—I smile back. A warmth blooms inside my belly that has nothing to do with the amount of food that's in it.

I discover I kind of like messing with Cade. He can be a total asshole, but perhaps this is a better way of dealing with him than trying to fight him all the time.

21
laney

I OPEN my eyes in the early morning light to find Reed crouched in front of me. He's holding a small packet of cookies with a tealight candle balanced on top and is grinning at me manically. Has he lost his mind?

I push myself to sitting. "What's this?"

"It's the tenth," he tells me. "It's your eighteenth birthday."

I blink in surprise. "I'd completely forgotten about my birthday."

"Congratulations," Cade says with his customary smirk. "Looks like you're an adult now."

There's something about his words that makes me catch my breath. An adult. An equal to all three of them. No longer underage.

"And I've got this for later." Cade produces one of the miniature bottles of champagne that he'd taken from the plane.

I can't help laughing. "I'm still not twenty-one."

"If we're over the Canadian border somewhere, the drinking age isn't twenty-one anymore." He screws up his nose. "I think it might be nineteen, though I could be wrong. But who gives a shit, anyway? Who is going to know with us being out in the middle of nowhere? No one can tell us what to do."

I glance over to Reed, who also shrugs.

"You're eighteen now. I guess that means, legally, I'm not your guardian anymore. You're free to do what you want."

"You're still my stepfather," I point out. "Legally, anyway."

"Yeah, I guess I am, though I don't feel it." He glances away, a shadow passing across his handsome features, suddenly troubled by something.

I get the same feeling passing over me as I did when Cade mentioned that I was legally an adult now. It's like threads of restraint are pinging off me, and a new sense of freedom settles in my soul. Though I feel like I've been independent from a very young age—out of necessity rather than want—now I don't need to explain myself to anyone else. I can live my life how I want to live it.

Then I remember where I am. Okay, maybe not quite how I planned on living it, and honestly, if we don't find a steady source of food soon, I'm not sure how long we'll have left, but it still gives me a kind of power among the men.

I purse my lips and blow out the candle, and then lift my gaze to find Reed staring down at me.

I smile back. "Thanks."

"Happy birthday, Laney," he says, and then he leans in and kisses my cheek. The kiss is so fleeting, like a brush of a feather against my skin, that a part of me wonders if it even really happened.

His jaw is covered in stubble now, though I know he has shaving cream and razors in his bag. The other two are the same. I guess I can understand not being bothered about shaving considering where we are. I'm just grateful that I've always been a fan of waxing, so I don't have to worry about hair growth, at least for the minute. When things start to get out of control, I'll have to ask one of the men if I can borrow their razors and cream.

I catch myself. Are we really going to be here that long that I'm going to need to worry about things like that? It's only been a week since the crash, and though this has been one of the longest weeks of my life, I'm sure it's not that long when it comes to search times. With each passing day, the search teams must be getting closer and closer to us narrowing down the area where we crashed. I refuse to believe that no one is looking for us or that they have just given up. Darius is a big name, and though people might not give one shit about what happened to me, I'm sure his disappearance is pasted all over social media and the news. I imagine there being big campaigns done to raise funds to try to find him, and there might even be search groups made of his fans trawling through the forest. I try not to think about Cade's comment about how the search area would be made up of a hundred square miles. He can't possibly be right about that. I also don't want to give any thought to the fact that the plane's computers weren't working properly when we crashed. How do we even know that the last time it pinged off our location it was giving the right readings? The fact of the matter is that we don't, but if I think on this too hard, I will lose hope.

Right now, hope is the only thing I've got left.

"How do you want to spend the day?" Reed asks.

"First, I want to eat these cookies."

"Sounds like a plan. What would you have been doing if you were home?"

I shrug. "Probably nothing different than any other day. It's not like my mom would have remembered, anyway. I mean, she wouldn't if she hadn't died."

Reed winces. "I'm sorry."

"To be honest, if she'd realized it was my eighteenth birthday, she would have thought it was a good excuse to have a party, and things would have been even worse than normal. She'd probably have gone to a bar and picked up a couple of random men and brought them back. I hate to think what they'd have done if they found out I was eighteen."

His expression darkens. "Had that happened before?"

I can't look at him, my cheeks warming. "Yes, plenty of times. I was younger then, of course, but plenty of them were too drunk to care." I give a cold laugh. "Or maybe it had nothing to do with how much they'd drunk and they just didn't give a shit about my age."

Reed's face is thunder. "Did they—"

He can't even say the word.

I lift an eyebrow. "Rape me? No, things never went that far. They were normally so wasted I could slip away from them when I saw what direction things were heading, but there were plenty of times I had to deal with them groping me and trying to kiss me."

I shudder at the memory, immediately nauseated. I can almost smell the stale alcohol and cigarettes on their breath, their clammy hands pushing up under my clothes.

Reed clenches his fists, and a muscle in his jaw ticks. "I've never even met any of these men, but I swear if one of them was standing in front of me right now I would tear his head from his shoulders."

I offer him a smile. "That's no use to me whatsoever, but I appreciate the sentiment."

Reed covers his face with his hands and then lowers them again. "Fuck. I should have been there. I could have fought those bastards off for you."

"Well, you couldn't have been there. You had Darius and Cade to look after."

"I wish I'd been there for all of you."

"You're here now."

I unwrap the cookies. The sweet scent of sugar fills my senses, and my mouth waters.

I have no intention of eating these without sharing. I break the first one in half and give the other half to Reed, and then share the next one between Cade and Darius.

"It's your birthday," Darius says. "You don't have to share."

"I want to. I wouldn't enjoy them unless I knew you were, too."

Silence, other than the sound of crunching, falls around us.

"You know," I say thoughtfully, "I don't know when any of your birthdays are."

"Darius is a March baby," Reed says.

Darius nods in agreement. "March the fifth."

"What about you, Reed?" I ask.

"Just had my birthday. August the twelfth. That's when I turned forty. Lucky me."

"Old man," Darius throws at him with a grin.

"Hey, less of that," Reed says, but he's laughing.

I don't think of Reed as being an old man at all. I know he's older, but if I saw him in the street, I wouldn't have put him in his forties. Clearly, he's older than Cade and Darius—I can see it in the faint lines around his eyes and across his forehead, and in the flecks of gray at his temples—but I'd never have thought of him as being old.

"You're a Leo, then, Reed," I say, "and Darius is a Pisces. That makes sense. Pisces are creative and imaginative and sensitive."

"So, what are Leos like?" Reed asks.

I try to remember. "Hmm…they're natural born leaders."

Reed grins, clearly liking the description. "Like a lion leading the pack."

"Exactly. It also means you like drama and being the center of attention."

He roars with laughter.

"What about you, Cade?" I ask.

"December twenty-third," Cade says, lifting a hand as though he's asking permission to speak in school. "Yep, I'm a Christmas baby. Lucky me. No one ever wanted to come to a birthday party when Christmas was almost here."

"You're a Capricorn, then. The goat. Determined and sometimes a bit ruthless."

His lips quirk. "Sounds like me."

I think for a minute, chewing at the inside of my mouth. "Do you think we're going to be back to civilization by Christmas? What about Thanksgiving?"

Reed offers me a smile of empathy. "I hope so. It's not going to be easy surviving here when it starts to get cold."

It's still warm right now, but I dread to think what it's going to be like here in a matter of only a month or two. We have the wood stove to help keep the cabin warm, but we're going to need to stack a lot of wood to keep us going. There's an axe out the back, but even if we start chopping down wood now, it won't be seasoned. Plus, we won't only have staying warm to worry about. The forest has been a good source of food, but once everything is covered in a blanket of snow, that sustenance will vanish. It's not as though we've got anything stored up to last us over winter.

I want to kid myself that we'll be found by then, but trying to convince myself of that when it might not be true could ultimately lead to our deaths.

What's more likely to kill us? Trying to hike to safety, or trying to last out the winter here?

Right now, I have no idea. Both options feel like suicide missions. If we try to hike and get even more lost and the weather turns, we won't even have any shelter. Perhaps freezing to death will be a kinder way to go than starving.

"What do you want to do for the rest of your birthday?" Reed asks.

"Let's go and hang out down by the river. It looks like it's going to be another nice day. We can swim and soak up some sun."

He grins. "Your wish is our command, birthday girl."

22
CADE

I DON'T WANT to like Laney, but she's growing on me. I try to imagine how things would be here without her and can't.

Is it because the money factor has been removed now? Yes, I thought the only reason she'd latched onto our family was to drain us of our dough, but, out here, we're all broke. Money doesn't matter. I also thought that she was a cold-hearted bitch. Her mother had literally died that afternoon, and she'd gotten all dressed up and gone to a concert with my father. Who the fuck does that? It brought back memories of my own mother's death, of how traumatic it was to watch her get weaker and weaker, and then completely waste away. She was like a skeleton in the end, and I'm so fucking ashamed to admit it, but I was frightened of her. Her fingers were like bones and her eyes had been hollows in her skull. She'd needed the comfort of her eldest son and, instead, I'd kept my distance. I'll never forgive myself for that.

There is so much I'll never forgive myself for.

So it was hard watching Laney swan around on my father's arm in a five hundred dollar dress only a matter of hours after her mother had died. Didn't she care? I thought I could be cold, but then I thought she must have been a fucking ice queen. It's only since we've been here that I've seen the other side of her. She's not cold—she's just protective of her heart. She doesn't want to show her emotions to anyone. To be vulnerable with us.

I get that.

We're more comfortable and confident around the cabin now. We spend a lot of time down by the river, trying to catch fish, or just bathing or swimming. Laney doesn't have a swimsuit, of course, but she's comfortable around us now in a plain bra and a pair of panties. She tells us to think of it like she's wearing a bikini, but it's not that easy for me to do. Darius can't see her, of course, but I catch Reed staring at her when he thinks no one is looking. Her body is long and lean and elegant, with just the right curve to her hips and breasts. She doesn't seem to be aware of it, but she's like a fucking supermodel.

I pick up a flat pebble, and in an area of the river where the boulders have created a shallow pool, sheltered from the rush of the water, I toss the stone. It skips on the surface—once, twice—before sinking to the riverbed.

Laney has been lying sprawled out on the bank, catching some sun, but now she sits up and looks in the direction I threw the pebble.

"How did you do that?" she asks.

I turn toward her. "Do what?"

"Make the pebble jump across the water like that."

"Make it skim, you mean? Haven't you ever skimmed stones before?"

"Nope."

I laugh. "You've led a sheltered life."

She gives me a look that tells me I don't know what I'm talking about but doesn't argue with me.

"So, teach me what I need to do."

Darius climbs down from the rock where he's been sitting and joins us. He drops to a crouch and feels around until his fingers close over a flat, dark gray stone. He picks it up and rises back to standing, and then flicks his wrist skillfully and lets the stone fly. It jumps across the water, once, twice, three times, before sinking.

"All right, bro," I say. "You trying to show me up?"

He grins. "You're showing yourself up."

Reed joins us. "What are you guys up to?"

"Stone skimming competition," I tell him. "Think you can compete, old man?"

He chuckles. "Compete? I can wash the floor with all of you."

"I'd like to see that."

"Oh, you will."

Reed hits four skips, and he turns and holds one hand up for a high-five. We all leave him hanging.

"My turn," Laney says.

She throws the first stone. It hits the water and sinks straight under.

I'm about to clap and jeer, but she turns around with such disappointment in those light blue eyes that the laughter dies on my lips.

"What did I do wrong?" she asks.

"You need to skim it. It's all in the wrist action." I demonstrate without a stone in hand, flicking my wrist.

"I guess you're good at wrist action," she teases, a note of flirtation in her tone.

It lights up my entire body, my blood sparking. "Be good, Cuckoo," I warn her.

She doesn't want to go down that route with me. She's far too innocent, and I will corrupt every inch of her.

"Let me show you."

I stand behind Laney, my chest pressed to her back. I wrap one arm around her tiny waist and take her right hand in mine, so the back of it is in my palm. I can't help myself. I press my nose to her hair and inhale deeply. She's been washing her hair in the river, but only every few days, so she smells more like her than any kind of fake fragrances in the shampoo. I have to create space between us from the waist down or else she'll feel my erection lengthening. I fight the urge to jam myself up against her, to grind against her ass. She's only in her underwear, and it's fucking with my head and my body. It wouldn't take much to snap open the back of her bra and toss the item away. I picture her standing there, her breasts bare, and I get even harder. Fuck. It's going to be difficult to focus on skimming a stone when all I'm thinking about is the noises she'd make if she let me go down on her.

Maybe I should be telling myself that she's my stepsister and I shouldn't be thinking about her in such a way, but I don't see her as a stepsister. Plus, she's eighteen now.

What would Reed do if I fucked her? He'd lose his shit, I'm pretty sure about that. But would he be mad because he's supposed to be protecting her, and technically we're related? Or would he only be angry because he'd wish he got there first?

Of course, I'm forgetting one important thing. Laney might not want to fuck me. But I consider myself a good judge of these things, and there have definitely been moments between us.

"Ready?" I ask her.

She nods.

I pull back her hand and then flick it forward.

Nothing happens.

Laney giggles. "I forgot to let go of the stone."

I find myself laughing, too. "Muppet."

She spins in my arms, her eyes wide with amusement. "Muppet?"

I shrug. "Better than Cuckoo."

"I was getting kind of fond of Cuckoo."

Her gaze travels down my bare chest, and I watch her expression morph once more as she catches sight of the way my shorts are tented by my erection. I lean in and speak low, so the others don't hear. "Like what you see?"

She takes a sharp breath and her lips part. "Show me again."

I smile and pull her back up against me in the same position I had before. Only this time, I don't keep the space between my cock and her body. I jam myself hard up against her, grinding, but not enough for the others to notice. With the arm that's around her waist, I hold her even closer. My fingers are itching to slip down the front of her panties, to travel down between her thighs and then push up inside her, but Reed is glancing over with a slight frown, as though he's picked up on the sexual tension between us.

We flick the stone together, and this time she remembers to let go. It skims across the surface twice.

"Whoohoo!" she cries. "Now let me do it by myself."

She does and gets another two jumps on the stone.

"You've got it," I tell her.

She throws me a smile, and my heart tightens. Fuck. That smile.

I'm suddenly filled with the certainty that I would do absolutely anything for her to smile at me that way again.

23
laney

A WEEK HAS PASSED since my birthday, and there's still no sign of rescue.

I want to do my part, so I go around to the woodshed at the back of the cabin to chop up some kindling. I've been doing my best to bring back fallen branches that I come across in the woods, but I'm fully aware that I can't haul the large logs around that the men do. I don't like feeling as though I'm somehow inferior to them, or that they're having to carry me. I want to do my part.

I might not be able to lift a log, but I can lift an axe and chop one. We got lucky in that an axe had been left in the woodshed. It was old and a little rusty, but one of the guys had done their best to sharpen the blade using a rock from the riverbank. There are still some orange spots on the metal, but it's sharp enough for wood.

Lifting the axe, I get to work, splitting the wood down into smaller slivers. It doesn't take long before my arms, shoulders, and back are aching. Sweat runs down my spine and from my hairline, stinging my eyes. In the time since we've been here, I can already see my body changing, and not only that I'm probably thinner than I used to be. I've got muscles where I'd never noticed them before. The men are also ripped with muscle from all the physical work, and it's highlighted by the loss of body fat from no longer having access to all the hotel room service they'd been living on.

Something large and buzzing flutters around my ear, distracting me, just as I'm bringing the axe in a downward arch.

I strike the wood at the wrong angle and the blade glances off the wood

The axe slips and catches me in the leg, at the spot right above my ankle.

I let out a cry of pain and shock.

Dammit!

I take a couple of shaky breaths and drop the axe to check my leg. It could have been a lot worse. I'm lucky I didn't lose my foot or chop off a couple of toes. I sit on the ground and check the wound. It doesn't look too deep, but it's bleeding, the blood soaking into my sock.

"Shit."

I use the bottle of boiled water I've got with me to wash out the cut. In regular society, I might consider going to the ER to get stitches, but we're nowhere near a hospital. I'm just going to have to wrap it up in a piece of torn t-shirt and hope for the best.

I don't want to tell the others what I've done, which means I don't want them to see me either, at least not until I've got my leg sorted.

I check for any sign of them and hurry back into the cabin. I find the first aid kit we took from the plane and carry it with me into the bathroom. I also grab a pair of jeans so I can change out of my bloodied ones. I'll have to hide them, or the men are going to ask questions.

I slip back in through the cabin's front door, go to my bag to grab what I need, and then hurry to the bathroom. I'm walking with a limp, and I'll have to disguise that when I'm with the guys. I'd tell them that I twisted my ankle, but then they'll probably demand to see it. Maybe I'll say it's my hip that's hurting, that I slept wrong on it. They wouldn't ask to see that, would they? I think of Cade and his flirtatious nature. Maybe he would?

I change my jeans and check my ankle. Spots of red appear through the piece of material that I've wrapped it in, but it doesn't look too bad. As long as the bleeding stops and I don't ruin another pair of jeans, I'm sure it will be fine.

Reed enters the cabin just as I'm exiting the bathroom. I shove the bloodied jeans behind my back.

"Oh, hi," I say.

He stops and studies me for a moment. "Everything all right, Laney?"

"Yeah, sure. Why do you ask?"

He angles his head slightly, lines appearing between his eyebrows. "You look kinda pale."

"Do I?" I flap my hand in front of my face. "No idea why, 'cause I'm boiling."

He gives me another curious look but seems to accept me at my word. A tiny thread of guilt winds into my heart. I shouldn't be lying to him, but I know he'll kick up a stink if he knows I've hurt myself. He'll decide I'm incapable of doing anything and will try to stop me walking into the woods or going down to the river. I'm already trapped in a small cabin with three large men.

I don't want to lose what freedom I have just because of a stupid accident.

I wake the following morning and instantly know I'm sick. Fuck. My head is pounding and, though I feel hot, I can't stop shivering. I still don't want to let the others down though. There are chores to be done. I hope if I get up and start moving around, have something to eat and drink, that I'll feel better.

I swing my legs out of bed and pull on my jeans, wincing. It's like every muscle in my body aches and my skin is hypersensitive. I go to the wood stove. The logs have burned down overnight, leaving only embers, so I grab some kindling and toss it on.

Darius frowns in my direction. "Something is wrong with you."

"I'm fine, honestly."

"Bullshit. I can hear your teeth chattering, and something else is different as well." He sniffs the air. "I can smell it."

My cheeks are already burning, but now they turn molten. I've done my best to stay as clean as possible, given the circumstances, but have I been skimping too much on the soap, in the hope of eking it out?

"Look, we've been stuck out in the middle of nowhere with only the river to wash in, so I don't really think—"

He raised his hand to cut me off. "I'm not talking about you not washing. It's something else."

He's garnered the attention of Reed and Cade now.

"What's going on?" Cade asks.

"There's something wrong with Laney." He says it as an absolute fact. He doesn't doubt himself for a second.

Reed turns to me. "Is that true, Laney? Is something wrong? Are you sick?"

"I-I'm not sure. I have a headache, and I guess I'm a bit feverish."

Darius speaks without doubt. "She has an infection."

I snap at him. "Christ, what are you, a damned bloodhound?"

Reed and Cade exchange a glance.

Reed places his hand on my forehead. "You're burning up. How long have you felt sick?"

I press my lips together and don't meet his eye. "Only since this morning." There's no point in lying. "I nicked my leg with the axe when I was chopping wood yesterday. I thought it was fine."

His eyes widen. "You did? Why didn't you say anything?"

"I didn't want to make a fuss."

"Let me see it. Now."

I don't dare disobey. I lift the cuff of my jeans and expose the spot above my ankle where I caught it with the blade. The material is blood-soaked.

"Jesus." Reed shakes his head. "Sit down."

I plonk myself on a wooden chair, and he crouches at my feet. He lifts the cuff of my jeans again and then carefully unwinds the makeshift bandage to expose my skin. There's a red circle around the wound, and it looks angry and bigger than it was before.

He makes a disapproving *tsk* sound with his tongue. "That's infected. Why didn't you say anything?"

"I poured some alcohol onto the wound to clean it. I thought it would be okay."

The muscles in his shoulders and the back of his neck are tense, standing out beneath his skin. He's tanned over the past couple of weeks, his skin deepening to golden.

"It's clearly not." His tone is terse. "That axe blade is rusty. You could have given yourself tetanus or something. When did you last have a shot?"

I find myself blinking back tears. I feel like shit, and now he's angry with me. Not only that, he's frightening me.

"I-I haven't."

"You haven't had a tetanus shot?"

I shake my head. "Not that I can remember, no. You know what my mother was like."

He softens a fraction. "Shit, yeah. I'm sorry, Laney."

Despite my best efforts, tears spill down my cheeks. I can't help it. My head hurts, and I feel like shit, and I'm stuck out in the middle of nowhere with an infected leg. What if it gets worse? I can't get any medical help out here, and it's not as though we have antibiotics on hand. I have visions of my leg and foot turning black. Will I even know or care by that point? Or will I be so sick I'll wish I'm dead.

"I don't want to die," I whisper.

"Oh, baby," Reed says and pulls me into a hug. "You're not going to die. We're going to take care of you. I promise."

Baby. It's the first time he's ever called me that, and for some reason it makes me cry even harder.

I cling to him and sob against his broad chest. My shoulders shake, even as he holds me tight, and I dampen the front of his t-shirt with my tears. His body feels so big and strong, and, for a moment, he makes me believe I will be okay.

But then a wave of dizziness sweeps over me, followed by a rush of cold that starts my teeth chattering again.

"Come on, let's get you back to bed."

He untangles me and scoops me up in his arms and carries me over to the mattress that's become my bed. My eyelids are impossibly heavy, and I struggle to keep them open.

"You're going to have to stay awake a little longer," Reed says. "We need to clean your leg up again, try to stop the infection."

Cade moves closer. "Won't it be in her bloodstream now?"

He sounds worried, and that worries me even more. I don't think he's ever been concerned about me in any way before, but now his tone is low, and I can sense the tension in it.

Darius crouches at my shoulder and his long fingers sweep my hair away from my sweaty brow. "There's no reason her immune system won't be strong enough to fight it. We just have to keep the wound clean, and make sure she's hydrated."

His touch is gentle and soothing, and, as though he can read what my body needs, he strokes my hair over and over.

Reed reaches for my waist. "I'm going to need to take your jeans off so you're more comfortable. Is that okay?"

I nod. He can do whatever he likes. I'm completely in their hands.

He pops the button and undoes the zipper, and then lifts my hips slightly to pull down my jeans. My panties are dragged with the material, but I don't even have the energy to be embarrassed when he pulls them back into place.

"Here, I've got the alcohol and one of the swabs from the first aid kit," Cade says.

I'm fully aware that I'm lying here in just my tiny, black lace panties and a t-shirt, surrounded by three men. Darius can't see me, of course, but I'm sure he pictures me just fine. I don't even care. His touch feels so good as he continues to stroke my hair. I never want him to stop.

Cade hands the items to Reed.

"This is probably going to sting," Reed tells me.

I nod. "It's okay. Do whatever you have to."

To my surprise, Cade takes hold of my hand.

"Squeeze as hard as you need to."

I find myself smiling at him, despite the pain I'm in. "I might hurt you."

He returns the smile. "I doubt it. You're as weak as a kitten right now."

I don't like being told I'm weak, so I squeeze his fingers as hard as I can to prove my point. He doesn't even flinch, and the effort it's taken me to try to hurt him has sapped the last residue of my strength. I fall slack against the mattress but don't let go of Cade's hand.

"Ready?" Reed says from down by my feet.

Weakly, I nod.

Cold wetness hits my skin and, a split second later, red hot fire shoots up through my leg. I cry out and grip Cade's hand and grit my teeth. Darius's palm remains on my forehead, and I break out in a fresh sweat.

I thrash and kick. "Ow, stop, please!

"Hold still," Reed instructs, his firm hand pinning down my shin. "I'm not done yet."

Tears spring to my eyes. "No, please. It hurts."

"I know, baby. Try to breathe. It'll be over soon. But I have to do a good job of flushing this wound out, okay? It's important."

The initial wave of agony has subsided into a dull throb. I sink into the mattress again and prepare myself for the second wave. It hits just as hard as the first, and I cry out. I try to yank my legs away, wanting to curl into a ball, but Reed has a solid hold on me and doesn't let me budge.

"Almost done now. I'm going to put some antiseptic cream on it and bandage it up to keep it clean."

"Okay," I whisper.

I hold still while he bandages my ankle. I'm still holding Cade's hand, and Darius's palm remains on my forehead, stroking my sweaty hair from my face. I take comfort in their presence, and, at some point, I must fall asleep.

I have no idea how much time has passed when I come back to. I feel awful. I don't think I've ever been so sick in my life. I'm only vaguely aware of my surroundings, and I struggle to stay with the real world, the darkness beckoning me back under.

I don't know how many times I repeat this process, waking and sleeping. It's a strange kind of sleep, almost as if I'm trapped somewhere between my dream world and the real one, but I can't quite get fully to either.

I'm aware of the men moving around me, of low voices filled with concern. They drip water into my mouth, but I struggle to swallow.

Am I going to die like this?

24

REED

THE ONLY TIME I can ever remember being this scared about another person was when Darius was seven and came down with the measles and ended up in the coma that would eventually lead to him losing his sight.

Cade was the one who'd brought the virus home and gave it to his brother. I had no idea their mother hadn't vaccinated them. I didn't even know they were supposed to have had vaccines. I hadn't been a father long at that point. I was completely clueless.

Cade hadn't been too ill with it—a bit of a rash and a high temperature—but Darius was a whole other story. Maybe it was because he'd been a few years younger, or just that his immune system was different than Cade's—but the whole experience had been terrifying.

I'd wanted to run away so many times during that period. I'd fought the urge to go straight to the nearest bar and drown myself in a bottle of liquor. If it hadn't been for the boys, I probably would have. But I had Cade to take care of while Darius was in the hospital, isolated, and Cade had been frightened that he'd somehow managed to kill his little brother. I'm not sure it's

179

something Cade has ever really gotten over—blaming himself for Darius's illness and his disability—though of course it was never Cade's fault.

Now, looking down at Laney so sick, I can't help but be taken back to the horrific days, and the weeks and months that followed, with Darius having to learn how to live in the dark. It had been heartbreaking, and I'd wished over and over that their mother had still been alive so she could have been the one to deal with it all. Those poor kids, losing their mom and getting landed with me as a father, and then going through that.

Life isn't fair.

Bad shit happens to innocent people who don't deserve it, and that's why I know there's a chance she won't make it.

Laney barely seems conscious. She moans and thrashes in a fever-state. The three of us hover around her, all of us equally anxious. I don't think I've ever seen Cade worried about another person, other than his brother, but I can tell seeing her like this is getting to him.

"How much longer before the fever breaks?" he asks me.

"I have no idea, Cade. It might not."

He balls his fists, his shoulders going rigid, then he turns and storms out of the cabin, banging the door behind him as he goes. Knowing Cade, he'll be out punching a couple of trees any minute now. I swear under my breath. He'd better not break his hand. We have enough to deal with without him adding to it.

Darius sits on the edge of the couch that's closest to Laney's mattress. His head is bent over her, his forearms resting on his knees.

"What do you think?" I ask him. "Does she seem any better?"

He places his palm to her forehead and twists his lips. "No."

I want to punch something myself. "Fuck."

"Is it worth trying to carry her out of here?" Darius suggests. "Maybe we can get her to a doctor."

I shake my head. "If I thought there was any way of us walking out of here, I'd have suggested it before Laney got sick. To try it now while she is so weak would be suicide."

"What if just one of us goes to get help? The others can stay here with Laney?"

"No. I won't have us splitting up. It's too easy to get lost in these forests. You might think you're headed in one direction only to find you've been walking around in circles. I don't want to lose Laney, but I'm not losing you or Cade, either."

It occurs to me that I could offer to go, but I hold my tongue. It's not that I'm afraid to go, or to be on my own. It's more that I don't want to leave the three of them alone. I don't think I've imagined the tension between them all. When Laney is sitting with Darius, I catch Cade staring at her. I haven't missed the way Darius will find any excuse to be near her. Cade might be rude and dismissive when she's around, but he forgets that I've seen what he's like around women he doesn't really care about. He's all smiles and compliments, telling them what they want to hear. The fact he hasn't turned on that charm with Laney tells me he's uncomfortable with his feelings about her. That he even has feelings for a woman is uneasy for him.

What would happen if I left the three of them alone, and I'm unable to return? I worry the brothers would tear each other apart for her.

Wouldn't I do the same myself?

I push the thought from my head. She's my stepdaughter. I'm responsible for her. That she's now eighteen and fragile and beautiful shouldn't make any difference.

Cade returns an hour later with a freshly caught rabbit, already skinned and gutted.

"I know she can't eat right now," he says, "but I thought I could make a broth for her for when she wakes. She'll need to get her strength back. She's already too thin."

Laney is too thin. I can't help my gaze drifting down her

long, bare legs. She's kicked off the blanket, and we've left it off, thinking it's better that she's cooler since she's still running hot. She didn't have much body fat on her before the plane crash, and now I can see her hipbones jutting out. I tear my gaze away before it drifts to her panties and the area below the lacy material.

"Good idea," I manage to say, my voice hoarse.

Darius has got a cloth and some cold water and is placing it on her forehead to try to keep her temperature down. It occurs to me that I've never seen either of them caring for another person —other than each other—before. While I'd never want Laney to be sick, there's something comforting in how they're acting. Maybe I can trust them more than I thought.

The hours pass, and Laney continues to sleep. When Darius isn't wiping her forehead, her skin prickles with sweat and she moans and twists her head in her sleep. I tell myself that it's good she's resting, that's how her body will heal itself, but I watch her anxiously. I resist the temptation to remove the covering I've put on her wound, wanting to check if there are any further signs of infection. If I lift the gauze, germs could get in, and then I'd have to change it again. We only have a limited number, and I can't risk wasting any. Still, I watch her leg above and below the bandage, keeping an eye out for any change in color. If the red spreads, then I'll know the infection is also spreading.

What we need is antibiotics, but there's no chance of finding such a thing out here. All we can do is watch her and pray her body is strong enough to fight it.

Day turns to night, and we take it in turns to sit with her while the other two get some sleep. I'm not sure any of us can really switch off, though, and even when I try to get my head down, I'm unable to close my eyes for fear of waking to find Laney has taken a turn for the worse.

At some point, I give in to sleep. I'm unsure how long I doze, but when I wake, hazy daylight streams through the windows.

The others are awake, too.

Cade rubs his hand over his face. "Laney's still not woken up." His lips thin. "What if she dies?"

Darius spins to face him, his face contorted with rage. "Shut the fuck up, Cade."

"I'm just say—"

Darius shoves him in the chest. "Don't say it!"

"Stop it, both of you."

I don't want to get between them, but I will if I have to. It isn't the first time they've fought. I guess it's only natural, what with them being brothers. But when we're in a small cabin with a sick girl, now isn't the time. I also don't want them to cause any damage to each other. A broken nose or cheekbone won't be easy to fix out here.

I grab Cade's shoulder and place my other hand against Darius's chest. I'm well over six feet, and while not quite as big as Cade, I am around the same height and size and Darius, but I might as well not even be there.

"What the fuck, Dax?" Cade yells. "This isn't my fault, you know. You might still blame me for you getting sick when we were kids, but you can't blame me for Laney getting sick as well."

"I don't blame you. I just don't want you to tempt fate. And I don't blame you for what happened when we were kids. How many times do I have to say it before you believe me?"

Cade scowls, though Darius can't see his expression. Darius knows his brother well enough to not have to see him.

"Since when have you started giving a fuck about women?" Darius throws at him. "You never have before."

Cade stiffens. "I just don't want us to have to deal with another body, that's all."

Darius scoffs. "Bullshit. I can sense how you are around Laney. You like her."

"So what if I do? She's my stepsister, isn't she?"

"I think she's far more than that."

A weak, feminine voice comes from behind us. "Why are you fighting?"

25

laney

THEY'RE FIGHTING.

Reed is standing between Cade and Darius, using his hands to keep them apart. I'm sure I heard my name mentioned, but I've been so out of it that I can't be sure. Why would they be fighting about me? The last thing I want is to come between them.

Upon hearing my voice, Reed drops his hands, and instantly each of their body languages changes. Shoulders drop, expression soften, and their focus is now on me instead of each other.

"Laney?" Reed says, crossing the room to drop to a crouch beside me. "Baby. How are you feeling?"

"I-I'm not sure."

He places his hand to my forehead, and a tentative smile touches his lips. "I think your fever has broken."

"That's good, right?"

He takes his hand away. "Yeah, it's good."

"How long was I out?"

"Twenty-four hours. We took turns sitting up with you to make sure you didn't take a turn for the worse."

I wonder what they'd have done if I had gotten even more sick. It's not as though they'd have been able to call an ambulance.

"That was good of you," I say.

Reed takes a lock of my hair in his fingers and tucks it behind my ear. "You gave us a scare."

The tenderness of his touch makes me want to cry.

"Sorry."

"I made you some broth," Cade says. "Do you think you can manage a little?"

I gaze up at the big, tattooed man. "You cooked for me?"

Pink touches his cheeks, and he shrugs. "It's only broth."

"I think I can manage some. Thanks, Cade."

Darius brings me a glass of water. "Broth is good, but you need to hydrate, too."

I am incredibly thirsty. My throat burns, and every time I swallow it's like eating glass. I cough a couple of times and groan.

"I'll get you some Tylenol," Reed says.

Darius holds the glass to my lips, and I take a couple of grateful sips. It's cooling and soothes my throat.

"Thank you."

Reed returns with the pills, and I take them with the water. Then Cade brings me the broth. I'm not really hungry, but I'm sure it'll do me good, and I can't stand the thought of seeing the disappointment on Cade's face if I refuse it.

My leg still hurts like a bitch, and I ache all over. I barely have the strength to sit up. I'm nowhere near better yet, but at least now I can tell the difference between being asleep and awake. I go back over the conversation I overheard as I was emerging from unconsciousness. Darius was accusing Cade of having feelings for me. Could that be right? Cade hasn't always been exactly kind toward me.

I smile.

"What?" Reed asked.

"You three are flapping around me like mother hens."

"We're taking care of you, that's all."

"You're doing a good job."

"Thanks."

Cade spoon-feeds me the broth. It's rich and savory and goes down surprisingly easily. He's calm and patient, and even when I half cough as he puts the spoon to my mouth and I spray him in broth, he only chuckles and wipes my face with the corner of his sleeve.

"Sorry about that." I'm embarrassed.

"Don't worry about it. You had enough?"

I nod. "Thanks."

I'm suddenly exhausted again. My limbs are heavy, and I don't think I can sit up any longer. My leg is throbbing. I hope the Tylenol will kick in soon.

"She needs to get some rest," Reed says.

It's only when I go to pull the blankets back up around me that I realize I'm only in my t-shirt and panties. Something else dawns on me, too, and a fresh sense of mortification heats me from the inside. Though I'm aware that I'm dehydrated, my bladder is so full it's almost painful, and there is no way I can get to the toilet on my own.

"Can someone help me to the bathroom?"

"Of course," Reed says.

He scoops me up as though I weigh nothing. He carries me to the bathroom and literally places me on the toilet. He doesn't leave.

I find the strength to raise my eyebrows at him. "I think I can manage this part alone."

"Oh, sure. Shout when you're done." He leaves the small bathroom and closes the door behind him.

I really don't want Reed helping me off the toilet. I know

they've been caring for me since I've been sick, but I'd like to keep at least a fragment of dignity.

I finish up and pull my panties back up and use the wall to stand. My thighs tremble, and I struggle to put weight on the injured leg. I have no choice but to stop.

"Reed?"

I feel utterly pathetic. He opens the door and comes back in, then he scoops me up again, holding me against his chest. I wrap my arms around his neck and bury my face in his shoulder. Maybe I should care more that he's just practically had to carry me on and off the toilet, but honestly, I don't have the energy to care.

Just that tiny thing has sapped all the energy from me, and I'm thankful to be back in my bed, even if it is just a bare mattress on the floor. I note how I've got a couple of extra blankets and realize the men have donated theirs to me. I don't want them to go without, but I know if I try to give them back, they'll only refuse, and I don't have the strength to fight them.

A whole week passes before I finally start to feel like myself again.

The cut on my leg is still healing, but no longer looks sore and angry, and I'm able to bear weight on it. I hate that I haven't been able to help with any of the chores while I've been sick, and that the guys have been carrying me.

I want to do my part.

First, though, I need to wash. I've been brought wet rags and soap to clean up as best I can in the bathroom, but what I really want is to submerge myself in the cold, rushing water of the river. I know I'll feel so much better after I've ducked my head under. There's something revitalizing about it. It makes me understand why people are submerged in water to be baptized.

Reed and Cade are both out, checking the traps and gathering firewood. Darius stayed with me, though I told him I didn't need a babysitter. They're all still worried that I'll take a sudden turn, though. I won't forget how they took care of me when I was sick. They could have written me off, but instead, they nurtured me. I never would have thought them capable of being so caring. I have no doubt that I wouldn't have made it if it wasn't for them. I owe them my life.

"I guess I don't smell great," I say to Darius apologetically.

His sense of smell is far better than any of ours. He uses his other senses as his eyes.

He throws me a grin. "You're fine."

"That's sweet, but I'm really not." I lift an arm to sniff at my armpit and grimace.

"Do you want me to help you down to the river?" he offers.

"If that's all right?"

"Of course it is, Laney."

I can have Darius there and not worry about him spying on me. I trust his hearing is sharp enough to alert me to any sign of danger, such as the local wildlife.

I gather up my towel and washbag, and we leave the cabin together.

Darius no longer moves with the hesitation he did when we'd first arrived. We stick to the same rules he always had at the various hotels—we're not allowed to move anything without telling him first, and then it always has to be put back exactly where we found it. Over the weeks since we've been here, he's learned his surroundings. Of course, the woods aren't as predictable as anything manmade, but Cade and Reed always take care of any foliage that might have shifted due to bad weather, though we've been lucky on that front so far.

We reach the river, and Darius hangs back to allow me to wash.

He leans against a tree, one foot planted on the trunk. He's found a twig, or perhaps a matchstick, and is flipping it between his fingers, trying to act as though his attention is on anything other than me.

I study him in detail, knowing he's blissfully unaware of my gaze traveling up and down his body. What does he look like naked? I've seen him with his shirt off, and in only a pair of shorts, but I'm greedy for more. I remember how he'd looked on stage, playing his violin with an entire orchestra behind him, and holding the audience captivated.

I've been a pent-up ball of sexual frustration ever since we've been at the cabin. Having three gorgeous men living in such close proximity to me hasn't been easy to deal with. Especially when they're all out of bounds like Cade, Darius, and Reed are.

Aware that I haven't moved for a few moments, I strip off my clothes and fold them up on a rock on the bank of the river. I pick up my soap and wade into the water, the cold hitting my calves. I clench my teeth and hiss air in between my lips.

Instantly, Darius is alert, his head turned in my direction. "Everything okay, Laney?"

"Yeah, just cold, that's all."

He nods and goes back to the stick, tipping it from finger to finger with surprising dexterity.

I know he can't see me, but being completely naked in front of Darius sends a dirty little thrill through me. Despite the cold water, heat coalesces between my thighs. I squeeze them together, intensifying the sensation. I tear my gaze away from my stepbrother and try to put the thought out of my mind.

I fail.

Trying to distract myself with the job at hand, I tip a little of the body wash into my palm and then click the lid back on.

We've still got a good supply, for the moment, but it will run out before we know it and then staying clean will become a whole lot harder. I dip my soapy hands into my armpits and then across my breasts. My nipples harden beneath my touch, and I linger, enjoying the sensation of my cold fingers on the sensitive peaks. I find my line of sight returning to Darius. His head is rested back against the tree trunk, his eyes lifted skyward. Can he see the difference in the pattern of sunlight created by the branches? His long hair hangs past his shoulders. I'm sure it's grown since we've been here.

God, he's so beautiful.

I capture my lower lip between my teeth. I know how wrong this is, but I can't seem to stop. I pull and tweak my nipples, hard enough to cause little shocks of pain that seem to have a direct route to my pussy. Tension builds at my core, and I squirm, wanting more. Needing more.

I allow my hand to drift lower, running across my flat stomach and then down between my thighs. I'm submerged, so I can't tell how wet I am, but the brush of my touch over my clit has me gasping.

Fuck. I want more.

I check Darius. He isn't paying me any additional attention. If he has any idea what I'm doing, he isn't showing any sign of it.

I wade to a slightly shallower point, so that water is only mid-thigh, and toss the bottle of bodywash onto the shore. It hits with a soft thud, and Darius glances my way again.

"Everything is okay," I assure him.

He nods and lifts his head skyward again.

With my eyes on him, I press my fingers inside myself. That contrast of cold and hot hits me again, like I'm penetrating myself with an ice-pop, and I have to bite down on my lower lip to stop myself groaning. I keep my gaze locked on Darius as I slide my fingers in and out of myself and caress my breasts with my other hand. In my head, I'm picturing it's his hands on me.

Can he hear the change in my breathing? Can he smell my arousal on the air? Can he hear the wet sucking of my pussy on my fingers? If he can, he shows no sign, except maybe a slight slowing of the way he flips the stick between his fingers. I imagine him knowing exactly what I'm doing. In my head, he's naked as well, and is standing there with his cock in his hand, touching himself in time with me.

"You sure everything is okay?" he calls.

He's standing straight now, the twig dropping from his fingers. His head is turned in my direction and his eyebrows pull together.

"Yes!" My voice is too high pitched. "It's just cold."

I gasp, but not from the chill.

My orgasm builds, heat and tension growing deep in my core. I struggle to keep my breathing steady, but I don't want to stop. I'll reach my climax even if I have to lie through my teeth to my stepbrother while I'm coming.

26

CADE

REED HAS GONE BACK to the cabin with the wood, but I want to check some of the traps I'd set out a couple of days ago.

My path brings me near the river, and I hear voices. Instantly, I stiffen, my ears sharpening.

One of the voices is light and feminine, ringing out through the trees. I exhale, and my shoulders drop. It's okay. It's only Laney, and since Reed has gone back to the cabin, I assume Darius is with her. She's been so sick and weak lately that she wouldn't be stupid enough to go down to the river alone. Some areas are deep and fast, and all it would take is one stumble to end up in trouble. I'm kind of pissed that she's only taken Darius with her. While he's perfectly capable of taking care of himself, would he be able to help her if she was swept away? He'd say he could follow the sound of her just as easily as I could follow her by sight, but I'm not completely sold on that.

I make my way through the trees, ducking low branches and hopping over rocks. The rush of the river grows louder. We're lucky to have it so close by, both for our drinking water and for washing in. In the next few weeks, however, it's going to get colder, and at some point the river will freeze and be covered in snow. What will we do then? We can bore holes in the ice to get to the water below, but we definitely won't be able to swim in it.

I want to believe we'll have been found by then, but weeks have gone by now. Will there even be search teams still looking for us? Or will they have given up, assuming we're dead? They don't know that we were able to find shelter, or even that anyone survived the crash.

I break through the trees and come to an abrupt halt.

Holy fuck.

Laney is in the river, completely naked. And that's not all. She's got her hand between her thighs and is touching herself.

Her eyes are open, but she's not looking in my direction. I follow her line of sight to discover Dax leaning up against a tree. Laney's getting herself off while eyeing up my brother.

A surprising stab of jealousy hits me, but it doesn't last long. She looks incredibly sexy standing in the river, her feet planted wide enough to give her access to her pussy, her tits jutting out. The ends of her hair are damp and hanging down her back.

Blood rushes to my cock, and I lengthen and harden beneath my jeans.

If she gets to masturbate over my brother without his knowledge, then that sure as hell gives me the green light to do the same to her. She's taking advantage of my brother's disability, after all. That's a shitty thing to do, so when she finds out about me—and I fully intend for her to find out—she won't have a leg to stand on.

I free myself from my jeans and run my hand down my length. I pause at the tip to flick my piercing. It sends an electric shock of pleasure through my body, and I grow even harder in my hand.

Laney's working herself faster, and I meet her pace, my hand traveling up and down my cock. She tilts her head back and her lips part, the position creating an arc in her spine. She bites her lower lip, and her beautiful features contort as she reaches for her climax.

A tiny groan of arousal escapes my lips, and instantly, I realize my mistake.

Darius frowns, his head snapping in my direction.

"Cade?"

Laney lets out a gasp and makes a feeble attempt to cover herself with her hands—one arm across her breasts, her other hiding her pussy. There's no point in me continuing to stay out of view, so I approach, still casually rubbing my cock. It's not like my brother can see me.

I let out a chuckle. "Bit late for that, Cuckoo."

She rushes for shore, water splashing up her slender thighs, and when she reaches dry ground, she bends and scoops up her towel. "How long have you be—"

She suddenly notices that my jeans are open and my heavy cock is resting in my palm. "Jesus, Cade. What are you doing?"

"Same as you. Got a problem with that? I was enjoying the show."

Lines appear between Darius's eyebrows. "What's going on?"

Laney widens her eyes at me, silently begging.

I've got no intention of keeping her little secret.

"Our sweet little stepsister was getting herself off while staring right at you, Dax."

Darius's expression changes, morphing from confusion into a smug smile. "So, that's what she was doing. I did wonder."

"I bet you did. You must have known she was naked in the river. I bet you were picturing exactly what that looked like. I guarantee your imagination was nowhere near as filthy as what she was actually doing, though." I run my hand up and down my erection as I describe the scene to my brother. "She had one hand jammed between her thighs, her fingers inside her pussy, while she touched one of her tits with the other hand."

Her cheeks are bright red as she stares at me. She seems to struggle to keep her gaze on my face, and it drops down my body to fix on my cock. Her pink tongue darts out and sweeps across her lower lip.

I continue to narrate to Darius. "And now she's staring at my dick."

Darius raises an eyebrow. "And why can she see your dick?"

"'Cause I figured if she thought it was okay to masturbate over someone without their knowledge, then she wouldn't mind me doing the same to her."

Her mouth opens to protest and then closes again. She grips the towel around her, but she still hasn't made any attempt to get dressed.

"Did you come, Laney?" I ask. "Did you orgasm over my brother?"

She shakes her head.

"No?" I check. "Then how about I finish you off?"

I reach out and pluck the towel from between her breasts. She doesn't even attempt to keep hold of it.

Her eyes widen. "Wh—"

I continue to describe what I'm doing for Darius's sake. "I've just taken her towel from her, so now she's naked again. She didn't even fight me for it." I lick my lower lip. "Fuck, Dax. I wish you could see her. I swear she's fucking perfect. Legs that go on forever and will look incredible wrapped around my hips, a tiny waist, tits that are small but high, nipples hard and pink."

I drop the towel to the ground, and then fall to my knees directly in front of her. She's staring at me like I'm a bomb that might explode at any moment.

I reach around her and take the globes of her bottom in each hand and pull her toward me. She's clean from the river, but still damp, and the scent of her arousal fills my senses.

"I'm on my knees in front of her," I tell Dax. "My face is at her pussy, and I'm going to lick her until she screams."

Before I give her the chance to protest, I cover her pretty little cunt with my mouth. I use my tongue to separate her pussy lips and then lick her long and deep, right up her slit to her clit.

Laney gasps and steadies herself with her hand on my shoulder. I curl my tongue around her clit and then suck it into my mouth.

My mouth is occupied, but to my absolute fucking delight, Laney takes over. Her voice is breathy and sexy.

"Cade is sucking my clit." She breaks off to give a sexy little moan. "And now his hand is on my inner thigh, and he's using his fingers on me as well. He's just pushed a finger inside my pussy and he's licking my clit. Oh, God. Oh, fuck, that feels so good."

She's rocking her hips against my mouth, as though she's desperate for more. I glance up at her, but she's not looking down at me. Instead, she's watching Darius.

Darius has his cock in his hand now. All his focus is on Laney—though it's not about what she looks like. He'll be desperate to get his hands on her.

This isn't the first time Darius and I have shared a woman. There have been plenty we've picked up and brought back to a hotel room to be played with all night. The women in question certainly don't mind.

There's a safety in it, for Darius, at least. If he can't see what the women are doing, what is there to stop them robbing him? He wouldn't even be able to give the police a description.

I keep licking her, the taste of her arousal coating my tongue. I curl my fingers inside her to stroke her inner walls, and she rides my hand, desperate to reach her peak. Her breathing grows ragged, and her thighs and stomach muscles tremble. I can tell she's close, but I'm not going to let her come just yet.

Sitting back on my haunches, I put some space between us.

She stares down at me in dismay. "Cade…"

I lift my hand to stop her.

I already know that Laney wants my brother. I'm confident she wants me as well, but since it was Dax who, albeit inadvertently, started this, I figure it's only fair he gets to end it.

"Do you want to finish off our little stepsister, bro? Do you want to be the one to make her come?"

27

DARIUS

I NEVER EXPECTED today to take this turn.

I want to learn every inch of Laney's body, trace her skin with my fingers and tongue. I want to inhale her scent, and taste her pussy, and suck her tongue into my mouth. I want to know how responsive her nipples are under my touch.

Had I considered that Laney was touching herself in the river when I heard her breathing change? Yes, I had. Had I considered that she was masturbating over me? Definitely not.

We won't fuck her. Not yet. There's plenty of time for that. Besides, in the back of my mind, I'm considering what Reed will say. He's the one who brought her into our lives. It doesn't seem right that we claim her first that way.

Counting the number of steps I believe will take me to where Laney is standing, I pause in front of her, sensing her body heat, hearing her rapid breathing. I reach out my right hand and am pleased to find her face exactly where I'd expect.

Her cheek is like velvet, and I trace my way down the soft pillow to her lips. She parts them for me, and I push a finger into her mouth. She sucks on it gently, and I get even harder.

I take her other hand and place it around my cock.

"Do you feel how much I want you, Laney?" I ask her. "Were you thinking about my cock in the river?"

Her fingers tighten around me, and I draw a breath. God, that feels good. My little stepsister's hand on my dick. She rubs me, running her hand up and down my length.

"Yes." Her voice is barely a whisper, a breeze in the leaves of the trees overhead. "I was thinking about you touching me."

"Do you want me to touch you for real?"

I care for this girl, for everything we've been through together, for her resilience and her gentle nature, for the hurt she's dealt with in her life. I want to make her feel good.

"Yes," she says again.

"Then lie down."

I know from Cade's description that she had a towel. She releases me, and I drop to a crouch and pat the ground until my fingers close around soft material. Then I spread it out, ready for her.

I take Laney's hand and help lower her to the ground. I might not be able to see her with my eyes, but I can picture exactly how she looks, spread out beneath the blue sky, breathtakingly naked, her small breasts rising and falling, her lips parted, her pussy wet.

I hover over her, holding myself up on my elbows. I trail the tip of my nose across her forehead, inhaling her scent, and then brush my lips down the bridge of her nose, to her mouth, where I claim her. She kisses me back with intense passion, pushing her tongue across mine. God, I can't believe she's naked beneath me. It takes every ounce of self-control I have not to part her thighs and sink my cock into her. But I remind myself who this is—our sweet Laney, the girl we'd all been terrified we might lose only a week ago—and I hold myself back.

My lips leave her mouth, and I kiss my way down, taking small nips at the sensitive skin of her throat. I palm one of her breasts and lower my face to her other one. Her nipples are already hard, and I draw one to the roof of my mouth and suck hard. She moans and arches her back, pressing into me. Her body is so lithe and supple, I want to drown in her.

I suckle on her, licking and biting, feasting on her perfect breast, before applying the same attention to its twin. Then I reach down, between her thighs, finding her swollen and ready.

I push my middle finger inside her and groan as she clamps around me, so tight. My cock is insanely hard, and all I can think about is how her pussy will feel wrapped around me. Sensations mean so much to me, since I don't have use of my sense of sight. I'm sure it makes sex even more intense. Where other men would be distracted by staring down at a fine pair of tits or watching the expressions a woman makes while she comes, I'm all about how it feels. I believe it helps me understand a woman's body better, too. I'm more in tune with the sounds she's making or the gasp of her breath or the way her pussy contracts when I hit a certain soft spot inside her.

Maybe other men would argue that I'm missing out, too. A part of me agrees, though I try not to dwell on it. I hate that I can't make eye contact with Laney. I wish I could see her face, though I believe I have a good idea what she looks like from touch alone.

I thumb her clit, eliciting a breathy moan from her, and then add my index finger, so she's stretching around two of my digits. She's so incredibly tight, the image of my cock inside her refuses to leave my mind. I'm not sure I've ever wanted to fuck anyone so badly.

I give little thought to my brother, though I know he's standing nearby. He's most likely getting off on the scene.

Laney's breathing grows faster, and sexy cries emit from between her lips. She's riding my hand now, pushing back on me as much as I'm driving into her.

She reaches for me again, her small, slender hand wrapping

around my cock. I'm so built up, I'm surprised I don't just come at her touch.

"Fuck, that feels good," I tell her.

She pumps her fist up and down my length, and I slip my fingers from her and settle between her thighs. She still has hold of my cock, and she rubs it at her entrance, coating the head in her arousal. I duck my head and kiss her neck and tits. All it will take is a nudge of my hips and I'll sink deep inside her. Fucking heaven.

"Wait," she suddenly gasps, freezing beneath me. "What about Reed?"

I lift my head. Having my father's name mentioned in the middle of sex isn't normally the direction I like things taking, but I understand why she's concerned.

"He doesn't have to know."

I duck down again, but she pushes her hand against my shoulder. "No, that's not what I mean." She hesitates. "Reed is… important to me—you all are—but I feel like…" She searches for the words. "I feel like if I'm going to fuck any of you first, then it should be him. He's our patriarch."

Hadn't I thought the same thing myself? Maybe other men would focus on the fact she'd been considering fucking my father, but I heard it differently. If she was going to fuck any of us *first*… If there was going to be a first, then that implies there will also be a second and a third.

Cade speaks from somewhere over my shoulder. "Reed wants you, too. It's been obvious from the first moment you came into our lives. He's battling with himself, though. He's telling himself it's wrong to want you like that."

"I can make him come around," she says with confidence. "I just need a little time with him."

She's right. She's a part of *all* of us, not just me and Cade. Reed is our patriarch—the head of our family. To exclude him in any way simply feels wrong.

"In the meantime, we can still make you come," Cade says. "You ever sucked cock before?"

She's so close to me, I can feel her shaking her head.

"Then how about you start with Dax?"

I'm honored that Cade is letting me be the one to get head from her. He's always been generous with the women we share. I don't know if it's 'cause he always feels he needs to make things up to me because he was the one who got me sick when we were younger, but in this case, I'm not complaining.

"I'll lick your pretty cunt again," he says. "I want to feel you come around my tongue."

We shift positions. I get to my knees and sit back, my ass on my heels, so my cock protrudes from my lap. Laney gets to all fours, so she can suck me off, and I hear Cade move in behind her.

"Oh, God," she cries, and I know Cade is already behind her, sucking and licking and fingering that precious pussy of hers. She doesn't move for a moment, her hands resting on my thighs, and I know she's lost in the sensations Cade is creating in her. Then she grips the base of me with one hand, and her sweet, hot mouth circles my erection. I groan, my head tipping back on my shoulders. She reaches beneath me with her other hand and cups my balls, then runs her fingers along my perinium. I don't know how experienced Laney is, but her instincts are good, because right now she's doing everything right. Her mouth is sheer perfection.

I can hear Cade lapping at her pussy. He must be on his hands and knees and desperate to take her like that. I can hardly believe we're saving her for our father, but it feels right.

She moves her mouth up and down on me, but I can tell she's struggling to keep up the momentum when she's so close to climax herself.

"Just relax, Laney," I tell her. "Don't think about what you're doing. Focus on Cade's tongue in your cunt, and I'll fuck your mouth. Pretend I'm not here."

At my words, I sense her relax a fraction. Her jaw goes loose, her tongue slack, and her throat opens up.

"Good girl," I tell her, stroking her hair. "Breathe through your nose. And when I come, I want you to swallow me down, okay? You're not to spill a single drop. Think you can do that?"

She nods again, my cock still between her lips.

I touch her cheek with the backs of my knuckles. "That's a good girl, my sweet little stepsister. Now orgasm for Cade, and I'll come down your throat at the same time."

I knot my fingers in her hair to keep her in place and nudge my hips forward. Her lips circle my girth, creating just the right amount of friction, and the inside of her mouth is pillowy, heated, and wet.

Cade's heavy breathing meets my ears, as does the sound of his hand working his cock. He's eating out Laney, while he's jacking himself off. Sometimes I wonder if I'd struggle to share like this if I could see my brother. I don't really want to get an eyeful of his cock. But since I can't see them, it's a non-issue.

Laney moans and whimpers around me, but I don't hold back. I fuck her mouth, lost in the sensations. Her muffled cries build to a crescendo, and I move faster, ramming myself down her throat. Every muscle in my body is wound tight with the promise of impending bliss, and I know I'm going to come at any moment.

As I sense her reaching her orgasm, I let go, too. My balls draw tight into my body, every nerve ending focused on my cock, and I release in a jolt of intense pleasure. Hot cum spurts from me into her mouth and down her throat, and I feel like I'm giving her a part of me, that, in this moment, we're joined. I feel her throat work as she swallows me down.

I give us a moment to catch our breath, and then I reach out and touch her cheek.

"Good girl," I tell her. "You took me perfectly." I wipe either side of her lips, to ensure she didn't spill any of my cum. "Swallowed it all down."

She releases my cock from her mouth, and I'm instantly bereft.

"That was intense," she says.

Cade chuckles. "I can't believe we just did that. Makes being stuck out here a hell of a lot more interesting."

On that, we definitely agree.

28

Laney

I CAN'T BELIEVE we just did that.

I'm drenched in guilt as we make our way back to the cabin. Is Reed going to take one look at us and know exactly what we've been doing? What's he going to say? I remind myself that I'm eighteen, and he can't tell me what do to, but that doesn't ease my remorse.

It's because a part of me knows he should have been there, too.

If anyone is going to be my first, it needs to be him.

I test how that acknowledgement sits with me. He's my step-father, if only legally, and I really shouldn't be thinking about fucking him.

That didn't stop you from masturbating over one stepbrother and letting another lick you out, a voice says in my head, the tone accusatory.

I think of all the moments I've had with Reed, how safe he makes me feel. I picture waking up with his erection pressing against me, and this time, instead of wriggling away, I shift myself into a different position, so I can rub myself up against it.

Instead of the thought filling me with revulsion, that familiar heat builds inside me.

God, what's happened to me? I've gone from an innocent virgin who barely gave a thought to men or sex, to a total nympho who's imagining getting it on with her stepfather.

"Are-are we going to tell Reed?" I ask as we're almost at the cabin.

Cade turns to me. "Are you fucking joking?"

I blink. "No. I mean, it doesn't seem right to have secrets, not in the situation we're in."

He gives a cold kind of laugh. "Everyone has secrets."

"Do they? I don't."

"You do now."

I stare at him and then turn to his brother. "Darius? What do you think?"

"He'll know," Darius says.

"So we should tell him?"

"Fuck, no. We deny everything, at least until you can work your magic on him. If you can make him understand how things could be so much better for us all here, then he'll come around."

They know Reed far better than I do.

"Okay." I let out a slow breath. "Okay."

I'm nervous as I enter the cabin, but at least now I have a bit of a plan forming. Reed can't be angry with us if he's involved, too.

Reed is placing wood on the fire, laying smaller sticks diagonally across each other, and larger ones on top. He glances over his shoulder as we enter.

"Thought I was going to have to send a search party out," he says, half-joking. He sees the three of us, and something flickers in his blue eyes. "Where did you get to?"

I speak hurriedly. "I needed a dunk in the river. Darius came with me to…make sure I was safe."

"I thought I could use a swim as well," Cade says. "I was sweaty after the walk."

Reed doesn't say anything else, but his gaze darts between us. He can sense something is off, some kind of tension, like electricity sparking through the air between us.

We go about our usual chores. I hang my damp towel on the railing of the porch outside and then use some river water to wash some laundry.

The creak of a floorboard comes behind me, and I turn to find Reed standing there, his hands on his hips, glowering down at me.

"What's going on with you and the boys?"

"Why?" I throw back. "Are you jealous?"

Something flashes in his eyes, and my heart misses a beat. He is. He's jealous.

"Don't be stupid, Laney. No, I'm not. I just don't think it's a good idea for you to get too close to them."

"Why not? They're my family, aren't they? Aren't I supposed to be close to them?"

"You know what I mean. Cade doesn't exactly have a good record of relationships with women. He uses them up and spits them back out again. I don't want that to happen with you. You deserve someone who is kind and gentle, and who actually gives a shit about your feelings."

I see my moment.

"What? Someone like you?"

His eyes soften. "I care about you. These past few weeks have been...intense. I'll be honest, I had no idea what to expect when I got the call that day to say you needed a guardian, but it definitely wasn't this. I thought you'd still be a little girl."

"I'm not a little girl," I tell him. "I might have only turned eighteen recently, but living with my mother meant I had to grow up fast."

His gaze travels down my body, then he catches himself and yanks it back up to my face. "I'm aware of that."

I reach out and take his hand. It's warm and solid. "So, you have to trust me to make my own choices."

He folds his lips into a thin line, unable to meet my eye. "That's not so easy, Laney. I'm supposed to be protecting you."

"And you are. I'm still alive, aren't I? We all are. You were the one who found this place. Who knows what we'd be living like now if you hadn't."

"I don't want to take advantage of you. I don't want the boys taking advantage of you either."

I play the innocent. "How are any of you taking advantage of me?"

"You're young and vulnerable, even if you don't realize that yet. When you get older, you'll look back and see this completely differently."

I consider this for a moment. "Maybe I will, but don't I get to make that choice? I deserve to make my own mistakes."

I'm not sure either of us really understands who or what I'm referencing now. Does he still think I'm talking about Cade? Or does he understand that I mean him?

I take a step closer, wanting him to comprehend exactly what I'm talking about. There's only a sliver of air between our bodies, but he doesn't move away. My body is still humming from the orgasm I had with the boys, and I discover I want more. Reed can give that to me; he just doesn't know it yet.

"What are you doing, Laney?" he asks, his voice guttural.

"We might never get out of here. If we're still here when winter approaches, we probably won't survive. What's the point in denying ourselves simple pleasures that can make this experience bearable?"

"Because what happens when we do get out of here, Laney? What questions will be asked then?"

"No one ever needs to know."

"Laney..." There's a warning in his voice.

"It's okay, Reed. We're just two people. Two *adults*. Feeling a certain way about someone isn't wrong."

He touches my face, his thumb brushing over my cheek, then down to my lips. "Being near you hurts," he admits. "I'm not going to lie and say I haven't thought about you that way. But it can't happen, Laney, and this doesn't help. Wanting someone so desperately and knowing they can never be yours is a special kind of torture."

I lift myself on my tiptoes, bringing our faces closer, willing him to let go and just kiss me. "Why can I never be yours?"

He doesn't back away. "You know why, baby."

We hold each other's gaze.

His hands slip down my sides, capturing my waist. I lean in closer and then drop my hand to stroke the length of his erection over his jeans. He's big and hard, and I imagine how he'll feel when he pushes inside me.

"Fuck." He releases me and steps away.

My heart drops.

"This can't happen." He shakes his head and turns away and storms off into the woods.

I stand on the porch, watching him go, holding back my tears.

29

Laney

WHAT HAPPENED between me and the boys at the river, and then my failed attempt to seduce Reed, doesn't get mentioned again.

Cade and Darius act as though nothing has happened, treating me as their kid sister, and nothing more. Reed is different, though, and I can sense he's still avoiding me and seems unable to meet my eye. The rejection hurts, but I don't believe it's what he really wants. I just need to convince him to give in.

We still sleep side by side on the mattresses on the floor, and when he's sleeping, he forgets the distance he's trying to put between us. I often wake with him wrapped around me, but the moment he wakes up and realizes, he releases me and turns his back on me.

It's been a few days now since we last caught anything to eat, and we're all feeling it. We've managed to forage berries and some edible roots from the woods, and we've collected freshwater mussels, but they haven't gone far to filling us up. Finding food is our current priority, and so I do my best to push thoughts of sex and relationships out of my head. I know I have bigger things to worry about right now, but it's hard not to have thoughts of them all crowding out my brain.

This morning, Cade and I take on the job of checking the traps. We've set out as many as our meagre supplies will allow us, and I'm praying that one will bear fruit. Everyone's mood is low when we're hungry, and conversations tend to revolve around all the different foods we miss from home and what we'd order if were able to get takeout. Darius dreams of tacos, while Cade wants pizza. Reed fantasizes about a rare steak done on the grill, while I'd gorge myself on sushi. But all the dreams of the different foods we love only serve to make us hungrier.

We hike together through the woods, but each trap we've checked so far has come up empty. I can sense Cade's mood growing darker with each empty trap, and it worries me.

I'm still a little wary of him and what our relationship is meant to be now. He's not as hard on me as he was when I first came into his life, but I know he has the potential for cruelty inside him.

Up ahead, a loud squeal meets our ears.

We exchange a glance.

"That sounds like rabbit to me," Cade says.

We pick up our pace, and sure enough, we discover a rabbit with a noose around its back legs. I feel bad for the poor thing, but we need to eat. This isn't hunting for pleasure's sake. Cade doesn't hesitate, and dispatches the animal quickly and cleanly, breaking its neck.

"Looks like we'll be eating tonight," he says with a grin.

It's a beauty, too. Big and fat.

I let out an almost primal whoop of joy and throw my arms around Cade's neck. He swings me around before setting my feet back on the ground. I sweep my hair from my eyes, suddenly breathless. He doesn't let go of me, his arms still around my waist. Something inside me tingles, heat flowing through my body. He stares down at me, his lips parted. The air seems to spark with tension between us. His touch burns through the thin material of my t-shirt.

I make a move, just a tiny, subtle lifting of my chin, a parting of my lips, and it's all he needs. His mouth crashes onto mine, hungry, unforgiving. He yanks me back, so our bodies are so tightly meshed, it's impossible to see where I end and he begins. My arms have already wound around his thick neck, and I jam myself even harder against him.

His tongue pushes between my lips, seeking mine. I nip at his lower lip, and he lets out a moan of desire.

Roughly, Cade grabs my hand and shoves it down the front of his sweatpants. Automatically, my fingers close around him. He's impossibly hard, the skin silky soft. And hot. I run my fingers up the shaft to the head where I find the ring pierced through it. I can't help myself. I'm curious, and I run my thumb over the top, applying pressure. His breathing grows ragged, and I can tell he likes it.

His mouth is on my throat, kissing, biting. I don't want to experience the arousal surging up through my core, but I do. Cade can be a total asshole, but he's also hot as fuck, and it's not like I'm completely innocent anymore. I masturbate him, loving how big he is, feeling him grow even harder.

We part again, both breathing fast, staring at each other.

"Fuck, little Cuckoo," he says. "I've wanted to fuck you from the first moment I laid eyes on you. Wanted to part your legs and taste you and push my fingers and cock inside you and watch you squirm and moan. My little sister."

"Only by marriage," I tell him, breathless. "A marriage that happened a very long time ago. It barely counts."

I squeeze his shaft, then run my thumb over the head and lightly flick at the ring piercing he has through it.

"Do that again," he says.

I comply and he groans.

"Ah, fuck."

"I want to know what it feels like," I say, "to have you inside me."

I'm nervous, but my pussy is soaked and swollen. My clit throbs. But I remember how I'd made the decision that Reed should be first, even if he doesn't know it yet.

Cade is thinking the same way. "What about Reed?"

"I don't know if he'll ever come around."

"Maybe," Cade says. "Maybe not. As much as I want to be inside you, I don't want to fuck things up with my family. There are other things we can do, though."

I nod, eagerly. "I want to rub your piercing against me, can I do that? I won't let you go inside."

"You want to rub yourself with my cock?"

"Can I do that?"

"Fuck, Laney. You're killing me."

I give a self-satisfied smile. "Good."

I kick off my sneakers, and he quickly rids me of my jeans and panties. He reaches between my thighs and presses his fingers inside me, and I arch my back. My eyes roll with pleasure. Fuck, that feels good.

He kisses the side of my neck.

"Fingering my dirty little stepsister. What will Daddy say?" he growls. "Or maybe he wants to get a taste too, huh? Suck on his naughty stepdaughter's clit."

I let out a moan and grind down on his hand.

"Are you ready for my cock now?" he asks.

"Just the tip," I tell him.

He repeats my words. "Just the tip."

Cade bends at the knees and positions his piercing at my clit, holding his shaft in one hand. He rubs the metal against the delicate bundle of nerves. It's cooler than his fingers and instantly sends fireworks sparking through me.

"You like that, huh?"

I cling to his shoulders. "Oh, God, yes."

"I want to be inside you, so bad. I want to feel your pussy clamp around my cock."

He continues to rub me with his cockhead, over my clit and then down between my pussy lips. I buck and arch my hips, wanting more but knowing I can't take it. Not yet.

He keeps going, rubbing me harder and faster. He pauses at my entrance and nudges the head just slightly inside. I feel myself stretch around his cock head.

"No deeper," I tell him. "That's enough."

His forehead falls to my shoulder as he pants, his hand working his cock.

Then he moves back to my clit again, and, perhaps to prevent himself from fucking me for real, plunges two fingers hard and deep inside my cunt. The invasion feels raw and brutal, but with his piercing rubbing my clit, sends me skyward. I'm spiraling, caught in a whirlpool of insane pleasure.

"Oh, God. Oh, fuck."

I want to watch him touching me, but my orgasm takes over, and I squeeze my eyes shut, focusing on the rising wave of bliss powering through me.

He clamps his hand over my mouth, preventing my cries being overheard by the others in case they're near. I wonder if Darius will have heard me anyway. Will he smell me, even, smell my arousal, my cream on my thighs? Will he smell me on his brother? Shit. I hadn't even thought of that.

But my thoughts turn to dust as my climax wipes out all my worries, and I shudder and jolt beneath Cade's touch, lost in the moment.

Cade comes with a grunt, spattering my stomach with milky white cum. I stare down at his cock, the cum still leaking from the slit. He's so big, and I wonder if I'll even be able to fit him inside me when the time comes.

Cade clears his throat and steps away, tucking himself back into his sweatpants.

He jerks his chin down at the rabbit. "We should get that back to the cabin. The others will be hungry."

No pillow talk, then?

"Oh, of course," I say, reaching for my clothes.

I look around and pick up a handful of dried leaves to wipe myself down with. Now we're no longer caught in the heat of the moment, I'm self-conscious.

Cade gathers up the rabbit while I dress, and within less than a minute, we're hiking back through the woods as though nothing happened.

I remember Reed's words of warning to me, about how Cade chews women up and spits them out. I'd somehow convinced myself I was different from those women, but am I, really?

He only wants me because I'm off limits—or at least I would be if we were still in normal society. If we were back in Los Angeles, he probably wouldn't have given me a second glance. I'd seen how he'd had women hanging off him. But we're not back in LA.

We might never see the city again if we're not rescued or find some way out of here.

30
DARIUS

I CAN TELL something happened between Cade and Laney in the woods.

Laney came back with her breathing all over the place, and Cade is basically ignoring her. Did he fuck her out there when neither Reed nor I was around? Laney has the right to do whatever the hell she wants, but I'm kinda pissed that Cade would fuck her when we'd already discussed that it would be best if Reed was the one to take her first.

I accost him the first moment we're out of earshot of Reed and Laney.

"Have you been fucking our sister?" I demand.

Cade laughs. "Don't be a fucking moron. She's not our sister. She's not even related."

"Legally, she is."

He grabs my arm and sweeps it toward the wide expanse around us, the never-ending ocean of trees that I know exists but can't see, and then drops it again.

"What law is there out here? Huh? There is none. No one to ask questions or judge us. We can do whatever the fuck we want.

We're probably going to die out here. You realize that, don't you? So we might as we take whatever comfort and pleasure we can get from each other before that happens. No one is ever going to know."

"We might get resc—"

"We're not going to get fucking rescued. When are you going to accept that fact? This is it for us now. They're probably not even looking for us anymore. They'll think we're dead."

"We won't survive here through winter," I say.

"Exactly, so we might as well make the most of what we've got."

"You did fuck her, then?" I check.

"No, brother, I didn't. I just made her come with my cock."

My face burns. "What does that mean?"

He chuckles. "Relax. I just rubbed her pussy with it. I didn't breach her precious little cunt...at least not by much."

I drag my hand through my hair. "Jesus." I'm jealous. I want it to be me who made her come. "She needs to push Reed harder."

"He backed off when she tried last time."

"He's a red-blooded male. He'll break eventually, and then he'll understand how right she feels."

Cade lets out a huff of air. "We all need to be in on this if it's going to work."

I nod. "Agreed. I'll see what I can do."

31

laney

DUSK IS APPROACHING.

I sit on the porch in our lookout spot. We've long since given up watching out for rescue helicopters or planes. Now it's just a peaceful spot to sit and look out over the forest.

Movement comes nearby, and I turn to find Darius joining me.

"Hi," I say.

"Hi yourself."

He settles into the chair beside me. "Cade told me about you and him in the woods today."

My cheeks heat. "Oh, right. Does it bother you?"

"Only in that I wish I was there."

I'm not sure what to say. Instead of going over what happened today, I take the opportunity to change the subject.

"What was it like when you lost your sight?"

It's a question I've been dying to ask him ever since we first met, but I never wanted to intrude before. Now we've grown closer, and I want us to be closer still. I want to know everything about him. I want to understand how his mind works, and what

221

he's feeling, and all the events in his past that made him the man he is today.

There's something intensely masculine about Darius, but in a different way than Cade. He brings a calm sensitivity with it, and while I know he loses his temper, it's mainly at his own frustrations than directed at anyone else.

"Terrifying," he admits. "I was just a little kid, and I couldn't get my head around the idea that I wasn't going to get better again. My mom had only died a year or so earlier, and in my mind, when people got sick, they either got better or they died. That I'd gotten sick and was never going to make a full recovery simply refused to sink in. It didn't help that when I dreamed, I still could see in my dreams. It was like when I was asleep, I had a whole world opened back up to me again, but then when I woke up, I was back in the dark."

I reach out and take his hand, my heart breaking for the little boy he'd once been. "That must have been awful."

"It was. I know people say kids are adaptable, but that didn't mean I didn't struggle. All I could think about was all the things I was missing out on, that I couldn't go to school with my friends, and that I'd never play sports again, and that everyone would treat me differently."

"Oh, Dax."

"Cade was amazing, though. I swear, I don't know what I'd have done without him. I know he blames himself for bringing the virus into the house and giving it to me, but it wasn't his fault. He stuck around the whole time, except for when he had to go to school. He fought with Reed, trying to convince him to let him stay home with me and get homeschooled as well, but Reed put his foot down. He said I needed the one-on-one time with the tutor, which I did, and that Cade needed to get a regular education. Cade fought him so hard about it, but Reed didn't back down."

I picture them both as boys, a slightly older Cade fighting to be with his little brother. Cade has acted like an asshole toward me on plenty of occasions, but I find myself softening toward him.

"Did Cade really believe it was his fault you went blind?"

"He did."

"Does he still?"

Darius twists his lips as he thinks. "Honestly, I'm not sure. I hope not. Besides, I wouldn't be who I am today if I hadn't lost my sight. I might have never picked up the violin."

"What if you had the choice between being able to see and never playing the violin again?"

He doesn't respond for a moment, but then he lifts his hand to my face and trails his fingers lightly across my features, pausing at my lips. "Before I met you, I'd have always chosen the violin. But there are moments where I believe I'd give up everything I hold sacred if it meant I could truly see your face for just one moment. To be able to look into your eyes and see what you're thinking...I'd give up anything for that."

I grab his hand and cup his palm to my cheek and then turn my face slightly to kiss it. I close my eyes, fighting back tears, a painful lump caught in my throat.

He pulls me into a hug, and we just stay that way, wrapped in each other's arms. I bury my face against his neck, his hair tickling my nose, while he presses his face to my shoulder. Our hearts meet, beating in one rhythm. There's something so completely fulfilling about this moment, about the sense that he's taking as much comfort from me as I am from him. To think I'd once felt him unapproachable, untouchable.

In this moment, there's a part of me that doesn't want to go back to the real world. I picture Darius swept back into the life of fame and glamor, of women throwing themselves at him, and I'm sure I'll lose him if that happens.

I also know how we'll be judged back in society. Because of Darius's fame, the nature of our relationship would be all over social media and the papers. The news would get out that I was a whore and they were all perverted.

With this in mind, I carefully untangle myself from Darius and turn back to the forest.

"Are you okay?" he asks.

I sniff and nod. "Yeah, I just started thinking what life will be like if we get rescued."

"You make it sound like you don't want us to be saved."

"I do…" I hesitate. "I just don't want things to change between us all. I want to stay with you. All of you."

He bites down on a bit of loose skin on his lower lip. "Cade and I were talking about that earlier."

I twist to face him. "You were?"

"We want to be with you, too, but…"

"Reed," I finish for him.

He nods. "Without him on board, it makes this whole thing even more complicated."

I give a small laugh. "Funny how bringing another person into this makes it less complicated rather than more."

"It's because he's already involved. But unless he can start thinking of you as a woman, instead of his stepdaughter, he's going to fuck things up for all of us."

I understand what he's saying.

"Okay." I lean in and place a kiss to Dax's mouth and then speak against his lips. "I'll try harder."

32

Laney

I WAKE EARLY the following morning with Reed in his customary position, asleep, but wrapped around my body from behind. It's not quite light outside the window, but the deep indigo of the night sky has lightened to a hazy gray.

Remembering Darius's words, I push my ass out, making contact with Reed's pelvis. He has his usual morning wood, and I smile to myself and grind a little more.

Reed stirs. From the change in his breathing, I can tell I've woken him.

"What are you doing, Laney?" he whispers.

I feign sleep. The hard line of his cock is pressed to the crease of my butt. I'm only wearing panties and a camisole to sleep in, and the flimsy material does little to cover me. He's in sweatpants, though, and I wish he wasn't.

He still hasn't pulled away from me, and I let out a deep sigh, and push my bottom out more, creating an arch in the small of my spine.

Reed gives a low moan and drops his forehead to rest lightly on my shoulder. He rolls his hips a tiny amount, pressing against

225

me. He's fully awake and knows exactly what he's doing. Does he truly believe I'm asleep? I can't help wondering how far he'll go if he thinks I'm sleeping and don't know.

I shift my position, and pretend I've got an itch at the spot where the strap of my camisole sits. I scratch the spot, and catch my fingers beneath the strap, pulling it down to expose the vast majority of one breast. Any woman who's ever slept in a tank top knows it's almost impossible to sleep in one of these things without at least one tit escaping overnight.

Reed sucks in a breath and freezes. I keep my eyes shut, my breathing even—though that might prove to be a struggle if this keeps going the way I think it will. I feel the motion of his hand as he lifts it over my body. He hovers it above my exposed breast and then brushes so lightly across the top I almost think I could have imagined it.

His breathing quickens, and he pushes his cock against the top of my ass again. He brushes his hand across my nipple, and it hardens for him.

He falls still.

"Laney?" he whispers, aware the boys are still asleep in the same room as us. "You awake?"

I don't react.

The weight of his hand falls on my breast and he lightly fingers my nipple, teasing it into a tight knot. God, that feels good. Arousal fires between my thighs, and my pussy floods with wetness. I want him so bad. Would he claim to be sleeping if I were to wake and demand to know what he's doing? He grinds against me again, his breathing growing hoarse as he massages my breast.

He needs to know I want this.

"Reed," I breathe, turning my face toward him, twisting my neck only so I don't shift where the parts of his body meet mine.

He goes to snatch his hand away, but I cover it with mine and pin it in place.

"It's okay," I tell him.

I reach behind my body for him, slipping my hand beneath the waistband of his sweatpants.

"Laney, no. Stop."

I shake my head and keep going. I'm happy to find he's not wearing any underwear, and I already know he's as hard as stone for me. I wrap my fingers around his cock and give him a tentative squeeze. He groans again and shakes his head against me.

"You need to stop."

"Do I?" I whisper. "Why?"

"You're my stepdaughter, and you're only eighteen years old."

"What does it matter? We might die out here. No one will ever know."

"I'll know."

"Are you saying you don't want me?"

"No, baby. I want you. God, I want you."

"Then take me," I tell him, still rubbing his erection. "I'm yours. I want to feel your cock in my pussy."

"What about birth control?" he asks, ever the sensible one.

"It's okay. I'm on the implant. You can come inside me. I want you to fill me up."

He groans at my words but pushes his erection into my palm. Then he uses his other hand to pull the sweatpants down his hips slightly, allowing his cock to spring free.

"Yes," I encourage him. "Fuck me. Please, Daddy. Make me come."

I don't know where the name comes from. It just slips out, but I can't help myself. It feels right on my tongue and turns me on even more. Maybe it's because I never had a father in my life, so I don't have any other connection with that name except with him.

For a second, I think I'm going to have triggered all his

morality issues around being my stepfather, but then he groans again.

"Naughty, baby-girl."

He slips his hand beneath the back of my panties, his palm cupping my ass. Then his fingers slide between my cheeks, graze over my asshole, and then slip between my folds. I groan and tilt my hips to give him better access. I can't believe how wet I am already—wet and needy.

He pushes one finger inside me, and I draw in a breath, my eyes rolling and hips pushing back on him. I can't believe how good that feels. He pumps his finger in and out of me, and I whimper with pleasure.

"Shh," he tells me.

He reaches around me with the arm pillowing my head and covers my mouth with his hand. Then he pulls the blanket up over us, so to any outside observer, at first glance, it might look like we're just hugging tightly. It would only be after hearing my muffled gasps and groans and the filthy words whispered against the shell of my ear that they'd realize there was far more going on.

It turns me on even more knowing Cade and Darius are in the room with us. They're still sleeping—I assume—but knowing they might wake at any moment only increases the thrill.

Reed takes his fingers from my pussy and positions his cock against my entrance. "Are you sure, baby-girl?"

"Fuck me, Daddy," I whisper. "Fuck me slow and deep."

He rubs his cockhead back and forth, covering himself in my lubrication.

I have no intention of telling him that this is the first time I've ever been penetrated by a man's cock.

He nudges his hips forward, penetrating me by just an inch or two. My body tenses at the invasion, but he kisses my neck and shoulder, and I relax again.

"God, baby-girl. You feel so good. You're so fucking perfect."

I stretch around him. It's uncomfortable, but not painful. I'm so wet and swollen, ready for him. He pushes himself fully inside me and holds himself there, as though sensing my need to grow accustomed to his size and girth. I've never felt this way before, so utterly full, and I close my eyes to imprint this moment on my memory.

I let him know that I'm ready for more by moving my hips, and he takes the signal, pulling out of me by a couple of inches before driving back in.

He fucks me like I'm an extension of his body. He's fully wrapped around me, his face buried in my neck, his arms pulling me closer. One hand is between my legs, working my clit and the other is over my mouth. Just as I'd asked, his movements are slow and deep inside me.

Tension builds in my core and spreads through my thighs and stomach. I think I'm going to explode, or possibly lose my mind. It's impossible to be quiet when I want to scream his name. He keeps his hand clamped over my mouth, and I bite down on the fleshy pad of skin. I must have hurt him, but he only fucks me harder, his fingers rubbing my clit with just the right speed and pressure.

It builds and builds, taking over me, mind and body.

I come hard, shaking and trembling, and crying unintelligible words against his palm. My pussy contracts and ripples around his cock, urging him on. He buries his face in my neck and lets go, too, filling me up with spurt after spurt of his semen, hot inside me.

He holds me tight, like he's afraid if he lets go, I'll explode. He kisses my throat and shoulder.

"That was amazing," I tell him with a happy sigh when I can speak again. "Thank you."

He gives a small laugh. "I should be the one thanking you."

"We need to get cleaned up before the boys wake up."

He slides out of me, and a gush of hot wetness follows.

Reed frowns down at the spot where we'd been lying. "You bled." Understanding dawns. "Jesus, Laney. Was that your first time?"

There's horror in his eyes, an expression I don't want to see there.

"Yes, but it doesn't matter."

"You said you're on the contraceptive implant. Why would you be if…."

He's baffled at my need for contraception if I wasn't sexually active.

"Heavy periods, that's all. I don't really have any now because of it."

"Jesus," he says again.

I glance nervously at the others. Did they realize I was a virgin? Would they have handed me over to their father if they'd known? I'm amazed they haven't woken up. Perhaps they have, and they'd just pretending, much like I'd done not long ago.

I turn my thoughts back to Reed and reach out to touch his face, his jaw bristly under my palm.

"I'm glad it was you," I tell him. "It was what I wanted. I'd much rather have been in the hands of a man who knows what he's doing and who cares about me."

My alternative might have been some teenager who only fucked me for a dare, or who sneakily filmed me on his phone and posted it to social media, or who used me for one night and never wanted to see me again. I trust Reed completely, both with my heart and my body.

He'd never do anything to hurt me.

33

REED

Even through my post-orgasmic haze, I can't help but worry about how this will look when we get back to normal society.

It won't go down well.

But what if that never happens? What if this is it for us now? I try to look into the future, at the four of us living together in this cabin. Will Laney decide one day that she prefers one of us to the others? How will that work? The jealousy will surely tear us all apart. I hate to think of either of my sons going through that kind of heartbreak, but I don't want to give her up either.

Maybe I'm lying to myself, but I don't see her age. I don't look at her and see anyone other than Laney. I hope she feels the same way about me.

No matter how I think or feel, the truth of it is that the outside world won't see it that way. They'll see a young woman, grieving for her recently dead mother, who's been trapped with three grown men who've taken advantage of her.

I fight off the knotting in my gut that says this is exactly what we've done. Especially me. I'm her guardian—or at least I was for that first week before she turned eighteen—and I'm supposed to protect her.

How will things work when we get home? Laney is young, and she needs to be able to live her life. She needs to do all the things she's missed out on, not only since she's been stuck here, with us, but all the years she's been looking after her mother, too.

That is if we ever do get out of here.

Something else occurs to me. Laney said she had the contraceptive implant, but at some point that will stop working. We can't have a baby out here. It won't be fair to any of us, but especially not Laney or the baby. Women die in childbirth. We can't risk it.

I know I'm getting ahead of myself, but if there's one thing we have out here, it's plenty of time to think.

Laney gets herself cleaned up, and I head outside to check our traps. The boys are awake, but they're acting as though they have no idea what has just taken place between me and Laney. I'm sure they know, though. Darius, in particular, must have been able to smell sex on the air.

The weather has taken a turn for the worse.

Black clouds gather on the horizon. We've been lucky so far, but it looks like a storm is going to hit.

When that happens, we'll all be stuck in this cabin together. Me, Laney, and the boys. It's not as though we can put on a television to distract ourselves or surf the internet.

Laney will be our distraction.

34

Laney

I ACHE PLEASURABLY between my thighs, and I can't wipe the smile off my face.

When I emerge from the bathroom, I find Cade sitting on the couch, his elbows on his knees, watching me.

"What?" I say, though my cheeks are heated.

"You know what." He arches a thick, dark eyebrow. "Had a busy morning?"

"Stop it, Cade."

"Why? I'm having too much fun. Did you think I wasn't awake and listening and watching the whole thing? I loved hearing all those sexy little moans you made while his hand was clamped over your mouth. I want to hear you make those noises again for me, little Cuckoo, except this time I want to hear them with my cock rammed inside you."

He clearly thinks that now I've got Reed out of the way, it's his turn.

"Not now, Cade, okay? It's too soon. I'm…sore."

He folds his arms across his chest and one corner of his lips lift. "Dirty little girl who fucks her stepdaddy now gets to fuck her two stepbrothers."

I shouldn't like how he speaks to me. This is what he wanted, and now he's trying to shame me for it, but my body responds. My core clenches and my nipples tighten beneath my t-shirt. I know I can't take any more, though. My body needs time to recover.

I decide to give as good as I'm getting. "You can't fuck me now. I still have your father's cum inside me. It's dribbling down the inside of my thighs. I assume you don't want to dip your cock in that."

His expression drops. "Fuck, Laney. How to ruin a moment."

I laugh, the sound slightly cold. "Sorry, Cade, but learn how to pick the right time, and let me give you some advance warning...it won't be any time today."

He pouts but gets up and crosses the room. To my surprise, he loops his hand around the back of my neck and ducks his head. He kisses me, demanding, pushing his tongue between my lips. Then he shoves his hand up my t-shirt and cups my breast, pinching my nipple hard enough to hurt.

I gasp and pull away. "Cade!"

"Just making sure you remember that you're mine as well. Your mouth is mine, your tits are mine, and your pussy is mine, even when it is filled with another man's cum. Got it?"

I don't dare do anything but nod.

"Good," he says. "Now I'm going to help with the chores. Hopefully, we'll find something to eat today. You need to keep up your strength."

"Where's Darius?" I ask.

"I think he went out back, to the woodshed."

"Does-does he know what's happened?"

Cade appraises me as though I'm stupid. "Yes, Laney. I think the fucking birds in the trees heard what happened, and Darius's hearing is better than most."

"Oh. I thought I was being quiet."

He chuckles. "You definitely weren't, but I enjoyed hearing it, and so did Dax. He's probably whacking one out now."

I roll my eyes. "Do you have to be so crude?"

"Only when I want to watch you squirm."

I ignore Cade and leave the cabin to go and find Darius. I want to make sure we're good. Even though he practically pushed me onto Reed's cock, knowing it's actually happened might change things between us.

I find him chopping wood and pause to admire him. He's shirtless, his long hair hanging down his back. He places the log on the block, lifts the axe above his head, and brings it down in exactly the right spot. His skill amazes me. The crack reverberates through the air, and, as though answering it, I hear a distant roll of thunder.

"I know you're there, Laney," Darius says. "Why are you lurking?"

"Sorry." I step forward. "Just admiring the view."

He swings back his hair and puts down the axe. "The forest or me?"

I smile. "What do you think?"

Darius lifts his face skyward. "A storm is coming. It's going to be bad. I figured I'd get as much wood in as possible before it hits."

I frown and lift my gaze as well. The sky does look threatening, the clouds low and gray and bulbous. "If we get a lot of rain, is the river likely to burst its banks?"

"Possibly, but I don't think it'll affect us. We're up too high. It'll affect our chances to gather food and wood though. We need to prepare."

My mind has been all sex and relationships recently, but it suddenly hits me that we're in survival mode.

"I'll go and gather kindling while it's still dry," I tell Darius.

No matter what happens between us all, surviving is the most important thing.

35
CADE

The storm rages outside.

I'm restless, pacing back and forth across the cabin. Sideways rain lashes against the already cracked windows, and I wonder if the glass will hold. I have no idea how long the cabin has been standing, and I figure it's probably seen storms as bad, or even worse than this one, and remained upright, but it's still a concern.

The rain on the roof sounds like a giant's fingers drumming. The roof is only corrugated steel, and the volume is insane—like constant roar filling my ears. It's too loud for us to even talk.

Hours have passed, and the storm shows no signs of abating. I think of the tall trees surrounding us. If one of those is brought down by the wind and lands on the cabin, it will cause some serious damage.

The walls feel like they're closing in. The space isn't big, and with four of us now trapped inside it, it seems to be getting smaller with every passing minute.

Just the presence of the others is frustrating me. They all

237

seem to be taking up too much space—even Laney, who probably only weighs a hundred and twenty pounds. Though I'm the biggest by a good couple of inches, my brother and father seem too broad and tall.

I want to go out onto the porch, if only to breathe some fresh air, but opening the door will only allow the horrendous weather into the cabin, and I'm concerned that I might not be able to get the door shut against the wind.

Instead, I leave the living area and go into one of the bedrooms. There are only the wooden structures of the two single bedframes in the room—minus the mattresses, which are on the floor in the living area—so I perch on the edge of the one closest. I put my elbows on my knees and exhale a long breath, tipping my head back.

Something catches my eye, and I frown.

Is that a hatch in the ceiling?

It certainly looks like it. There's even a small hook that's keeping it shut.

Happy to have a distraction, I stand on the bedframe so I can reach the ceiling. My height means I can reach it easily, and I unhook the hatch. It drops open, and instantly the noise of the rain on the corrugated roof becomes deafening. I even find myself ducking, as though it's a violent force that could strike me.

I jump down off the bedframe and go back into the living area and find one of the candles. With no electricity, and the batteries on the flashlights having waned a long time ago, it's the only light we have.

Reed says something to me, but the storm drowns out his voice. I ignore him and take the candle back into the bedroom, shutting the door behind me. Holding the candle, I climb back onto the bedframe and slide the candle up into the roof space. It illuminates the iron roof, but I can't see much else. If I'm going to get a better look, I need to go up there.

I'm strong and physically fit. The time we've spent stranded in this place and the lack of food means I've also dropped some weight. My jeans already hang off my hips. I'm not sure what I hope to find up there, but I hope it'll be supplies of some kind. With no sign of us being rescued any time soon, we need as much help as we can get.

I hook my fingers over the edge of the hatch, brace myself, bending my knees slightly, and jump. My momentum allows me to hook my forearm onto the roof space and then the other, and then I'm pulling myself up, hauling my body into the space. I hope the ceiling is strong enough to hold my weight. I'd prefer not to go crashing through it, though I imagine the others' faces as I make my arrival into the living area that way. They'd probably think I was a tree crashing through the roof or something.

I pick up the candle from where I'd placed it and use it to peer around. Something white is reflected back at me and I lean closer…

"Oh, fuck."

I jerk back again, hot wax spilling from the top of the candle and hitting my fingers. I barely feel it.

Is that what I think?

My heart beats faster than I'd like to admit, and even the candle flame flickers as my hand trembles. I get a hold on myself. The combination of the dark and the storm, and the thing I believe I've just seen has spooked me, and I'm not the kind of man who gets spooked.

I take a breath and look again.

The smooth curve of a white skull greets me, twin hollows where its eyes used to be. Its jaw is slack, the teeth still in position. It's lying on its side, the long bones of its arms out straight, the smaller bones of its finger lying on the boards as though uncovered by a paleontologist.

Who the fuck is he? Or who *was* he?

Above, the rain continues to pound and the wind howls

around the eaves. It's just me and him, confined in this low, dark space.

The candlelight wavers, and I'm suddenly gripped with the fear that it's going to go out and I'll be left here in the dark with a dead fucking body, but then it grows steady again.

"What the fuck are you doing?"

I jump at my father's voice. He's had to shout to be heard over the storm.

"Fucking hell. You just scared the shit out of me."

"I thought you'd vanished. What are you doing?"

He must be standing on something—most likely the bedframe—his head and shoulders protruding through the hatch.

"Look," I yell and hold up the candle again.

His eyes widen at the sight of the skeleton. "Oh, shit. Who's that?"

"How the fuck should I know?"

I've been focused on the remains up until now, but now I'm no longer alone, I lift the candle to look around the rest of the roof space, checking for any more human remains. To my relief, there are no others, but there are several cardboard boxes, their sides sagging. I remember the reason I came up here in the first place—to look for supplies—and get to my feet. The space isn't tall enough to allow me to stand straight, so I move hunched, careful to tread on the rafters so I don't go plunging into the room below. I reach the nearest box. Cobwebs hang in thick strands from every surface. I might be six-four and covered in tats, but spiders are not my favorite. All those legs creep me the fuck out.

I pull open the top of the box and hold the candle closer to see inside. I'm hoping for a shit ton of canned food, and maybe even a beer or two, but something completely different meets my eyes.

Guns. Semi-automatic, from what I can tell. They don't look

like hunters' guns to me, and there are far too many of them, all stacked on top of one another.

I go to the next box and repeat the process. Sure enough, it contains the same.

"What's in there?" Reed shouts from the hatch so to be heard over the storm.

"Guns. A fuck ton of guns." I open one of the boxes and lift out one of the weapons. "This isn't the only one. These boxes are full of them."

"Hunters?"

"If this is hunters, I don't know what the fuck they're hunting."

Carefully, I carry one down to inspect. I'm relieved to be out of the crawl space and away from my new skeletal friend. The storm hasn't abated any, and, for the first time, I'm thankful for it. Though it means no one will be out searching for us, it also means that whoever the guns belong to and, potentially, whoever is responsible for the skeleton, also won't be coming back for them any time soon.

I hand the gun over to Reed, and he inspects it, frowning.

"This isn't a good sign," he says.

"What is it?"

"The serial number has been filed off. If this gun was legal, that wouldn't have been done."

"People don't keep boxes full of guns in a roof space if they're legal," I point out.

It had never occurred to me that they were. The moment I'd seen them, together with the skeleton, alarms had gone off in my head.

"Whose cabin are we staying in?" Reed wonders. "Who does the skeleton belong to? We probably need to get a better look at him, see if we can figure out how he died."

I frown his way. "How are we supposed to do that?"

"Look for bone breaks, maybe, a fractured skull. What we really need to know is did he die by accident, or did someone kill him?"

I draw air in through my nose. "The same *someone* who owns all those guns, you mean?"

Reed shrugs. "He wouldn't have crawled into the roof space by himself and just stayed there until he died."

I offer another explanation. "He might have been injured and hid himself up there, and ended up dying?"

"If he was hiding, who was he hiding from?"

I think again. "Or he was already dead and whoever those guns belong to hid the body up there, maybe as a warning to anyone else who finds them?"

Reed clicked his tongue against his teeth. "Anyone like us, you mean. But why wouldn't they have taken the guns with them?"

"Maybe they meant to come back for them and something or someone stopped them?"

"Or they still plan to come back?"

His words are ominous.

Up until now, it's nature that we've believed we need to protect ourselves against. What if we have even more to worry about?

The bedroom door opens, and I find myself turning guilty. Darius and Laney stand there, both of them frowning at us.

"What's going on?" Darius asks.

I exchange a glance with Reed. Are we going to tell them? I guess we don't have much choice.

Reed holds up the weapon. "Cade found a gun in the roof space."

Laney widens her blue eyes in alarm. "What was it doing up there?"

I clear my throat. "That's not the only one. There are boxes of them."

"Shit," she curses.

I continue, "And there's something else. I found a skeleton hidden up there as well."

36

Laney

"WE SHOULD LEAVE," I say, alarm sirens blaring through me.

This isn't good. This isn't good at all. We'd always wondered who the cabin belonged to, but we'd never considered it might be used by a criminal, or maybe a whole gang of criminals.

Cade stares at me. "And go where?"

"I don't know, but it can't be safe here. What if someone comes back for the weapons?"

"We don't know that anyone is going to do that. It's not like this place was locked up or anything when we arrived. For all we know, the person the skeleton belonged to is the same person who owns the guns. It might be that no one is coming."

I shudder, hating to think that we've been sleeping beneath a man's final resting place. "And if they do? What then?"

"Then they'll have some kind of transport and we'll be on our way out of here."

I shake my head. "If they don't kill us first."

"How will they know we've even found the guns or the skeleton?" Cade says. "We put the gun back, close the hatch again, and no one is any the wiser. We just explain we were in a crash, and hopefully the gunrunner will help us out of here."

I arch an eyebrow. "Hopefully? We're pinning our lives on *hopefully*?"

"Given our current situation, even if we take the whole box of guns and dead person out of the equation, I'd say the best we've got is hopefully."

"Or we leave and try to walk out of here," I suggest.

He gestures around him. "Walk where? We have no idea where we are or how far away we are from any form of civilization."

Reed steps in. "Well, we're not going anywhere while this storm is still raging, and we can be pretty confident that whoever owns the guns won't be back while the weather is this bad either."

"Do you think they *will* come back?" I ask him.

"I've got no way of knowing that, Laney."

We all fall silent for a moment, considering this turn of events.

"How did they get here?" Darius says suddenly. "If gunrunners have been using this place, they must have been able to access it, but we haven't seen any roads nearby."

Reed considers this. "They definitely don't get here by car or truck, and I think there's too much tree coverage for a helicopter."

"Boat, then," I say. "The river is close enough. They must be using a boat to transport the guns."

"It's possible," he agrees. "It makes the most sense."

We certainly haven't seen any sign of either helicopters or planes. It makes me wonder if the authorities have given up looking for us. The thought is terrifying. What will happen to us if we have to spend a winter out here? How will we survive? I know the men are strong and capable, and I'm thankful every day that we all made it through the crash, but even the local bears will hibernate over winter because of the lack of food. We've already started smoking and storing meat, just in case, but we're barely getting enough calories in us to keep us going each day as it is. I can't imagine there being even less.

I think of the river again.

"If the gunrunners did get here by boat, it must mean that if we follow the river far enough, we might come across some kind of civilization."

"You think we should try to walk to safety?" Cade asks.

I hesitate, considering my response. "Right now, we have food and shelter, and, if we tried to walk upstream, we'll be leaving that behind, but perhaps we'll get to the point where it'll be worth the risk."

Cade's lips thin. "When winter comes, you mean?"

I nod. "Yes."

Reed looks between us. "Trying to walk out of here could be suicide. We have no idea where we're going, or if we'd even be walking in the right direction. How do we know if the gunrunners travel up or downstream? It's better to stay where we have food and shelter and wait for a rescue."

"Or wait for men with guns to turn up and shoot us all in the head," Cade throws in.

Reed turns to him. "We have no way of knowing that will happen. Besides, we have guns now. Maybe we can just step up our lookout, watch for anyone who might be coming. We've got it good here. I don't want to change that."

I jump in. "We might not have any choice when winter arrives."

He holds my gaze. "We'll deal with that then."

Darius takes my side. "We can't wait until winter arrives. If we do that, trying to walk will definitely kill us. If we're going to try this, then we need to do it while food is still plentiful and it's warm enough to sleep outside."

"No!" Reed's shout makes me jump. "We are not leaving the

cabin. I'm the head of this family and my word is final. No one is going anywhere."

With that, he storms from the room.

37

Laney

THE STORM PASSES without too much damage, and none of us broach the subject of walking to safety to Reed again.

I can tell the guys have it on their mind, though. Cade knuckles down with his traps, catching as much as he can, and Darius is increasing the amount of meat he has drying for jerky.

I find myself spending more time on the porch, sitting and looking out over the forest. A low-lying mist hangs over the trees this morning, the green triangle tops of the spruces appearing through the white.

I'm not so much looking out for rescue helicopters or planes —my hope for those died some time ago—but instead am watching out for any signs the gunrunners might be on their way.

At least things are good between me and Reed, and me and the boys. They each take every opportunity to be with me. I feel like I always have one of them touching me, and not always in a sexual way, either. They put their arms around my waist and shoulders, kiss the top of my head or the back of my neck, and hold my hand. They playfight about who gets to pull me onto their lap, or whose shoulder I rest my head on.

I've never felt so wanted or cherished or adored.

It's during the night that I'm closest to Reed, when we're snuggled up together, and hidden by both darkness and the blankets. That's *our* time. It's during the day, out trapping with Cade or down by the river with Darius, that I spend time with them.

Darius comes and joins me on the porch.

"You haven't played your violin since we've been here," I say to him.

He shakes his head. "No. It doesn't feel right. I promised myself that the next time I played would be when we're back in civilization."

"What if that never happens?"

"Then I guess I'll die without ever playing it again."

I'm filled with sorrow on his behalf. "That's so sad, Dax."

He smiles, but I can tell it's not a full smile.

"I've got something else to fill my time."

He means me.

"Wait here," I tell him, and go into the cabin. I find his violin and bow and bring it back out to him. I place the violin in his lap, and the bow in his hand.

"Play for me."

His brow furrows. "You touched my violin?"

There's a coldness to his tone that I'm unused to.

"Umm…only to bring it out to you."

"I already told you I wasn't going to play here. Why didn't you listen to me?"

My stomach sinks as I realize I've done the wrong thing. "I just thought—"

"Thought you knew better than me. Would you have done the same to Cade? Gone against his wishes like that?"

"I-I don't know." I do, though. If Cade had told me he didn't want to do something, I would have accepted it.

He sets the violin down beneath his chair but keeps hold of the bow. "Come here, Laney."

I'm unsure what's going on, but I edge a little closer.

"Now take off your pants and lie down over my lap."

I blink. "What?"

"You heard me. Do as I say. Now."

There's no room for argument in his voice.

"What are you—"

"Pants off, Laney." He taps his thighs with the bow, and I gulp. "Don't keep me waiting."

I glance around for the others but see no sign of them. Quickly, I unbutton my jeans, and kick off my sneakers. I've still got my panties on, but he never said anything about taking them off.

I slide across his lap, so my legs are on one side of his thighs, and my head hangs down the other. My pelvis rests across his legs, my ass sticking into the air.

He uses the tip of the bow to trace from my nape, right the way down my spine, to rest at the top of my ass. He hooks the tip underneath the elastic waistband and gives them a flick.

"What are these, Laney?"

"My panties. You never said to take them off."

He gives a strange kind of laugh. "Of course I want them off."

He rolls them down my thighs, and off my feet, and then bunches them in his fist. He brings them to his nose and inhales deeply.

"Fuck, I love the scent of you. That alone gets me hard. I'm keeping these for later." He pockets my underwear. "Did you know this bow is worth thousands of dollars?"

I shake my head. "No, I didn't."

"It's made from the very best brazilwood and has a solid gold button. It's made to fix my exact hand and body size, so it's one of a kind. If it were to break, I'd be extremely pissed."

So that's why he's angry? He thought I might break his bow?

Darius continues, "But even knowing what you do now about

this bow, I also want you to know that I'll happily break it across your sweet little backside if you go against my wishes again."

I bite my lower lip, tears threatening. "I'm sorry."

"I'm going to spank you now, Laney, and I'm going to use my bow, even if it breaks. Do you understand? You'll get five strikes, and I want you to count each one."

I'm trembling now. His erection is a hard ridge beneath my pubic bone, and even though he's punishing me, it's turning him on. How much is this going to hurt?

"I want you to count each one," he says. "Ready?"

It occurs to me that I could get up and run away, but I don't want to displease him any more than I already have. I can take this, and then, by the feel of his cock beneath me, I think he'll make me feel good again.

"One," he says.

There's a whip in the air, and a crack, followed by a sharp sting.

"Ow!" I cry out.

"Count it, Laney."

"One," I whimper.

He strikes me again, this time in a slightly different place.

I squeal. "Two."

Heat blooms where he's hit me. He uses his hand to rub the places on my bottom that I imagine must be striped with red.

To my surprise, I feel myself getting wet. I grind down on the spot where his cock is beneath me, trying to apply pressure in exactly the right place.

"That's right." I can hear the smile in his voice. "Now you're getting the idea."

He lifts the bow and strikes me again.

"Three."

"Part your legs for me."

I do, and he strokes down, over my asshole, to my pussy. He dips his fingers inside of me, and I moan in pleasure. Then something else makes contact with me, and I stiffen. It's solid wood, tipped with metal. He only uses the very tip, but it's enough to feel like an invasion.

"Dax!" I cry.

"Shh. This will feel good." He's fucking me with his bow now, playing my body as though it was his instrument. My breathing is fast and frantic, and I grind my clit against his cock.

Then he slips it back out of my body and whips me again.

"Four!"

I choke back a cry. I don't know how I feel. A part of me is humiliated, and even angry with him, but the other part is so incredibly turned on, I can't even think straight.

He smooths over the spot where he's struck me again. "Do you know why spanking feels so good, even while it hurts?" He doesn't bother waiting for my reply. "It's because right now your body believes you're in pain, and it's flooding your system with all these feel-good hormones to help to alleviate it. Except, you're not hurt. In fact, I'm making you feel good."

I'm not so sure about the not being hurt part, cause it fucking stings when he hits me, but I also totally get the feeling good part. My head is woozy, as though I've been taking drugs, or I haven't quite woken up yet.

"Last one," he tells me. "Are you ready?"

I nod and clench my hands into fists.

"Spread your legs a little more for me, Laney," he says.

I comply, feeling the slipperiness between my thighs. I'm completely open for him, exposed.

He brings the bow down for the final time, but instead of hitting my ass, he strikes my pussy from behind. I jolt as though someone has just wired me up to an electric shock machine. All my inner muscles clench and my pussy floods with wetness.

"Oh, God," I cry. "Oh, fuck."

Then his fingers are in the same place he struck me, smoothing over the spot before pushing inside me. I buck and grind against his cock, and he pumps me, fast and hard, not letting me come down from the high of being whipped with his bow.

My entire body is wound tight, and I climb higher and higher, until I finally topple over the edge, my pussy pulsing around his fingers. Then I go slack over his lap, panting hard.

"Well, that was fun," Darius says.

He helps me up, but instead of releasing me, he spins me around so I'm straddling his lap. Then he drags my t-shirt over my head and tosses it away. I haven't bothered to wear a bra—it's not like my tits are huge and the only people who see me out here are definitely ones who prefer me to go without. I love being naked while he's still fully dressed. There's something so wanton about it.

"Take out my cock," he tells me.

Eagerly, I reach for him, freeing him from his jeans. His cock is so perfect, long and not too thick. I run my hand up and down him, taking a moment to swipe my thumb over the slit, gathering his precum.

"Now ride me. Fuck me hard and fast," he instructs.

I position my pussy, so wet and swollen from my prior orgasm, at the head of his cock and then sink down. I groan as I impale myself and wrap my arms around his neck. I go as deep as I can, stretching around him, taking all of him.

He reaches for his bow again.

"No, Dax. I can't take anymore spanking."

He gives a slow grin. "That's not my plan."

He trails the tip of it back down my spine, to my ass, and then between my cheeks. I realize what he has in mind and whimper.

"This will feel good. I promise."

He tickles my asshole with the tip of the bow. Automatically, I clench against the pressure and inadvertently clamp around his cock as well.

"Shh, relax."

He pushes the end of the smooth wood inside my ass. It's not big at all, and he must only be using the first inch or so, but the invasion feels huge. It also feels...good. All my senses are directed down there, focusing me completely.

I'd kept completely still while he played with my ass and the bow, but now we start to move again. I lift myself up and down, my thighs trembling with the tension. He holds the bow high up, close to my body, to ensure he controls how much of it penetrates me as we move.

He fucks me with the bow as I ride his cock. I don't think I've ever felt so utterly uninhibited. We're on the porch with the whole forest at my back, and I'm being fucked in the ass with an inanimate object while being impaled on a man's cock. I tip my head back, my hair falling down my spine. He ducks his head and covers one of my nipples with his mouth.

Unintelligible sounds peal from between my lips, joining the sounds of the forest, and then I curl back into him, slamming down on him, faster and faster, until I lose all rhythm.

I come hard for the second time, and Darius climaxes with me, jerking inside my body, filling me up.

I cling to him, my arms around his neck, my face buried into his shoulder. We're both breathing hard, our bodies rising and falling as one. He slips the bow from my body and places it to the floor.

"How are you feeling?" he asks.

"Incredible," I admit.

He touches my face, trailing his fingers down it in the way he does when he wants to learn my expression, and then kisses me, slow and deliberate. His cock, still inside me, jumps.

"You know," he says, "it's moments like this where I think I'll be happy if we never make it home."

I press my forehead to his and close my eyes. I know exactly how he feels.

38

Laney

I'M deep in sleep when a loud creak comes from the porch.

I bolt upright, clutching the thin blanket around my body. I have no idea what time it is, but it's still dark. The nights are cooler now, but the fire continues to smolder in the wood stove, red and orange embers illuminating the room enough to see, but only just.

The men are all still asleep. Reed is lying on his back and is snoring lightly. Cade is on his side, one arm hanging off the edge of the sofa. Darius is on his front, his hair covering his face.

The creak comes again, and adrenaline shoots through my veins. There's someone out there, and it's definitely not one of the guys.

I smack Reed's hard shoulder with my balled fist and hiss, "Wake up. Someone's here!"

He lets out a groan and his eyelids flutter open. "What?"

I shush him to keep his voice down, and he sits up.

"What's wrong?" he whispers.

"Someone is—"

The noise comes again, and his head spins toward the door. "Shit." He turns to the others. "Wake up. We've got company."

Cade is instantly awake and on his feet, as though he's been expecting this moment to come. Darius takes a moment longer to come around, but in a matter of seconds, we're all awake and focused on whatever is going on outside.

As well as the creaking floorboards, there's another sound, a heavy shuffling, someone moving slowly and laboriously. Outside the cabin windows, there's only darkness. There's no light from the moon tonight, a blanket of cloud cover blocking both that and any starlight.

If we try to use any light to look outside, we'll alert whoever is out there to our presence. Right now, they might not have any clue that any one is inside the cabin.

I try to remember what we might have left out on the porch —what evidence of our presence is out there. If someone knows this property, subtle changes such as the positioning of the chair will be enough to make them realize they're not alone.

Who would come out here in the middle of the night?

There's only one real explanation, and that's to do with the presence of the guns and the body in the roof space. Whoever left them there must be back for them. I can't imagine how far they must have had to travel in order to reach the cabin. Have they come via the river, as I'd suspected? If so, it means they have a boat, and if we can get it to, we'll be able to get to safety.

A loud scraping comes from the log walls, and I shoot a look at Reed.

"I don't think that's a person," he says, keeping his voice low.

I furrow my brow, not understanding what he means. The shuffling thump comes again.

Understanding dawns in Cade's eyes. "It's a bear."

Reed nods.

My mouth drops open. "A bear? Oh, my God." I'm not one

hundred percent sure if this is good news or not. While I'm glad it's not a group of hardened criminal gunrunners, a hungry bear could prove just as deadly. "Will it be able to get in?"

"I hope not," Reed replies, still keeping his voice low, "but if it presses against the windows hard enough, it'll break the glass."

"It must have been attracted here by the rabbit jerky," Darius says. "Meat is hanging in the woodshed to dry."

"I hope it takes it and leaves again," I hiss.

"Trouble is," Reed says, "when a bear finds a source of food, especially at this time of year, it'll keep coming back to it."

I widen my eyes. "You mean it won't go away?"

"Not without a little encouragement."

Cade gets to his feet. "I'll get the gun."

"You can't shoot it!" I cry, louder than I'd intended. "It doesn't deserve to be shot. It's in its own habitat, and it hasn't done anything to hurt us. Just wait for it to leave."

He stares at me. "And when it comes back during the day and you're sitting out on the porch and it decides you look like you'd make a good meal, would you still not want it shot then?"

"You don't know that's going to happen," I protest.

Reed eyes me. "You really want to take the risk?"

"You agree with him?"

Reed nods. "Yeah, I do. I'm not going to risk losing any of you to a bear."

I turn to Darius. "What about you? You think we should shoot some innocent animal because it's come close to the cabin?"

Darius links his hands between his knees and nods. "Sorry, Laney, but yeah. If that bear decides it wants in here, we'll be in trouble."

"If it tries to get inside, then we can shoot it."

While we'd been arguing, the noises of the bear had faded away.

I hold my breath, trying to hear over the thudding of my

heart. Has it gone? Perhaps it had overheard us discussing shooting it and decided to make itself scarce. Of course, I don't actually believe this, but there is a chance it heard human voices and instinctively knew we posed a danger. I imagine its huge furry butt shuffling from side to side as it lumbers its way back through the woods, and I hope it makes a sensible decision to never come back again.

"From now on," Reed says, "when we go out of the cabin, whether that's to hunt or forage or collect wood, you take a gun with you. Plus, we always go out in pairs, no going on your own. It'll be too easy to get distracted by something and not hear the bear coming."

"Umm, what about washing?" I ask. "Are you saying I can't go down to the river on my own?"

"Definitely not. Bears love to fish. It could easily be somewhere nearby."

I let out a sigh. I understand his reasoning, but I'll miss my time by the river. It's the only time I really get to myself, where I don't have to think about one of the men being around, and I'm reluctant to give it up.

"Okay," I relent.

While I'll miss my alone time, I also don't want to get attacked by a bear. I've seen the size of their claws and imagine the damage they would cause. For one of us to end up with the kind of injuries one might cause would be life-threatening, and I don't even want to think about the horror of it.

When morning arrives, we venture outside, Cade armed with one of the guns.

"Look," Reed says, jerking his chin at the outside of the cabin walls.

There are pale grooves in the logs, two sets, high up. It's clear the bear had been on its hind legs and used the side of the cabin as a scratching post.

"Was it trying to find a way in?" I ask, a tremor to my voice.

He twists his lips. "Looks like it. Bears will be thinking about fattening up for hibernation now, which is probably why we had our visitor last night. Make sure we don't leave any food waste or scraps near the cabin, and if we're gutting birds or rabbits or fish, do it down by the river so it washes away."

"What about the windows?" I ask. "They're hardly made from solid glass. What if it figures out it can break its way in?"

Cade holds up the gun. "Then we shoot it."

"I don't feel safe here anymore," I tell him, blinking back tears.

He puts his arm around my waist and kisses the top of my head. "I'll keep you safe, Laney."

I smile up at him, and as I do, I catch Reed frowning at us both.

39
REED

IT'S BEEN a few days since the bear incident, and Laney's comments about no longer feeling safe have been playing on my mind. She's the one who suggested that we try to walk out of here, and I'm the one who's made her stay. What if something happens to her here, and I could have done something to change it? I'm supposed to be the one protecting her, and I'm terrified I'm going to fail her. How would I ever forgive myself?

I walk into the cabin and stop short.

Laney is lying on one of the mattresses by the fire. She's naked. Cade is between her thighs, while her head rests in Darius's lap. Darius's hands are on her perfect tits, squeezing and pulling at her nipples, drawing them into tight peaks. Her eyes are closed and her back arches, the most glorious sounds of pleasure curling from between her lips. I don't know what Cade is doing with his tongue, but she's clearly loving it.

She looks beautiful and sexy…and young.

Too young.

I can barely control the rush of emotion that hits me. What the fuck are we thinking? I'd promised I would protect her, even if that meant protecting her from me and my sons. Now we're all using her body like she's some kind of fuck toy for us to play with.

I see this from the point of view of an outsider, of how the public would crucify us if we ever managed to get back to normality. Two big adult men feasting on a young woman. They're her stepbrothers, and I'm her stepfather, and I'm just standing by, letting this happen.

It's not right.

Only Darius shows any awareness of my arrival, his head twisted toward the door. Laney and Cade are too caught up in their pleasure to notice me.

I stalk across the cabin and grab Cade's shoulder and haul him away from Laney.

Before he's barely had the chance to get to his feet, I swing my arm. My fist connects with his jaw, and his head rocks back. The crack of the impact seems to echo around the room.

Laney's eyes spring open and she screams, unsure what is happening. She pushes with her heels to get to sitting, and backs straight into Darius's arms. She grabs a blanket and drags it around herself. I hate that she feels she has to cover her body from me. It hurts in a way I can't even explain. Darius wraps his arms around her protectively and holds her tight. She's staring at me as though she doesn't recognize me.

Cade is down on one knee, his hand clutched to the spot where I'd hit him. I'm sure I can smell Laney's arousal coming from her skin, and I respond to it like a man, not her stepfather. My cock tingles, heat forming in my balls. I don't want to have this reaction to her, and my anger rachets up a notch.

I'm a fucking hypocrite, and I know it.

Cade angles his face toward me, his brow knotted in anger and confusion. "What the fuck are you doing?"

"What the fuck am *I* doing? You're the one going down on your stepsister."

"And? Like you haven't fucked her as well. Why are you getting up on your high horse all of a sudden?"

"This is wrong. Can't you see that? Jesus Christ." I drag my hand through my hair.

Cade smirks. "Feels pretty fucking right to me."

I raise my fist again, and he pushes himself to his feet.

"You gonna hit me again, old man? For what? Huh? You jealous or something? You want Laney all to yourself?"

I can see why he thinks that.

I lower my arm. "I'm sorry, Cade. I didn't mean to do that. I just reacted. I—I just think this setup needs to change. This isn't good for any of us."

"Why are you doing this?" Laney cries. "Talk about hot and cold. You had no problem with me being with all of you yesterday."

"You're wrong," I admit. "I did have a problem with it. I always have. I just wasn't strong enough to resist. You're so sweet and beautiful and sexy, and we're trapped here in these crazy circumstances. We shouldn't be treating you like this."

"So, you stop sleeping with her, then, if you're the one having a crisis of conscience," Cade says. "Why the fuck should we?"

I shake my head. "You think this is going to work? You think she isn't going to prefer one of you over the other someday? What's going to happen to us then? Would you be able to forgive your brother for taking her away?" I turn and address Darius. "Would you, Dax?"

"What are you saying, Reed?" Laney asks, tears in her eyes. "Do you not want me to sleep with any of you because you think morally it's wrong, or because you think I'm going to break the family apart?"

I look at her. "Can't both reasons be equally valid?"

"I'm not going to pick one of you over the other." There's desperation in her blue eyes. "I would never do that."

265

"You can't make that promise."

"Yes, I can," she insists.

"You're too young. How you think about things will change as you get older?"

"I'd never want to come between any of you."

I harden my jaw. "Didn't you see what happened just now?" I throw my killer blow. "You already have."

She blinks a few times and then gathers the blanket closer, untangles herself from Darius's arms, and runs from the room. She slams into the bedroom and shuts the door behind her.

Darius gets to his feet to go after her.

"Leave her," Cade commands.

"Why the fuck should I?"

"Because we need to talk about this."

Darius gestures toward the closed door. "Don't you think Laney should be involved in the conversation?"

"She will be," Cade says. He turns toward me. "But first, I expect an apology. You've never hit me in your life, not even when Darius and I were kids. But you start now? Because of her?"

"He did it to prove his point," Darius says. "He's making his own prophecy come true."

I fold my arms across my chest. "No, I didn't. I swear it. I just reacted. But losing my temper like that has made me accept what lies ahead if we continue down this road."

Darius won't accept it. "This is Laney we're talking about! You can't ask us to give her up. Not now."

"I know who we're talking about. It's because it's her that this is so important. We shouldn't be living like this with her. It's not right."

"Why? Because some society we're not even part of anymore says it's not right?" He drags his hand through his long hair. "That's fucking bullshit, and you know it."

"We've shared women plenty of times before," Cade says. "It's never been a problem."

"Not like this," I say. "Not like with her."

Cade narrows his eyes. "So, what are you saying? That we're all supposed to start acting like we're some normal family? Like Laney actually *is* our stepsister?"

I draw a breath. "If we're going to think about walking out of here, then we need to focus on surviving that. If we make it to safety, then maybe we can look at this again."

Darius turns his head in my direction. "You think we should walk out of here?"

I swallow, feeling my Adam's apple working. "Laney is right. It's getting more and more dangerous here, and that's only going to get worse with winter coming. I don't know when we should leave, but I think we need to be prepared."

40

laney

DARIUS IS the one who comes to me first.

"Laney?"

I turn to him, tears streaming down my cheeks. "Why is Reed doing this? Why is he trying to hurt me?"

"He's not. That's the exact opposite of what he's trying to do."

"Well, if he's not trying to hurt me, he's doing a really shitty job. He's broken my heart."

The last thing I'd ever want is to come between them. I love them too much for that. But this is hell, and I'm trapped in it. How can we possibly go back to what we were before?

Darius cups my cheeks in his hands and lowers his forehead to mine, his eyes slipping shut.

"Laney," he whispers. "It's going to be all right."

My entire body aches to claim him, to stand on my tiptoes and press my lips to his. I could let this blanket fall so I'm naked again and take hold of his hands and run them over my body. I never had the chance to reach my climax, and I'm a pent-up ball of heartache and sexual frustration. He's so perfect, and I can't stand the thought that I'll never get to touch him the way I want again—the way I know *he* wants, too.

Darius still wants me, I'm sure of it. Cade, too, perhaps. But how can I be with them if Reed isn't in agreement? I *will* come between them all; I know I will.

Reed is right. I have to put a stop to this. It has already gone too far. It was one thing when it had just been sex, and I'd known that if we ever made it back to the real world, we could have all kept our secret to ourselves and no one would be any the wiser. But when feelings get involved, it complicates things. Keeping it a secret would mean us having to give each other up when we're rescued, but if I cared for them—if I *loved* them—I wouldn't just be able to walk away.

I would break my own heart if I did.

"Reed thinks we should try to walk out of here," Darius says.

That wasn't what I'd been expecting at all.

"He changed his mind?" I ask in surprise.

"I guess the bear was the last straw." Darius considers this for a moment. "Or he can see us tearing each other apart if we stay."

I wonder which is closer to the truth.

"If we manage to walk back to civilization," I say, "what will happen between us all then?"

"I'm not sure," he admits, "but at least then we'll be safe, and once we're safe, I'm sure Reed will see things differently. If he no longer thinks you're vulnerable, or that we're being too much of an influence on you, he might come around."

I try to picture what life will be like back in the real world with the three of them. We can't let people find out what's happened between us. I'll be branded a slut for sleeping with three men at once, and Reed will probably be questioned for abusing me, or some other such nonsense. No one will believe I'd been eighteen when he first laid a finger on me, or that I'd been perfectly capable of wanting him in return. He'll be branded a pervert for sleeping with his stepdaughter.

It suddenly hits me how selfish I've been. I wanted Reed, and I got him, but he's the one who'll lose the most if any of this gets out.

That doesn't change how I feel, but once we walk to safety, and the media storm dies down around us, and people forget that Reed is my stepfather, then we'll have the freedom to do whatever we want.

41

laney

IN THE DAYS THAT FOLLOW, as we prepare to leave the cabin and hike into the wilderness, I do my best to stay out of the men's way. I feel like they're doing the same to me—Cade in particular makes any excuse to leave an area when I arrive.

Sleeping in the cabin with them each night is like torture.

Cade has taken himself into one of the bedrooms, removing the cushions from the couch and creating himself a bed. Reed still sleeps on the mattress beside me, but it's as though he never really relaxes. Any time my hand or foot accidentally strays over to his mattress, he jerks away as though I've burned him. My heart aches for the easy way he was with me before. I miss his hugs as much as I miss his kisses and touch, though I miss them as well.

Darius has completely shut down from me. At least with the other two, I catch them staring at me when they think I'm not looking, but I can't have that with Darius.

I wish they would fight for me, and I'm brokenhearted that they don't. I tell myself that I'd never want to come between them as a family, but, if that was the truth, I'd accept what they'd decided, wouldn't I? I'd put my own feelings to one side for the sake of the family, but I can't.

I still want them. All of them.

Just as I did when we'd first crashed and came to the cabin, I do my best to hide my true emotions from them. I only give in to my tears when I believe I'm alone in the cabin, or when I shut myself in the bathroom and cry until my chest hurts, or sob silently into my pillow at night.

But no amount of anguish changes our situation.

We prepare as much as possible, gathering food and filling water bottles. We plan to leave the day after tomorrow. The weather is looking good, but we still need to be organized.

I'm going through the kitchen cupboards, making sure we haven't missed anything that might come in useful. I crouch at the cabinet under the sink, and something catches my eye. There's a metal object hidden behind one of the pipes.

A phone.

My heart jolts. I reach in and pluck it out. I assume it must belong to the gunrunners, a hidden burner phone that they use to organize their crimes. If I can turn it on, there might be the chance we can use it to call for help. We wouldn't have to hike after all.

I frown down at the screen, then turn it over in my hand. On the cover, a sexy cartoon woman in a red dress stares out at me from one eye, the other hidden beneath a swathe of hair, and my confusion deepens.

"Cade? Isn't this your phone?"

He lifts his head. "What?"

I hold it up. "Isn't this yours?"

"No, I don't think so."

"But it is. Look." I turn it around so he can see the cover. What would the chances be of one of the gunrunners having the same picture? "You said you'd lost it in the crash."

"I did."

His gaze shifts away, a muscle in his jaw ticking.

"You're lying. Why are you lying?"

Reed overhears. "What's going on?"

"I found Cade's phone."

"You did? I thought he'd lost it. What's going on, Cade?"

Cade's expression has turned dark, his brow furrowed, his lips compressed. Alarm spikes through me. Did he hide the phone under the sink? Why would he do that?

"Does it work?" Darius asks.

I push the button and hold it down, hoping to bring the phone to life, but nothing happens. My stomach drops in disappointment. For a moment there, I'd been picturing the phone screen coming on and us being able to dial the emergency services to come and get us out of here.

"Nothing," I say. "I guess the battery is dead."

"It was dead when I found it after the crash," Cade says.

Reed narrows his eyes at him. "Then why say you couldn't find it? And why hide it under the sink?"

"I don't know how it got there. It must have fallen out of something."

I stare at him, the understanding that he's lying sinking deeper into my gut. The phone had been wedged behind the outlet pipe. It wasn't as though it could have dropped out of a pocket and ended up there. Someone had to have put it there.

"Why wouldn't you want us to know you had your phone?" I ask.

Cade exhales a long breath then covers his face with his hands. "Fuck. I guess you were going to find out at some point."

"Find out what?" Reed says, his tone serious.

"I was in trouble, back in the States."

Reed frowns. "What kind of trouble?"

"Money trouble."

"What are you talking about?" Reed throws up his hands.

"We have money. That's never been a problem for us, at least it hasn't been since Darius's success."

"That's the thing, though, isn't it? It's Darius's success, not mine."

Lines of confusion appear between Darius's eyebrows. "I've always paid well. If you needed more money, why didn't you just say something?"

Cade turns to his brother. "I did, remember? That investment a couple of months ago."

"The one hundred K?" Darius checks.

"Yeah, that's right. Only, I didn't invest it. I paid off some debt."

"What debt?"

"Gambling debt," Cade admits.

"I don't understand," Darius says. "When did you start gambling?"

"Six months ago. I wasn't always out chasing women."

He shoots me a guilty look.

"But that still doesn't explain why you hid your phone," I say.

"I paid off that gambling debt, but then I ran up more debt. I borrowed money from the wrong people, and they were coming after me. I knew I couldn't ask you for more money, Dax. I hated that I'd already lost you a hundred grand. These people are not good men. They threatened me." He stares down at his hands, where they're twisted together. "They threatened *you*, Darius."

Reed's eyes are wide. "Jesus fucking Christ. So, you thought what, exactly? That if these people thought you'd died in a plane crash, you'd be off the hook for the money?"

"I wasn't thinking ahead. It's just that after we crashed, all I thought was that here," he gestures around us with his hands, "those men would never find me. They'd never find Dax."

Darius's scowl deepens. "So you decide we'd be better off

dying out in the middle of nowhere rather than you having to face these men?"

"They're not the kind of men you can just face. They'd have shot you in the back of the head if they didn't get what they wanted."

Darius throws up his hands. "So why not just ask me for more money? Tell me the goddamned truth for once in your life?"

"I was ashamed. Embarrassed. I fucked up, big time. I felt like I was just ruining your life. First, you lost your sight because I got you sick, and then I bring madmen to your door because I've got a gambling habit."

His brother glares at him. "And then you get us stranded in the middle of fucking nowhere when you could have called for help!"

"I thought I'd bought myself some time, but I hadn't expected for no one to find us. I was sure the plane would have some kind of emergency beacon on it that would alert rescuers to our location. I hadn't considered that the battery would die before I got the chance to call for help, and we'd still be lost weeks, or even months later."

Reed drags his hands over his face. "Fucking hell, Cade."

Cade keeps talking, as though he hasn't heard him. "Out here, as well, there's no temptation to gamble. I thought it would be like going cold turkey, you know. It would be a win-win. Those men would think I was dead, and I wouldn't be able to gamble anymore."

I opened my mouth, still confused. "But didn't it occur to you that they'd find out when you were found again? That it would be all over the news?"

"Honestly, I didn't even think that far ahead. I was just so relieved not to have it as an immediate problem—that I'd get a fucking break from worrying about it all the time. You all felt this was the place where you were in danger, but for me it was the one place I was safe."

I can't believe Cade has done this to us. Could we really have called for help on Cade's phone after the crash? Would the emergency services have perhaps been able to use some kind of tracking to figure out our location? I imagine an alternate universe where he'd made different choices, and none of the past month had happened. No illness. No finding a dead body in the roof space. No encounters with hungry bears.

But also no connection with the men. No experience of them taking care of me. No passionate sex and kisses. No sleeping with them curled up around me.

I never would have the kind of connection I have with them now if we'd been rescued right away.

What would that alternate universe have brought about? Would we have gone straight back to Los Angeles, only for these men Cade was talking about to find him? Find Darius? What if Cade had made that call, and we'd been taken back to LA only for those men to shoot Darius?

"You asshole," Darius snaps. "You selfish fucking asshole."

Darius launches at him, his fist swinging. His knuckles connect with Cade's jaw, and Cade flies backward. He hits a wooden chair as he goes down, the chair splintering. Then he's lying on the floor, with Darius on top of him, and he hits him again.

Cade doesn't even fight back. He just lets his brother beat him, taking every hit. Blood flies, spattering across the wooden floorboards.

"Enough!" Reed roars.

He grabs Darius by the shoulders and drags him off. All the fight has gone out of Darius, too, and he allows his father to pull him away from Cade.

Cade just lies there, his chest rising and falling, his handsome face a bloodied mess. The sight of him brings tears to my eyes.

"I never meant to get you all killed," he whispers to none of us in particular, staring up at the ceiling.

"You didn't," I say. "We're all still alive. Look at us. We're fine."

Fine might be pushing it, but we're not dead yet. We still have a chance.

What will happen if we are rescued, though? Will those same men still come after Cade? Come after Darius? If they learn of our relationship, maybe they'll even come after me.

I suddenly understand what Cade was thinking. Would I choose to sacrifice any of them for us to be back in civilization? Not in a heartbeat.

We might have our challenges here, but, for the most part, we're safe.

And we have each other.

42

laney

IT'S our final night in the cabin. Tomorrow, we leave, and I'm sick with heartache and sorrow. Though I'm frightened to stay, it also feels as though leaving the cabin means saying goodbye to the relationship I have with these three men.

The others are out collecting final supplies, but Reed comes home early and alone.

He stops short when he sees me. "Why are you crying?"

I lift my head and stare at him in disbelief. Can he really be this dumb?

He carries on speaking. "You've barely eaten all week. You don't talk to us anymore. What's going on?"

I widen my eyes. "Are you serious?"

His forehead crumples. "What do you mean?"

"For someone who is forty years old and acts like he knows his shit, you are really fucking stupid."

"What are you talking about?"

I shake my head and sit up. "No one in my life has ever really wanted me around. My mother barely even knew if I was there half the time. The men who came into her life—including you—left again just as quickly. I never even knew who my father was. I guess I shouldn't be surprised that you don't want me either."

He comes and sits beside me on the couch.

"Of course I want you around, Laney. We all do. But you don't have to give your body to us for us to care about you."

"I know that, but I want to be loved."

"You *are* loved. We all love you."

I shake my head. "Not that kind of love, Reed. I don't want to be loved as a sister or a daughter. I don't want gentle kindness. I don't want you to be fucking *fond* of me. I want intense passion. I want obsession. I want to be consumed by all of you. That's not the kind of love you have for a family member—step or otherwise. And every time I look at any of you, I can tell that I'm not the only one who feels this way, but you're making it seem like how we feel for each other is wrong or dirty. How can it be wrong to love someone so powerfully?"

"We're related, Laney," he says softly, but I hear the pain in his voice.

I throw up my hands. "By a marriage that was finished years ago. A marriage that you barely even remember taking the vows for."

"That's not how the rest of society will see it."

"What society, Reed? It's just us out here. You're killing all of us by denying us what feels right. Honestly, I've never known anything to feel more right than being here with all of you. It's been killing me, holding myself back from touching you, holding you, and I know you feel the same way. Who are you doing this for? A bunch of nameless people we might never even see again?"

He lowers his head. "You, Laney. I'm doing it for you."

"It's not what I want. I'm eighteen years old. I should get to decide."

"You'll regret it later."

The muscles in my jaw are clamped tight, and so much adrenaline is rushing through my body, I feel slightly sick. "First of all, we don't even know that we have a later. We all might still die out here. Secondly, so what if I do? I can't imagine how I possibly could, but if I do, don't I get to make my own mistakes?"

"I'm worried that you're going to grow up, and look back at all of this, and hate me."

"I could never hate you."

He put his head in his hands. "You say that now, but what happens when you're thirty and I'm already past fifty? You're going to think differently of me then."

I take his hand. It's so warm and rough and familiar. I love this hand. "I'll still love you. I don't see your age."

"But you will."

"Then we'll deal with it then. There are always going to be bumps in the road in relationships. Even people who are the same age have them, and Reed, we don't even know if we're going to get to thirty and fifty. We don't know if we're going to live past winter. Don't ruin what little time we might have with 'what ifs.'"

He twists his body to look into my face, and for the first time, I see hope in his eyes.

"God, you're so beautiful," he says. "From the first second I saw you, it was like something changed in my life. No one has ever affected me the way you do."

"Then stop fighting it. I'm yours, Reed. Take me. Take all of me."

He slides his hand up the side of my face, cupping the back of my neck.

"I'm powerless around you, baby. When I'm around you, all I want is to touch and hold you, and when we're not together, I can't stop thinking about you. It's like the only thing I exist for now is you, and keeping my distance from you is the hardest thing I've ever done."

I reach for him, touching his face, the bristle of his beard growth scratchy against my palm. "Then don't keep your distance. None of us want that. I feel exactly the same way about you."

He turns his head, planting a kiss to my palm.

I draw in a shaky breath. I don't want to push him, in case he withdraws from me again, but just that simple kiss has stoked a fire inside me.

"I want you, Reed. I want you to consume every inch of me. I want—no, *need*—to feel you inside me."

"Ah, fuck, baby." He has a new kind of intensity in his eyes. "You have no idea how much I want that. Every part of your body should be mine."

"It already is," I tell him. "You just need to take it."

He doesn't wait another second longer. He covers my mouth with his and kisses me with a fierce hunger, which I return. He breaks the kiss, both of us panting with need.

"I want to take this hole," he touches my lips. "And this hole." He pushes his hand between my thighs. Then he reaches around to my ass and growls, "and this hole. I'm going to pin you down and fuck you so hard you'll forget your own name."

I whimper, partly in excitement, partly fear. It's like I've unleashed a beast and I'm not sure I'll be able to put him back in his cage again.

He strips me naked, and then removes his own clothes. I love being naked with him. His body is different than Cade's and Darius's, thicker, more solid, with a spattering of hair across his chest. It makes him even sexier.

"Suck my cock, baby-girl. Get on your knees and suck Daddy's cock."

He's gotten over his stepfather issues, then...

I happily drop to my knees and open my mouth for him. He

fists my hair, holding me in place, and pushes his erection between my lips. I suck him until he's moaning, his hips thrusting, and then he tells me to stop.

"I'm going to come too soon," he says, "and there's something else I plan on doing to you. Stay on your knees."

I don't dare move, remaining on my knees on the floor, my hands in my lap, my head bent.

He's gone for less than a minute and returns with a couple of items.

"Now lie on your stomach and lift that sweet little ass for me," he says.

I do, and he shoves a rolled-up towel under my hips so my bottom is raised. I'm tense with anticipation.

He climbs between my legs from behind and clicks open the lid from a bottle of lube.

I wonder which of the men happened to have lube in their bag when we crashed. My money would be on Cade, but frankly, it could be any of them.

He runs his fingers across my ass. "You have marks on your skin."

"Dax whipped me with his bow."

"Did he, now?" Reed sounds impressed. "And how did you like it?"

"It made me come," I admit, my breath catching.

"I like how it looks."

He continues to touch me, his fingers trailing between my cheeks and skimming over my hole. I suck in a breath.

"God, I love this perfect ass," he growls. "How could I ever have convinced myself I could live without it in my life?"

I love how he worships me.

He ducks down to lavish affection on me with his mouth, and I'm thankful I went down to the river this morning to wash. His tongue trails over my asshole, a zing of pleasure shooting through me.

"Oh, Reed. Fuck."

"Relax, baby. This will feel so good."

He pushes his tongue inside my ass, and I squeal with shock. But then he's licking me and tonguing me, and my squeals turn to gasps and moans. God, I feel so dirty and embarrassed and humiliated, but also incredible. The feelings war inside me.

He lifts his head to use the lube and replaces his tongue with his fingers. He uses just the one initially, sliding it in and out, but then adds a second, stretching me. I'm sure I'm going to come, and I grind my hips against the rolled-up towel, trying to find some release.

His fingers withdraw, and the head of his cock presses against my tight hole. I tense again.

"Breathe," he tells me. "You can take it."

He's so big, I'm not so sure. But I want to please him more than anything. I don't want to let him down.

He applies pressure, and I feel myself stretch. A burning sting of pain goes through me, and I gasp.

"No, please, stop. You're hurting me."

I gulp back a sob as burning pain stretches my asshole. He's too big for that way; I know he is.

"Shh, baby-girl. It's okay. This is going to feel so good for us both, I promise you. You just need to get through this part, and then it'll all be better."

He shunts in a little deeper, and I whimper. My cheek is pressed to the floor. I try not to focus on the pain as his huge cock forces its way inside my ass.

"God, I wish you could see how beautiful you look right now," he tells me." Your ass is stretched so perfectly around my cock. I can't wait to see my cum leaking from your hole."

He's inside me, and I cling to that knowledge. It's what I've wanted more than anything these past few days. A part of me wants to cry because I've been terrified that this would never happen again. Reed and his sons mean everything to me, but not as a stepfather or stepbrothers. They're my lovers. My soul-mates. The men I want to spend my life with, however strange that may seem to outsiders.

A tear trickles from my eye, and he leans over my back to wipe it away. He brushes his thumb down my cheek, swiping away the tear, then lifts it to his mouth to suck off the salt. The movement changes the angle of his cock in my ass, and I moan.

He notices. "That felt good, baby-girl, didn't it?"

I nod.

He starts to rock his hips. The movement is slight, but my clit tingles, and the pain I'd experienced while he was forcing himself inside me fades.

He gives a guttural growl as he moves inside me, taking it super slow, still letting me get used to him.

"Tell me to fuck your ass, baby."

"Fuck my ass, Daddy. Do it. I'm sorry I cried."

"I like to see you cry. Do you know why? It means you're being honest about your feelings. There's no wall up or pretense that you're strong or being hard. I can trust those tears. They're real."

He reaches beneath my body to play with my clit. His first touch sends sparks through me, and I moan again, throaty and raw. He only applies pressure, giving me something to rub up against, like a goddamned cat in heat. But the combination of his touch, and his cock shunted deep in my ass, is driving me wild. I wriggle and buck, and I can tell he's loving it. He loves having this much control over my body. One moment, I was begging him to stop, and the next I'm using him like a strap-on.

"Tell me what you want me to do. Say it how I like it."

"Rub my clit, Daddy. Make me come."

I feel so filthy saying those words, but they turn me on so much, and I can tell it has the same effect on Reed.

He's moving faster now; we both are. I'm matching him with every stroke of his cock, pushing back on him, wanting more.

Our bodies slam together, and I know I'm going to climax at any moment.

"I'm going to come inside your ass, baby," he growls. "I'm going to fill your pretty ass up with my cum."

I climax, my body convulsing, and Reed releases himself in a hot rush inside me. I let out another sob, but it's because I'm overwhelmed and relieved, not because I'm sad.

He gathers me up in his arms, pressing kisses to my neck and shoulder, holding me tight.

"Are we okay?" I ask him, desperate for reassurance. "Will you tell the boys that we're all together again?"

"Yes," he says. "I'll tell them. From now on, we're all with you."

43

laney

IT'S EARLY MORNING, and we step down the cabin's porch steps and onto the ground.

We've gathered as much as we can carry, including bottles of boiled water, dried rabbit jerky, and blankets to keep us warm. We also have what we need to trap animals, fish, and light fires. We might not have the comfort or convenience of the cabin, but it's enough to ensure our survival.

What will we find upriver? Are our theories correct and whoever owns the cabin reached it this way? I want to find civilization, don't I?

My feelings are mixed.

Yes, I want to have hot running water, and be able to order pizza, and I'd kill for some new clothes, but I'm worried about what will happen when we're back in normal society. The media storm around Darius is going to be huge. We'll have every reporter on us, the general public will use their phones to take photos and videos of us, and everyone will be asking questions about how we survived.

I don't want to share Darius with all those faceless fans.

I'm worried about Cade, too. If he owes people money, will they come after him? Darius has already said he'll pay them what Cade owes, but will Cade be strong enough not to gamble again? It's an addiction.

Then there's Reed.

He's worried that people will find out what happened between us. Will they believe I was eighteen before anything happened? They most likely won't even care. It'll just be a reason to crucify him. Plus, I know neither of us wants this to end. We don't want to be apart. Any of us. But questions will be asked, and all it takes is for one member of a hotel staff to see something they shouldn't, or notice which bed I've been sleeping in, for word to spread.

But if we stay, we get to continue our strange but beautiful relationship, but we most likely won't last the winter. The chance of all of us surviving is minute, and the thought of losing any one of them just about kills me. How would we keep going with such a loss?

The thought alone has the power to punch my breath from my lungs.

It doesn't matter which scenario I look at, there are things I hate about it, but surviving has to be our priority.

I pause to look back at the cabin. Stupidly, my eyes fill with tears.

"You okay, Laney?" Reed asks.

I sniff and nod. "Feels strange to be leaving. I know we didn't exactly choose this place to be our home, but it's been one, hasn't it? The cabin has been the first place I've lived where I haven't been scared to come back to it. It's the first place I've felt loved and wanted, and I guess I'm sad to leave."

He offers me a smile. "*We're* your home, Laney. You've felt loved and wanted because you've been with us, not because of the cabin. When we get back to civilization, we'll make a new home."

"Is that what you want? Do you want me to still live with you all when we get back to normality?"

"Of course. How could you ever think that we wouldn't?"

"Because I'm not used to people wanting me around."

He pulls me into one of his big bear hugs. I love hugging this man. He's the best at it. I bury my face into his broad chest, and he kisses the top of my head. "Of course we'll want you around, baby. We love you. Don't you know that by now?"

My throat tightens, and I gaze up at him. "You love me?"

"I can't believe you'd ever think we don't."

I turn to Cade and Darius. They're both nodding. "Of course we love you," Darius says.

Cade agrees. "I definitely love you, little Cuckoo."

"I love you, too. All of you."

I want to cry again, but with happiness this time.

"It's time to go," Reed says.

I nod and shift my bag on my shoulder. Then together, we turn from the cabin and head down the much-walked trail we've created to the river. Sticking close to the river will mean we've always got a water supply, plus we can fish.

We walk in near silence, each of us lost in thought at the epic journey ahead. None of us can know what our futures hold, or if we'll even have one. I pray we'll find civilization within a matter of days, but really, we have no idea. We're working on theory alone—that someone has built that cabin in a location that must be accessible within a few days, though most likely by boat—but we could be wrong.

A couple of hours pass, and we stop to eat a little and drink some water. When we stop for the night, we'll build a fire and boil up some more for the following day. At least drinking the water means I don't have so much to carry. Already, my bag feels impossibly heavy on my shoulders. I've built up a fair amount of muscle from the physical work of living out here, but my back already aches, and I'm worried I'm going to get blisters. It won't be pleasant trying to hike for days and days with the backs of my heels rubbing off.

A loud crack sounds somewhere behind me.

I frown, stopping, and glance over my shoulder. "Did you hear that?"

Cade stops with me. "Hear what?"

"I'm not sure. Something big moving through the trees."

He removes the gun from where he's had it jammed into the belt on his jeans. It seemed sensible to bring one with us, just in case. "Might be the damned bear."

"Or a different one," I say.

"Hold up, you two," Cade calls to his father and brother. "There might be a bear around."

They both halt.

"Did you see one?" Reed asks.

I shake my head. "No, but I heard something. Like something heavy stepping on a branch."

We stay where we are, each of us straining our ears to catch another sound. It's like the whole forest in frozen, holding its breath, waiting for our next move. Only the familiar rush of the river meets my ears.

"Well, we can't stand here forever," Reed says. "Whatever it was must have gone in the opposite direction. We need to keep moving. Just stay alert."

I start to doubt myself. Had I really heard something, or had it been my imagination? I'll admit that I'm pretty wired, leaving the cabin to hike into the wilderness. I'm hyperaware of all the dangers that lie out here for us, and I'm terrified one or more of us won't make it. I keep reminding myself that we won't make it if we remain in the cabin over winter and that we have no choice but to move, but that doesn't make it any less terrifying.

We get back on the move.

"You know what I'm most looking forward to when we reach home?" I say. "Real coffee."

"Hell, yeah," agrees Cade.

"You'll be wanting coffee, too, won't you, Darius?" I call to him. "Black with no sugar, I remember."

Cade glances to Darius and snorts. "Black with no sugar? That's not how Dax drinks it. He's one of those freaking half skim soya latte orders."

"You are?" I realize something and laugh. "So, I'm not a coffee psychic, then?"

Darius grimaces. "Afraid not."

He'd just said it to make me feel better. Or maybe he'd been embarrassed about his half skim soya latte? Either way, I think it's cute.

Cade is leading us now, his head down, shoulders broad. I distract myself by watching the way the muscles of his back move beneath the thin material of his t-shirt. His brother sticks close by him. This isn't easy for Darius, but he doesn't complain. I'm frightened enough by what lies ahead, and I can see. I can't imagine being Darius, hiking into unknown territory. I appreciate how he and Cade work together, though, the synchronicity they have. Darius trusts Cade completely, and any time we reach an area that's harder to navigate—with fallen branches or rocky ground—Cade tells Darius. Darius then places his hand on Cade's shoulder and allows his brother to guide him through.

While of course I want us to reach safety, I'm also worried about what will happen when we're back in normal society.

Darius suddenly stops. "Did you hear voices?"

"Voices?" I echo.

"Are you hearing things now, Dax?" Cade teases. "Voices in your head telling you what to do?"

But Darius doesn't laugh. Lines appear between his brows, and he gives his head a slight shake. "I could have sworn I heard someone speaking."

"Could it have been the wind in the trees?" I suggest. "Sometimes it sounds like whispering."

His lips tighten. "I don't think so."

Another thought occurs to me. "What if it's a search and rescue team? What if they're still looking for us?"

Hope blooms inside me. If we've been found, then we won't have this terrifying hike ahead of us.

Are we about to be rescued?

I lift my face to the sky. "Hello? Is anyone out there?"

Reed catches my arm. "Laney, stop it."

"Why? What if Darius is right and he did hear someone? They'll be able to help us."

The others join in, shouting 'help!' and 'we're over here!' Then we fall silent, listening intently again. No response comes. All I can hear is the twittering of birds, buzzing of insects, and the constant rush of the nearby river. The hope I'd felt a moment ago dies as quickly as it arrived. No one is out here except us. Darius must have been mistaken.

Reed has clearly come to the same conclusion. "Let's keep going."

We all nod, put our heads back down, and keep walking. Though we're worried about winter drawing in, I'm glad it's fall now, and not summertime. At least it's not too hot, or that would make the hike even harder.

I call up to Cade, "Are we going to—"

In front of Cade, someone steps out from behind a tree, something lifted above their heads.

Before any of us get the chance to react, they bring the thing they're holding down hard and fast, making contact with the side of Cade's head. He goes down hard, and I let out a scream.

A second man appears from the woods. He stoops down and grabs the gun from Cade's belt. They both train the weapons on us. Automatically, I raise both hands in the air, and Reed does the same. Darius can't possibly know exactly what's going on, but I get the impression he has a good idea.

For the first time in over a month, we're no longer alone.

The two men look around.

"Well, well, well," one of them says. "Who the fuck do we have here, then?"

This clearly isn't a rescue team.

I believe we've just met whoever put the body in the roof space.

acknowledgments

I will admit that I felt a little daunted at writing a character who is visually impaired. Because of this, I roped in a lovely reader, Lilibet James, to read Immoral Steps and give me her thoughts on the chapters from Darius's point of view, which she did. So special thanks goes to you, Lilibet. Your advice and thoughts were invaluable.

Thank you so much!

Also, thanks to my crack team of editors and proofreaders—Lori Whitwam, Jessica Fraser, and Tammy Payne. I appreciate all your hard work whipping this book into shape.

Thanks to Wander Aguiar for another insanely hot photograph, and Daqri at Covers by Combs for the fantastic typography.

I must also give a mention to Silla Webb for her beautiful formatting. It makes me so proud to see the book in paperback and hardback.

And finally thanks you, the reader, for keeping my dream of making stuff up for a living alive.

Until next time!

Marissa

about the author

Marissa Farrar has always been in love with being in love. But since she's been married for numerous years and has three young daughters, she's conducted her love affairs with multiple gorgeous men of the fictional persuasion.

The author of more than forty novels, she has written full time for the last eight years. She predominantly writes dark reverse harem romance, but also writes dark m/f, paranormal romance and fantasy as well.

If you want to know more about Marissa, then please visit her website at www.marissa-farrar.com. You can also find her at her Facebook page, www.facebook.com/marissa.farrar.author or follow her on TikTok @marissafarrarwrites.

She loves to hear from readers and can be emailed at marissafarrar@hotmail.co.uk. To stay updated on all new releases and sales, just sign up to her newsletter!

Other Dark Contemporary Books by the Author

The Limit Series:
Dark Contemporary Reverse Harem
Blurred Limits
Brutal Limit
Broken Limits

The Bad Blood Trilogy

Shattered Hearts
Broken Minds
Tattered Souls

The Monster Trilogy
Defaced
Denied
Delivered

Dark Codes: A Reverse Harem Series
Hacking Darkness
Unraveling Darkness

Decoding Darkness
Merging Darkness

For Him Trilogy

Raised for Him
Unbound for Him
Damaged for Him

The Mercenary Series:

The Choice She Made
The Lie She Told
The Trust She Gave
The Trap She Faced

Standalone Novels

No Second Chances
Cut Too Deep
Survivor
Dirty Shots

Printed in Great Britain
by Amazon

40315937R00179